Vasily Mahanenko

NO MISTAKES

*Books are the lives
we don't have
time to live,

Vasily Mahanenko*

World of the Changed
Book#1

Magic Dome Books

This is a work of fiction. Names, characters, businesses, places, events and incidents are either the products of the author's imagination or used in a fictitious manner. Any resemblance to actual persons, living or dead, or actual events is purely coincidental.

No Mistakes
World of the Changed, Book # 1
Copyright © V. Mahanenko 2019
Cover Art © Ksenia Nikelson 2019
Cover Design © V. Manyukhin 2019
English translation copyright © Jared Firth 2019
Published by Magic Dome Books, 2019
All Rights Reserved
ISBN: 978-80-7619-110-5

All Books by Vasily Mahanenko:

Table of Contents :

Chapter 1

Congratulations!

You discovered a dungeon during the prerelease!

Once the official game version is released, you'll get a well-earned reward.

And you'll get an even better reward if you beat the dungeon!

YEAH, BITE ME, SIS! Like I was ever going to be getting you a new phone...you'll be fine with your old one. Next time you'll think twice before making a bet with your elders!

"Mark are you screwing around on your phone again? Doesn't that ever get old? You should try something useful instead of turning your brain to mush," Chris muttered angrily. Another time, hearing the boss say something like that might have gotten to me, but not right then. He wasn't mad at me or my phone; it was the trip. The road we were on barely deserved the name. The pavement had ended a couple kilometers back, and it was like the car had suddenly stumbled onto a set from an old war movie. Dirt, mud, potholes. I could practically hear the shells whistling overhead, the wounded groaning nearby. *Sheisse, sheisse, nicht kapitulieren...*

"You've got to be kidding me!" Chris exclaimed when something scraped against the bottom of the car, which shuddered to a halt. "Whatever, we're here. Time to walk."

"What about our stuff?" I hit the pause button begrudgingly and dropped my phone into my pocket. The release was just a few hours away, and I'd been counting on beating that dungeon. *Could the timing be any worse?*

"We'll get it later—the presentation isn't for another three hours. It's a kilometer to the village. Let's go."

I opened the door and glanced down sadly at my white sneakers. It wasn't the death they'd dreamed of. Anything but that. The grayish-red clay was almost up to the car's running boards. *That damn GPS and the skip traffic function! Where could there possibly be traffic here a hundred miles from the city?! And what kind of VIP village needs a children's entertainer? They didn't have enough money for their resort?*

There was a squelch, followed instantly by a string of curses from the boss. His shoes, which cost a month's salary for me, had just introduced themselves to the local scenery. That was my signal. If Chris saw that I was holding back, he would fire me and hire Joker. The bastard had been gunning for my job for a long time, and I wasn't about to let him have it. Ignoring the new hue my shoes took on, not to mention my quickly soaked socks, I went over to the trunk and pulled out two large bags. Chris was the entertainer. And a good one. The kind that was invited to perform even in the rarest of air at the top of the social hierarchy. And me? I was just the guy he had to carry everything around, strong, durable, and cheap. You don't have to pay much when you're talking about a student working a side job in their spare time. The only thing that cheered me up was that my extensive collection of autographs was going to pick up some new entries, making it even more valuable. Chris didn't accept just any invitation. Especially when it involved trudging through the mud.

The look on the face of the guard at the security checkpoint didn't bode well. Instead of the usual tubby character who'd been fired from government service for drinking and was happy spending the rest of his days doing crossword puzzles with the button to open the gate next to him, the guard was a hulking character with the figure of a young Schwarzenegger. Angular cheekbones played nervously, barely visible behind his collar. Pointedly sliding the bolt back on his automatic, he barked threateningly.

3

"No begging! Get out of here!"

I ducked behind the boss, not a fan of people pointing weapons at me. Chris, not quite the coward I was, just pulled out a piece of paper.

"We were invited. Here's the pass."

Another fighter stepped out of the checkpoint, that one a copy of the first. Just as powerfully built, he was rough-looking and dangerous. He leveled his gun at us and signaled to his partner, who only then stepped over to Chris. *They don't play around!* After studying the document and shining an ultraviolet lamp on it, the first character walked my boss over to the checkpoint. I found myself there a couple minutes later. Our bags were disemboweled, our pockets were turned inside out, we were stripped down to our underwear, and it was only then that boredom replaced the vigilance in the guards' eyes. Their job was done. We weren't terrorists, and they could return to whatever it was they'd been doing before we got there. As I stuffed everything back into the bags, I noticed the first guard pull out his phone. A familiar intro popped up on the screen. I wasn't the only one enjoying the new game.

The castle we arrived at was built with a clear hint at the owner's taste for *Beauty and the Beast*. The two structures weren't similar; it was that the master, having lost his true love, built himself a tower, locked himself up inside like the beast, and got to work waiting for his beloved beauty. Judging by the merry laughter coming from around one of the pools, there were quite a few beauties there auditioning for the role. The owner himself was a homely weed in the surrounding flowerbed: short, pudgy, and bald with sagging cheeks. When he saw us, he waved a fat hand welcomingly. A butler showed up instantly beside us to bow to Chris.

"The master asked me to help you freshen up. Come with me."

Then he turned to me.

"I don't have any instructions for you. Margot, please take our guest to the summer veranda and make sure he washes up. Scrub the path, too. We wouldn't want anyone getting dirty."

That last thing he said was a reference to the trail my wet pants were leaving behind them. I squirmed under the butler's gaze. It was like he was looking at empty space.

"Mark, can you get the drone ready?" Chris looked at me inquiringly. That was something he usually took care of, but we were running out of time before the event.

"I've seen you do it a hundred times," I replied frankly.

"Great. Get yourself ready and take care of that—and hurry."

"On it." I sounded better than I felt. It was one

thing to launch a toy; it was quite another to be responsible for a piece of professional equipment worth north of ten thousand bucks.

The girl with the beautiful foreign name of Margot coupled it with a clearly provincial nose spattered with freckles. She led me off to the veranda and handed me some clean clothes that were neither new nor my size, though I didn't have much choice in the matter. After washing up, I got to work on the drone. Four blades hummed rhythmically as the unit soared into the sky. The weathervane on the roof of the villa twitched from side to side, but that didn't worry me. The drone's powerful motors and 17-inch blades held its position even in a strong wind. I'd flown it before, so I took the liberty of giving it a test run around the villa, pausing above the pool to admire the beauties clustered there before coming in for a landing. And that was all that was needed from me until the end of the event. Chris' baggage had been hauled to the location, the drone was ready, and I wasn't standing out. Later, I'd have to collect it all and get the car out of the mud—the boss certainly wasn't going to deal with that. I was the perfect employee.

There was only one thing on my mind right then. Settling onto one of the couches, I pulled out my phone and frowned—the battery was down to 30%, and my charger was in the car. *Although...that should be enough.* I checked my email to find nothing urgent or important. Squirrel had texted me that she was off to see a friend and wouldn't be back until that evening. That meant there was nothing to eat at home, as the little one would sooner go hungry than make something. With no messages on social media, I tapped the icon with a tremor of anticipation. The intro flashed by, the rest of the world faded away, and my stalker stepped into the dungeon.

Congratulations!
You beat a dungeon during the prerelease!
Once the official game version is released, you'll get a well-earned reward.

A satisfied smile spread across my face. There were just twenty minutes left before the official release—I'd made it in time.

World of the Changed exploded onto the market out of nowhere, suddenly becoming all gamers everywhere could think about. The astounding graphics, the intuitive controls, the lack of microtransactions, the ubiquitous advertising... It wasn't an hour before World of the Changed was on every TV, every radio station, every bus. Millions and millions of users were awaiting the official release to jump in and start destroying mutants and monsters. Among them were my sister and me. We quickly made it to the tenth and final level available in the prerelease, after which Squirrel announced there was nothing else to do. Sure, it was interesting, but the real fun was coming later. I'd just proven her wrong, however. And not only had I found the real fun; I'd also been able to beat it, taking out a champion and collecting some kind of bonus for myself. Even if it was meaningless bells and whistles, it was still nice.

We were down to the final minutes before the release. The action was kicking up around the castle, laughter was breaking out, fireworks were soaring skyward, everyone was rushing over to wish the master a happy birthday, and girls were running around in their bathing suits. I was out of the action, the perfect place for me. Parties like that weren't my speed.

"Here you go." Margot appeared to place an enormous tray down on the table. Lids were lifted, and the savory aroma of meat hit my nostrils. My mouth watered treacherously. The last time I'd had food that good was... *Well...probably the last time mom cooked for us... When she was still alive.*

A lump formed in my throat. It had been two years since my parents died, and I still hadn't gotten used to it. Squirrel had been thirteen. They were going to take her away to a children's home, but my uncle stepped in and helped set up custody. As a twenty-year-old, it was hard for me to take on responsibility for the family. I did it, though. I didn't drop out of school, and I found a job. But there wasn't money for little joys like food and alcohol, which was why I used games to relax. The best were the ones where you didn't have to pay. And that's why World of the Changed seemed perfect—I'd spent the previous month investing all my free time in it.

"Who are you to Chris?" Margot asked as she sat down on the edge of the couch and brushed back her curls. I smiled carnivorously—it was the same as always. Chris got the fame and glory; I got the curious servant girls. There were no pangs of conscience, either, as I was a twenty-two-year-old not planning on giving up sex for at least the next forty years.

"Oh, that's a long story," I whispered back mysteriously. Margot scooched closer and bent over to hear me better. Her face approached, and I was measuring her up for a kiss when her pupils suddenly dilated. She let out a wild scream. I lurched backward—Margot was screeching so loudly that it sounded like she was being torn to pieces. The girl threw herself onto the floor in a fit of convulsions, her squeals continuing. Other cries came from the other side of the door. I jumped up and looked out the window—everyone was yelling and rolling around on the ground. Men in slick suits, girls in bikinis, guards, all of them. A chill ran down my spine. *What's going on?! Is it terrorists?*

Suddenly, my phone vibrated. An enormous green button reading *Activate antidote* and a countdown appeared on the screen.

30... 29... 28...

I shuddered and looked back at Margot, who was no longer making any sounds. Something strange was happening to her. She was still screaming, only her screams were silent. The convulsions were still there, too—she twisted her arm so violently that I heard the horrifying sound of crunching bones. But that wasn't even the worst part. Her pretty face was starting to swell, becoming blue, deformed, and engorged.

My phone vibrated so hard it jumped around the table.

15... 14...

Complete bewilderment came over me. I couldn't do anything to help Margot, but there was no point just standing there next to her. *What if it's contagious? A biological weapon, maybe?* I grabbed my crazed phone only to almost drop it. *I didn't know this model could vibrate like that.* To shut it up, I jabbed the damn button. The vibrations stopped.

But that didn't make anything better.

For a few moments, I forgot everything—Margot and her suffering, the people on the other side of the door, even myself. Because a small, two-milliliter syringe filled with a green liquid had appeared in my hand. It did so gradually, almost as if the product of a high-speed 3D printer. A fire burst into my chest, and I remembered how important oxygen is to humans. After taking a deep breath, I hurled the mysterious thing onto the couch. *What the...?!*

But the devil had gotten into my phone. Another green button appeared: *Watch video.* In hopes of bringing reason back to the device, I gave in and...

Yet another curse escaped my lips. It was hard to wrap my mind around the image on the phone.

It was me in the video. My face, the clothes I was wearing, even Margot twitching in the background. On the screen, I went over to the syringe, picked it up, and plunged it into my leg. A green check mark appeared, though that wasn't the end of the video. It rewound to the beginning. Once again, there I was, standing there with a grin on my face as I looked at the syringe. I turned away demonstratively, after which I dropped to my knees and started writhing around the same way Margot was. The camera dropped slightly lower to show the girl. My hair stood on end. Margot was gone, in her place some kind of beast barely reminiscent of a human. It had enormous teeth, long claws, spikes all over its body, and deformed, bulging eyes. The arms and legs had turned thick, stubby, and lizard-like. Snapping its jaws, what used to be Margot leaped up to the ceiling, threw the door open, and disappeared. The camera went back to show my bluish face. An X appeared to show that I'd failed the mission, and the video ended. It was replaced by another countdown.

30... 29... 28...

I looked over at Margot and nearly vomited. The girl's face was exactly like the one I'd seen in the video. Her body was also starting to change, turning from human into monster. Her right arm burned intolerably. I held a hand up in front of my face, and that time I couldn't hold back the spasm—my fingers were lengthening and turning blue. That did it. In one leap, I was next to the couch, where I grabbed the syringe and thrust it into my leg. There was a flash of pain, the world around me started to spin, and I was swallowed by an encroaching darkness.

Waking up suddenly, I found that I didn't even have a headache. The first thing that occurred to me was how much I had to have drunk to have a dream like that one. But that thought was quickly chased away when I looked up and saw the drooling beast staring hungrily at me from a couple meters away. I had to wonder if my underwear was still clean. The scraps of clothing and the beads around its thick neck told me that the beast really was what was left of the cute girl. A third thought hit me, and I quickly held my hand up to my face. A wave of relief washed through me—my fingers showed no signs of the bluish tint or deformation. *Hooray!* There was at least some good news in all the chaos.

Once again, my phone buzzed, and the monster

growled menacingly. It crouched like a cat ready to pounce, though something held it back. I pulled my gaze away to look at my phone. Wondering fleetingly if it really was mine, I ignored that idea. What was on the screen was far more important.

Welcome to World of the Changed!
Number of registered players: 105,778,331.
An additional 500 million former players were
selected randomly and added to the list of players
on Earth.
Have fun!

It took a while for that to register. *So, this is the release? What, is this an alien invasion? The whole thing was a plot to enslave Earth? But why wouldn't they just make everyone monsters then? Why make it so complicated?*

The game will begin in ten minutes.
Familiarize yourself with the status table for
your character.

I automatically tapped the button that came up, and it was followed by a small table:

Status table		
Name	Mark Derwin	
Coins	0	Level	0
Titles and ranks		
None		
Attributes		
Strength	1		
Stamina	1		
Agility	1		
Skills		
Pistol shooting		1

Before I really got a chance to study it, a new window popped up:

Because you did a great job during the prerelease, the following bonuses are available to you:

Beginner. For getting to the highest level (3 coins and 50% off all items at the store for two hours).

Small. For finding a dungeon (8 coins).

Medium. For beating a Champion (12 coins).

Large. For beating a dungeon (KORT-I energy pistol).

Skill: Pistol shooting +1 (1).

Loyalty bonus. The game was open on your phone when it launched (attribute syringe).

Would you like to accept your bonuses?

And there were the two bonuses, one a green

check mark and the other a red X. There was no doubt in my mind which I was going to pick—the green button swirled away. The space around me drifted oddly. Two items appeared in my palm: a familiar syringe filled with a green liquid and a miniature pistol. Almost like I'd slipped out of reality for a second, my heart stopped as I gazed down. *That's some kind of magic!* The pistol fit my right hand perfectly, almost as if made from an impression. Of course, it was unusual, with neither a bolt nor a safety. Something more like a blaster from a fantasy movie.

One minute until the game launch.
Careful! There's an aggressive monster within three meters of you.
Get ready for battle and remember that there are no respawns in World of the Changed!

Chapter 2

A PUNGENT SMELL hit my nostrils. I almost sneezed. The monster's saliva dripped onto the floor, bubbled, and hissed, kicking up a green mist. Its eyes fixed on me, it once again crouched, tucked its tail under it, and got ready to spring forward.

I aimed my KORT-I, but I couldn't pull the trigger. What if everything that was going on was a figment of my sick imagination? What if there weren't any monsters, and I had just lost my marbles? Margot might have been trying to tell me something. I was ignoring her, holding an arm out to protect myself. And I wouldn't have been holding a pistol since there was no way I could have found something like it around there. But which option was more realistic? The one my eyes were telling me was true or the one my brain was proposing?

Suddenly, there was a burst of automatic gunfire and a few explosions off in the distance. The monster perked up its ears like some kind of watchdog before turning to look out the window. I followed its example and...

That was a mistake. My chest sagged under the weight of a heavy blow, ribs crunched, and I flew backward against the wall, yelling from a pain in my leg. The carnivorous beast had ripped an enormous chunk of flesh off my hip and was swallowing it whole. Chewing be damned. I couldn't move as the pain shot through me, and with my last shreds of consciousness I pulled the pistol's trigger. Short blue rays shot out of the barrel. The monster shrieked, trying to jump away, but it just toppled back onto the ground. My first shot hit an appendage, my second slammed into the body, and my third finished it off. But more blue streaks continued pouring into the corpse—it took an effort for me to stop shooting.

A shiver ran through my body. The awful wound on my leg was bleeding. When I brought my sleeve across my mouth, it came away slick with blood, and my ribs were certainly broken. Breathing was difficult. Medical shows from TV popped inopportunely to mind—what if my lung was punctured and I was living out my last few seconds? *What a shame...* I was going to die from some chick-turned-monster, and not as the result of a heroic feat of valor. And she wasn't even that attractive... *Sis would definitely needle me for that one...*

My fading consciousness suddenly swung back into sharp focus. *Squirrel!* She'd gone off to see a friend, which meant she was somewhere out in the middle of the whole nightmare. I wanted to scream, but the only thing that came out of my mouth was a gurgle. I had to do something. If I didn't, I was definitely going to kick the bucket. My glance fell onto my phone, which was lying near the couch. An attempt to move just brought with it a new bout of pain that almost finished me off. In addition to the burning in my leg and chest, there was something wrong with my back. A chill ran over me again, the world started to darken, and I did the only thing I could. I stretched my arm out toward my phone. *If I have to die, I'm going to go down fighting.*

Something slapped lightly against my palm. I felt cold metal. Opening my eyes with difficulty, I stared dully at the phone in my hand. *Where did that come from?* There was nobody next to me besides the riddled monster, and I didn't think Margot's ghost had come back to help me out.

The screen blinked actively. I focused my attention, reading the text. If there was anything that could help me then, it was that lifeless pieces of glass and metal.

You won your first battle and affirmed your right to life.

Level +1 (1).

Attribute point available.

I'll deal with that later! My shaking fingers slipped across the screen, opening tabs that turned out to be useless when it came to the condition I was in. After closing yet another window, I went back to tapping and finally came up with a new inscription:

Welcome to the store.
You have 23 coins in your account.
50% discount active (1 hour 35 minutes).

Sweat and blood trickled into my eyes. They burned mercilessly, though I kept reading the product descriptions in the *Most popular* list. I had no other way to look for help. The items on the screen changed once again, and I finally saw something:

Small regeneration kit. *Completely regenerates your health in 8 hours. Single use. Cost: 10 coins (20 without your discount).*

I frantically jammed my finger at the picture. Some kind of confirmation popped up, but my tortured brain had enough on its plate trying to maintain consciousness. A syringe started taking shape in my hand. Unlike the first, this one was enormous, a good ten milliliters. It didn't come with instructions, so I went with the usual, burying the needle in my good leg and pressing down on the plunger. There was another flash of pain that proved too strong for me.

There was no way of knowing how long I laid there unconscious. All I knew was that there came a moment when I started hearing the world again, only I didn't feel any pain. I had to clear my eyes of dried blood before I could open them. And the first thing I saw was the monster. It hadn't gone anywhere. A glance down at the wound on my hip told me that the bleeding had stopped, and the hair on the back of my neck stood up when I took a closer look. A bunch of black dots were rebuilding my flesh basically the same way the pistol and syringes had appeared. I was being printed.

I felt some objects in my mouth. Spitting them out, I froze yet again—they were my teeth. Capped, yellow, and riddled with cavities. I hadn't had money for a good dentist, so I'd gone the free route, though that experiment had ended when they "accidentally" pulled the wrong molar. Judging by the size of the cavity on one of my teeth, I would have had a major problem on my hands in another two weeks or so.

Running my tongue along my jaw and expecting to find gaps there, I was surprised to no end when every tooth was in place. I ran a finger along them—all there, and even the two on the floor had been replaced. And it was only then that I noticed how well I could see the writing on a sign hanging on the far wall. There was no sign of my nearsightedness. Taking a deep breath and feeling no pain in my ribs, I had a hard time holding back a joyful shout. *It worked!*

I was healthier than ever.

On the other hand, I didn't have long to enjoy the feeling. My phone started going haywire again in an effort to grab my attention.

Low battery. If your phone turns off, you won't be able to earn coins.

That meant another visit to the store. This time, I knew what I was doing. The item I was looking for popped up right away:

Energy block. *+10 hours of charge. Universal device suitable for any energy consumer. Cost: 0.5 coins (1 without your discount).*

I had just 13 coins left, but I splurged on four blocks to have on me for a rainy day. Small dock stations that fit my phone perfectly appeared in my hand. Connecting one of them to the device, I just grunted—I was starting to get used to miracles. The dock station melted away the same way it came, and my phone's battery jumped all the way up to 100%. *Better than sitting next to an outlet for hours.*

Still unable to get up, I crawled over to the syringe. It was only when I got to the couch that I belatedly remembered the pistol. My KORT-I was over by the wall, nearly drowned in a puddle of blood. The episode with the phone sprang to mind. It too had seemed out of reach, only to appear unexpectedly right next to me. Stretching a hand out toward the weapon, I imagined it returning to nestle carefully in my hand.

Nothing. The pistol just laid there in the pool of blood, not moving a millimeter.

My inquisitive mind refused to take no for an answer, and I tossed my phone away from me. Just in case, I kept it fairly close. Reaching toward it worked— the device flew over and settled in my palm. *Ah-ha!* A second attempt with the pistol came up empty. Again, I sent my phone flying, this time all the way to the far wall. Again, it came back. *So that only works with my main device? Got it.*

The syringe finally in my hands, I sent its contents into my hip. My phone screen instantly reacted with new messages:

You used an attribute syringe.
Would you like to boost your current values or unlock a new attribute?

A new one! During the prerelease, I'd more or less worked out the principles behind World of the Changed. My character was a stalker, and I'd only gotten as far as I had because I'd been incredibly lucky: out of the hundreds of available attributes, I picked Regeneration, which had proven most valuable for me. The ability my character gained to lick even the deadliest of wounds had been what had let me beat the Champion, the final boss in the dungeon. And since that had worked on the phone, I figured it would work in real life. The only thing that had saved me after my first go-in with a monster had been the coins I still didn't really get. I couldn't risk that again, so...

Regeneration +1 (1).

I dumped my extra attribute point into Regeneration without a second thought, boosting the value to 2. The wound in my hip started itching; the number of black dots doubled. A couple minutes later, I was on my feet and even taking a few steps. I hobbled over to the pistol and picked it up, feeling much better. Three shots, practice showed, were enough to turn a monster into a corpse. There wasn't a description on the gun itself, so I turned to my phone:

KORT-I energy pistol. *Ignores physical armor. Blocks regeneration. Charge lasts 100 shots (92 left). Range: 25 meters. Cost: 50 coins (100 without your discount).*

That mention of blocking regeneration grabbed

my attention instantly. *What, those beasts can heal themselves, too?! How is anyone supposed to kill them if they didn't beat a dungeon?* I thought back to the automatic gunfire and grenade explosions. *That was probably the guard at the checkpoint!* I suppressed the urge to dash off in search of him, figuring wisely that the fact that the gunfire had ceased meant he was no more. At least, there was nothing I could do to help him right then.

As I continued exploring my phone, I found my way to the main menu. There were a few buttons at the top level next to *Store* and *Your character. Take picture, Call,* and *Share coins.* I wasn't about to be sharing anything right then, so I let that button be. Everything in me wanted to call Squirrel, but I waited on that, as well. I was afraid to learn that she was no longer in the land of the living. She hadn't beaten a dungeon, which meant she didn't have a weapon. And so, putting off that moment, I tapped *Take picture* and...

I stared in disbelief at the all-too-familiar functionality. There was the camera; there was the button to take a picture. *Seriously?* There I was in the most advanced game ever created, one capable of printing items out of midair and turning 90% of the population into terrifying monsters, and it had a selfie camera?

Catching the defeated monster in the frame, I took the shot. I wasn't about to carry my trophy around with me, and that was as good a reminder as any of my first victory.

You took the first picture of 1 dead inferior monster. 1 coin received.

There was a ding, and the number 12 appeared next to my battery indicator. The entire extent of my wealth. *You're kidding me! So they give you coins for pictures, and not kills?! That's ridiculous.*

Just in case, I touched the body, expecting to get some kind of loot. There was none. No flask of blood, no mage-epic machinegun, nothing. The only thing I got from the beast was a single coin, and I'd had to take a picture of it to get that. I looked at my pistol and went back to the store. *Damn it!* Surviving was going to be harder than it had seemed a few minutes before.

Charge block for energy weapon. *Charged energy block sufficient for 100 shots from an energy weapon. Works for all weapon types. Cost: 15 coins (30 without your discount).*

Deciding that there was no sense waiting any longer, I tapped the call button. There was only one contact, and she was marked as a relative: Squirrel Derwin. The game had deleted everyone else.

"Mark, is that you?" Squirrel answered after the first ring. My sister was speaking in a whisper, barely able to keep from crying, judging by her voice. Someone hushed her from the background. She fell silent.

"Where are you?" I tried to keep my voice low, as well.

"In the metro. Mark, what's going on... They're changing... They're... They're eating them!"

"Quiet, I know. What kind of bonuses did you get?"

"Dude, if you're going to be calling, I'll shoot her," came a rough whisper. "I'd rather sacrifice one than twenty. Short answer: we're in a metro train car underground. The changed are all around us, just not in here. If you want to help, send coins. We need food. Okay, that's it... Hey, don't touch that! The windows have to be covered!"

The line went dead. I felt better, even despite the rough call. Squirrel was alive, and someone there with her had adapted quickly. It was finally that *Share coins* button's turn to shine. Ten coins were subtracted from my account, and a few seconds later I got a kiss emoji and a thumbs up. Texting wasn't available. That just left the little moving pictures.

Okay... Sis is in a train car. They don't have food, and farming coins is difficult to impossible. I have to get her out of there, though that means making sure their whole group survives. I knew Squirrel would rather die of hunger than keep food from the others. Up came the store:

Food. *A supply of nutrients and water sufficient for 1 person to last 1 day. Cost: 0.5 coins (1 without your discount).*

They were good for that day, leaving me twenty-four hours to find another twenty coins. That was twenty pictures. *I can do this!*

The wound in my hip had nearly closed, which let me make my way over to the window and look around. The monsters were everywhere. A pair was taking on the kennel, where a German shepherd was whining in fear. Several others wandered the courtyard looking for food, with a new kind of monster, definitely different from the one by the couch, at their head. It was taller, stronger, and clearly in command. Almost as if it could sense it was being watched, the beast started sniffing the air. I crouched down and crawled away from the window, hiding behind the couch. As if it was going to do anything to protect me. The delicious smell of roast meat hit my nostrils, and my stomach growled—I hadn't eaten anything since that morning. Knowing that I was making a mistake, I still pulled the tray closer and started stuffing my face. For the first time in a long while, I both enjoyed the food and chewed it thoroughly with my new teeth. There was no reason to avoid particularly hard pieces.

After a satisfied burp, I realized that I was starting to feel human again. It was time to try killing monsters, and the most important thing there was figuring out how many and where they were. *Wait a second, I have the drone remote!* Chris hadn't had time to pick it up, and I had to assume that his distaste for video games meant he wasn't going to be coming back for it. The only thing I could do was hope he was in the half percent of lucky ones the system had selected.

New device detected.

Would you like to connect your Matrice-210 RTK drone to your phone?

As soon as I picked up the drone remote, my phone let me know that it wanted to be in charge. And that was fine with me—I didn't want to carry around any more devices than I had to. Something loaded quickly, and another button appeared on the screen: *Drone.*

Drone expansion functionality unlocked for the store.

Putting off the urge to check out the new tabs, I launched the machine. It responded beautifully, even better than it had with the old remote. Having adjusted to using the phone, I sent the drone on a familiar flight pattern around the villa. The monsters instantly reacted to the flying device. Shrieking with frustration at their inability to damage it, they leaped along behind, crashing through bushes and toppling statues. By the time I got to the pool, there were already a good twenty of the beasts in hot pursuit. Half of them were the big kind. More spikes, longer claws, and astonishing agility. One of them took a running head start before leaping into the air, soaring forward, and throwing out its arms. I had to send the drone shooting upward to barely avoid having it taken out. Of course, I couldn't get close to the villa, either—there were plenty of monsters on the roof. I also noticed a few patches of blood by the pool which told me that some of the guests had been players. They'd just gotten very unlucky with where they'd activated.

A couple minutes later, the drone was hovering over the checkpoint, bloody carnage stretching out below. The remains of monsters were everywhere, some even moving despite terrible wounds. The checkpoint doors were blown off, the walls were broken down in some places, and the only conclusion I could draw was that the guards had sold their lives dearly. Jumping, I turned the camera back toward the field of battle. There were at least thirty of the beasts lying on the ground. *If I can get over there and take a picture, I'll pick up thirty free coins!* That meant another day for Squirrel and another day for me to think of a plan.

But how was I going to get over there?

I brought the drone back toward the villa. The pack followed, though a couple stayed behind to chase some cats. Leaving the drone to hover out of reach, I started thinking. There was no way I was getting out of there without a pitched battle, so I needed eyes on the street. There was no counting on the doors—the beasts would take them out with their first pass. But a look around the area showed me the perfect spot for a stand: the bathroom. There was a long hallway leading toward it, and if I could set it up right, the monsters would have to make their way down it. I stepped into the bathroom, which was as big as a swimming pool, said a prayer even though I considered myself an atheist, grabbed a shampoo bottle, and hurled it at a mirror I'd set up in the living room.

The shards of glass fell to the floor. Instantly, the door flew off its hinges. Three beasts burst in, attracted by the sound and looking for fresh meat.

I took my time aiming—I needed to be careful about spending my pistol charge. Hurling another bottle to attract attention, I watched as one of the monsters caught it in midair and buried its teeth in the plastic. Shampoo flooded its mouth. Three pairs of dark eyes stared at my end of the hallway, and they tore down it a second later. But regardless of how fast they were coming, I was ready.

A headshot dropped one of them. It fell, holding up the other two. And while they were busy picking their way past the newfound obstacle, I took a second shot. There was no way I was missing from six meters away. The second body hit the ground, and a third clump of blue energy hurtled out when it did. Three shots, five seconds, a hundred nerve cells burned.

A glance at the screen told me there were no new opponents nearby. The main crowd hadn't heard my little diversion. Creeping out carefully, I went over to the clump of bodies and touched them again just in case they gave me loot before the picture. No such luck. Making sure the three all fit into the frame, I tapped the button.

You took the first picture of 3 dead inferior monsters. 3 coins received.

That raised several questions, only I didn't know who had the answers. The most important one was where my experience was. Since I had a level, killing three beasts should presumably have given me some. How else was I going to earn it? But there was no bar, no scale, nothing to give me an idea of how many monsters I had to destroy to level-up. The other unpleasant issue was the ability to take a picture of all the bodies at once. *So if some sly player out there hides until the end of the battle, they can just steal all the coins?* That "first" had me worried. While I'd been assuming I got coins because I'd taken a picture of the beasts for the first time, I was starting to wonder if I'd get coins for them if someone else had already taken a picture. *I'm going to have to be careful around other players...*

Ha! There I was, only three kills in, and already dreaming about surviving. There were at least thirty monsters out in the yard, which meant I was going to be busy. *Speaking of which, time for the next shampoo bottle.* A couple of the creatures looked to be close enough to hear the noise.

The bottle bounced off the couch, and my stomach dropped when I heard the sound of glass breaking. The entire crowd hunting the drone turned to find where the sound had come from. With a drawn-out yelp, they dashed toward the summer terrace. I hiccupped in fear and dropped onto the bathroom floor, my pistol clutched tightly in my hands. Adrenaline pumped through my veins. A shiver ran down my body.

Here we go...

Chapter 3

A BLOODY MESS, I wallowed in the bathtub, wishing for nothing more than an end to it all. There just wasn't enough energy to keep on fighting. I picked up my phone and used my one miraculously surviving eye to survey the gloomy messages on the screen:

Cannot restore eye. Regeneration level 5 required.
Cannot restore left arm. Regeneration level 15 required.
Cannot restore legs. Regeneration level 15 required.

I'd pulled off the win, but it was a Pyrrhic victory. There was nothing left of me. I needed a complete regeneration, but that cost twenty coins, not to mention a charge for my pistol. And there was no sense going anywhere unarmed. The monsters I'd taken out could give me the thirty I needed for an energy block, but that would have left me a legless, one-armed, and one-eyed invalid. The perfect fighter in a world of monsters.

And it had started off so well! The beasts had come piling into the hallway, more getting in each other's way than helping. That had let me gun them down one at a time until I started to think that I might even live to see the other side. Sure, the higher-level monsters took two or three shots each, but they died the same as the rest. The movement in the hallway stopped, and I looked away just for a second to catch a glimpse of the veranda using the drone. That was a mistake. Well, to be fair, nothing much would have changed even had I stayed focused. Despite my best-laid plans, the attack had come crashing through the ceiling. All I'd had time to do was hold up an arm to protect myself. A searing pain had scorched its way through my arm and legs, and the beast ripped a claw through my face. Almost crushing my skull, it left me bereft of an eye, a cheek, and part of my neck. I don't even know how I survived. How I fought off the attack. How I wasn't utterly demolished. Yes, I fired away, yelled, even jabbed the remaining stub of my arm into the mouth of one beast to use it as a shield against its friends, after which I'd fired a couple shots into its eyes. The last one met its end in the bathtub—my pistol had run out of charges. Even seriously injured, it had been in no hurry to die. I turned on the water, jammed the plug into the drain, and threw myself on top of the creature. It thrashed around in agony before going still. *At least they're not amphibious.* I slipped into the water, leaving just my head sticking out above it. A grin even spread across my face somehow as the icy water numbed my body. The burning wounds became bearable. My face was still on fire, but I wasn't about to submerge myself completely. I had my sister to think about, and she didn't have anyone besides me.

With a groan, I held out my arm and took a picture of the hallway.

The phone vibrated suddenly, too violently for me to hold onto it. But even after it splashed into the water, it kept going strong—there was some kind of report on the screen. Channeling my inner Jedi, I waited until the device slapped against my palm. It took some concentration for me to read the messages. That done, I stared blankly at a point on the wall, doing my best to wrap my head around the new information:

You took the second picture of 3 dead inferior monsters. 0 coins received.

You took the first picture of 23 dead inferior monsters. 23 coins received.

You took the first picture of 11 dead superior monsters. 55 coins received.

You took a picture of an interesting superior monster kill. Bonus received: 3 coins.

Somewhere deep down in my soul, even numbed as I was by the cold water, a flicker of hope was kindled. Without a single twinge of conscience, I spent fifty coins on a regeneration kit and an energy block for my pistol. The remaining thirty-six coins stayed in my account for later. *Squirrel needs to eat, too...*

Pulling myself out of the tub, I collapsed onto the floor. I really needed to stick the energy block in my pistol, but I just didn't have the strength. The pain returned with a vengeance the second I left the cold water. With my last remnants of consciousness, I buried the regeneration syringe in myself. My final thought as the darkness took hold was that I was happy I'd been able to attract all the beasts with the drone. There weren't any potential unexpected guests to worry about.

I only woke up that time when the healing process finished completely. It's hard to describe the feeling I had when I rubbed my regenerated hand across my regenerated legs. A tear might have escaped my eye. And even though my body craved action, there was no sense leaving even my flimsy cover without night vision. Another battery went to charge my phone. But that gave me an unpleasant thought—what if Squirrel's phone was dying, too? How was I going to get in touch with her? Ignoring the stranger's warning, I gave her a call. The answer came almost immediately.

"Mark?" came a whisper belonging to a man I

didn't know. All I could think was that the worst had happened. A white film settled in front of my eyes, my head buzzed, and I barked back at him.

"Bitch, if you did something to her, I'm going to—"

"Mark, it's okay, I gave him my phone," I heard my sister say in a muffled voice. "You need to talk to him."

"Buddy, I'm sorry, I didn't think about how you'd take that." It was the stranger again. "I'm Wart. Thanks for the coins—you seriously bought us some time. It's just that..."

"You need more."

"We do. My phone and Squirrel's are the only ones with any battery left. The rest are dead, we have those creatures everywhere, lots of them are superior, and I think there might even be a champion. They're wising up too quickly. We need a weapon, at least a pistol."

"A pistol? I don't have a coin machine over here, and the beasts don't like giving them up."

"I get it, I get it. But you have to understand, we're not going to survive without help. We could use a couple coins just to charge some phones—I'm hoping some of us have relatives that can share. I'd sell my soul to the devil for a few damn coins at this point."

"Can you make do with sixteen for now?" I asked begrudgingly. *I know, I need to worry about myself, but there are people there... And my sister...* I hated myself for my weakness.

"Buddy, you... Yeah, that would be great." Wart's breath even caught in his throat.

"You're responsible for Squirrel. If anything happens to her, I'll find you, even if it's on the other side. Got it?"

"Yep. I'll do everything I can. So, you found a dungeon, too?" Wart asked suddenly. Somehow, the picture in my head was of a guy around forty with the hefty midsection of an inveterate gamer. That was how he'd been able to so quickly pick up what was going on in the world.

"I didn't just find one; I beat it. Okay, hang tight, and I'll figure something out."

Sixteen coins found their way to Squirrel's account, and I went back to the store. To go from victim to hunter, I was going to need another purchase.

Strength field–I. *Protection from physical damage, up to 10 attacks. Cost: 20 coins.*

A small chain with a large red gem appeared in my hand. I fastened it around my neck, the hair on my body standing up from the static electricity. It was like a second layer of skin appeared. Of course, it wasn't a panacea, and the incredibly quick monsters could land ten blows in a matter of seconds, but it was something. I could buy something more powerful later.

One more time, I pulled up my status table. There weren't any changes besides that first skill appearing. *How do you level all this up? Just with injections?* But that still didn't explain how experience worked or how to get to the next level. There weren't any syringes for that in the store. *Damn, this is hard without help!*

Status table			
Name	Mark Derwin		
Coins	0	Level	1
Titles and ranks			
None			
Attributes			
Strength	1	Regeneration	2
Stamina	1		
Agility	1		
Skills			
Pistol shooting			1

Suddenly, something strange caught my eye, grabbing my full attention and making me quickly charge my pistol. The monsters were gone. There weren't any in the hallway; there weren't any in the bathroom. Not a one. The weak moonlight was enough to tell me that much, and I had no idea where they'd gone. *Did someone collect them while I was unconscious? Why didn't they do anything to me? Or do the bodies melt away after you take a picture of them?* I was going to have to check into that. The drone was on the ground not far from the veranda. When its battery died, just like any other professional piece of equipment, it carefully landed rather than dropping like a miniature meteorite. I had to see what was going on by the checkpoint. If the bodies there were gone, somebody was alive in the village, and I had to find them. Surviving in numbers is always easier.

It turns out that being a hero is no walk in the park, especially when there are dozens of mutants howling on the neighboring properties. I had to fight once again, that time with myself, before I could leave the veranda. And when I got to the drone, I let out a breath with a cloud of steam. The cold night air was brisk, invigorating. For a little while, I couldn't figure out how to use the docking station—the plugs were different. But when I held the thing up to the drone, a slender cord detached itself from the device, the dock station disappeared, and some condensation appeared on the drone's body. I very much hoped it wouldn't impact its balance. The drone's little lights blinked merrily, and I hurried back to the veranda. It was cold and dangerous outside. There was a bedroom on the second floor, and I wrapped myself in a blanket, shivering from the cold. *Ah, what I wouldn't do for a cup of hot tea right now...*

Nothing had changed at the checkpoint. The

bodies of the monsters were right where they'd been earlier. And that meant that they disappeared after being photographed, though I was still going to have to see that with my own two eyes. I kept the drone high in the air to make sure it didn't attract any unwanted attention. Flying over the town, I didn't see light in any of the villa windows. Either the survivors were hiding or there weren't any of them left. It was a good distance to the nearby villages, but I still pushed the drone higher to see what there was on the horizon.

I couldn't stifle a happy cry—somewhere off to the west where the city was, there were lights. And they didn't look like fires. Actually, my impression was that they were spotlights, lighting up the vicinity. *People! There have to be people there!* A warmth made its way through me. Talking with survivors on the phone was one thing; seeing them was quite another. I made up my mind to head in that direction the next day. Finding Squirrel from there was going to be a piece of cake.

There was nothing but complete darkness to the east and north, though my heart again skipped a beat when I looked south. Flashes of blue light told me that someone was firing game weapons. *Hooray!* Not only had the people there survived, but they were also fighting back. For a couple seconds, I thought about heading down there, though I quickly put that idea to rest. Squirrel was in the city, and that was all I needed to know.

I headed out to hunt as soon as the sun appeared over the horizon. To start with, I took the drone for a trip around the villa to attract the changed, though I was surprised when nothing took the bait. They had to be out there. If only judging by the number I'd killed, I knew they were.

Checking the veranda out was easier in the light of day, though I still wasn't able to find any clothes. I had to step outside barefoot and wearing nothing but my underwear. My phone and energy block were in one hand; my pistol was in the other. The cool air caressed my body, and I shivered. It was chilly. And quiet.

Almost as if reading my mind, a monster yelped on the neighboring property. The call was taken up by a second, then a third, a tenth, and soon the whole area was resounding with their howls. And just as I'd predicted, I could hear some coming from the villa next to mine. Four of the beasts peeked out of a first-floor window, threw their heads back, and joined the chorus. That was strange—I hadn't noticed that kind of synchronicity the day before. The doors burst open as the quartet piled out onto the street. One was superior, the other three inferior. They stopped to sniff the air, and the hair on my neck stood up, not at all from the cold. A new voice made itself heard above the rabble. Everything fell silent, and even the monsters who'd just come out of the villa pinned their ears back.

World of the Changed

They're scared!

Concealing myself behind some bushes, I made my way closer to the four. A few deep breaths oxygenated my blood and calmed my nerves. I sank to one knee. Aiming steadily, I took my first shot. One monster down. The rest froze and looked around, which gave me an opening for a second shot. Another inferior down, but they saw me that time. Letting out a deathly shriek, the remaining pair dashed toward me. They turned out to be incredibly, unexpectedly fast across the open ground, to the point that I paused and lost the upper hand. Sharp teeth flashed; jaws clamped down on my skull. That popped my ears, and the rest of the battle happened in complete silence. The monster wrenched his neck, throwing me to the side, though I crashed into the second one and sent it tumbling. That was a turn of events it wasn't expecting, and it didn't have time for an attack. We flew into the bushes, a bundle of arms and legs, but I was the only one to reemerge. One shot was enough to quiet the inferior monster forever. Its superior friend shook its head and tried to get a grip after its unsuccessful attempt at a bite. Dark blood trickled out of its mouth, shards of teeth coming with it. A couple shots put it out of its misery. I held out a hand, summoning the phone I'd dropped.

There were two charges taken out of my strength field, but I was happy. The experience had taught me that it wasn't worth taking on the beasts out in the open. They were just too quick.

You took the first picture of 3 dead inferior monsters. 3 coins received.

You took the first picture of 1 dead superior monster. 5 coins received.

You cleared the Initiation Zone of monsters. Level +1 (2).

1 attribute point available.

Finally! I was thrilled to level up, though I wasn't sure what I'd gotten it for. Was it killing monsters or clearing the location?

Without bothering to hide, I headed toward the pool. The dozen dried pools of blood left no doubt that there had been other players at the event. I bent over the only thing that was left of the first poor guy—the ubiquitous phone.

Player Chris Vertonen. Status: Dead. Cash: 3 coins.

You're kidding me! The boss had in fact played the game, never letting on. And the three coins were the bonus for getting to the maximum level in the prerelease. Who would have thought that Chris had been into the game?

Right next to the coins was a button that read

Collect, and tapping it rewarded me with a ding from my own phone. Plus three for me. Almost as if its work was done, Chris' phone disintegrated, slipping through my fingers and falling to the ground as a fine dusting. *See you, boss. You were a good guy.*

But that made me think—did I really want to go find other people? Human nature is a tricky phenomenon, and it's simpler to steal from whoever's closest to you than it is to go out and do the work yourself. *What if everyone takes the path of least resistance and starts killing other players, and not just, monsters in the struggle to survive?* If they did, other players would be the first targets. We were easier to take out, and we gave up coins with much more ease.

I didn't get lucky with the other phones—they were all empty. When I got tired of tramping around barefoot through the pools of blood, I headed back to the house. Careful steps around the shattered glass took me up the stairs to the second floor. It had once been luxurious up there, though most of the interior was demolished by that point. The monsters had apparently been so disappointed with the owner's poor taste that they'd gnawed the walls and furniture to pieces. I finally found a closet in one of the bedrooms and got to work picking out clothes.

Heading down to the kitchen, I got some food in me. There wasn't any electricity, so I had to eat it cold. And I grabbed a butcher's knife while I was there—

sometimes, good old physical damage comes in handy.

Incidentally, I wasn't thrilled with the ones in my strength, agility, and stamina attributes. While the following two were more or less on the money, as I'd never been that fast or good at running long distances, I definitely had some strength to me. Chris hadn't just hired me for my gorgeous eyes, after all. I was stronger than the other candidates for the job, having spent years working out. That was what made me a good pack mule for him. The problem was that the game apparently didn't count that, handing me those embarrassing ones everywhere.

Sighing deeply, I pulled up my attributes. I really needed to get my regeneration up to five so I could start healing serious wounds, my eye being a good example, but being as weak as I was meant there wouldn't be anything left to heal. The monsters could take me out with a sneeze. And so... A new syringe appeared in my hand.

Strength +1 (2).
Your body will need 8 hours to complete the change.

When I woke up, the sun was high in the sky. The process had been staggeringly painful, and my body twitched just thinking about it. There was no way I was going through that again. It felt like thousands of needles had been jabbed into me at once, tying my nerves up in tight little knots. I'd always thought I'd felt real pain when I visited the free dentist, as the only anesthetic he'd had on hand was the earplugs he'd used so he didn't have to listen to my screams. But I'd been wrong. Real pain was what I'd gone through eight hours before. It had been so intense, in fact, that my heart had stopped.

I stood up and gave myself a once-over. There was a lightness, and muscles had appeared. For instance, the biceps I noticed were bigger than anything I'd had even when I was working out. The six-pack abs were a pleasant surprise, too. My erstwhile belly had taken the brunt of student years spent playing video games, to the point that Squirrel had started calling it Peter and giving it a jiggle every time she walked by. But everything was perfect down there—I looked like one of the trainers at the gym. That was going to take some getting used to.

My phone buzzed so suddenly that I jumped. As I read the text on the screen, I realized getting to my sister was going to be anything but easy.

Congratulations!
You managed to survive the first day of World of the Changed.
Mission functionality unlocked.
Player ratings unlocked.

***

Monster levels increased by 1.

A level 1 larva appeared in your current location.

***

New mission: *Clear the village.* Description: Kill all the monsters in the village of Riverside. Monsters left: 183 inferior, 42 superior, 1 champion.

Chapter 4

JUST AN HOUR LATER, I was putting my new strength through its paces. And the pain was worth it.

The mission had me intrigued, especially that bit about the champion. It didn't take long to figure out that it was holed up in the enormous villa at the end of the road. That was the biggest building in the area, which made it no surprise that the monster had made it home base. Physically, the creature looked something like a triceratops—horns and spikes atop a beast the size of a trash truck. It just moved much faster than its cousin, and it also had bolts of lightning flashing periodically from its front horns. *Damn, a monster with abilities!* That was what I'd been most afraid of in the prerelease, what had sent me back to the respawn point over and over again. The smaller monsters dragged food over to the champion, the slower ones catching lightning bolts in their rear end. But it was when two women were dragged over that I realized the creature had to go. It sniffed them over, snorted, and, from what I could tell, decided that one of them was fit for consumption. She was scarfed down on the spot. Turning to the second, the champion bit off her limbs, licked her wounds to stop the bleeding, and had her dragged off into the garage. The beasts were acting in unison and with a purpose that surprised me. They weren't at all like animals. No, it was more like some kind of society, just a terrifying and alien one.

I wasn't about to send the drone into the enormous garage—there were too many monsters in the area. Bringing it back, I checked out the neighboring property and noticed about ten of them there. They really had changed overnight. The inferior beasts were bigger, with protective plates and additional spikes on their heads. Their superior friends hadn't fallen behind in the arms race, though it looked like their benefit was more intellectual. All of them were acting deliberately. And that scared me. *Could that be because there's a champion nearby?* That would have explained why Wart mentioned his suspicion that there was another one in the metro.

To take one example, the smarter changed didn't chase the drone around anymore. I had to take them on myself, though that gave me the chance to try out my upgraded strength. Three of them came at me. The first fell to a shot from my pistol, and I dodged the second, though the third was too much for me. As I watched the jaws slam closed around my neck, shattering the thing's teeth and taking a charge out of my protection, I did what any guy would have done in my shoes. I buried a smooth right hook in the monster's chin. The result exceeded my wildest expectations: there was a crunch, and the inferior creature's head snapped back. Its enormous hulk flew overhead and landed nearby. I was pretty confident it wasn't about to get back up.

In one fluid motion, I turned and sent a charge into the back of the beast that had missed with its attack. It screeched and rolled across the ground, digging in with its claws. My shot had severed its spine. Picking up the butcher's knife, I decided to see what it could do. One foot on the creature's back, making sure it couldn't crawl away, I reared back and slammed the blade home. My hand went numb; the handle slipped right out of my hand. And the whole thing turned out to be futile—the massive blade had only made its way a couple centimeters into the monster's body. I pulled it out with an effort and tried again, though the result was the same. Non-game weapons were practically worthless against the beasts in the game. A shot ended the monster's hopes of regeneration. One picture later, and I was staring unhappily at a couple new messages:

You took the first picture of 3 dead inferior monsters. 3 coins received.

You took a picture of an interesting inferior monster kill. Bonus received: 1 coin.

The beasts really were stronger and faster, which was why I'd been hoping for a concession from the system in the form of additional coins. But that didn't happen. *If they level-up again tomorrow, it's going to take multiple shots to kill each one.* There was no way I was going to be able to level-up myself—all my coins would go toward energy blocks. And what about Squirrel?

Clearing the property was easy—the creatures were running around on their own, and there weren't any superiors. But I sighed after taking the pictures. I was moving too slowly. No, it wasn't that my agility was holding me back; I couldn't take on more than one at a time, and that just got me one coin each. There wasn't much you could get for the chump change I was pulling in. Food, charge, a first aid kit. Everything else cost serious money. Taking a deep breath, I headed onward. The coins weren't going to earn themselves.

It took me the rest of the day and another cleared villa to reach the checkpoint.

You took the first picture of 12 dead inferior monsters. 12 coins received.
You took the first picture of 4 dead superior monsters. 20 coins received.

I was happy to get the coins, though I would have preferred more. Thirty of the thirty-two I picked up went toward an energy block for the pistol. That meant that I really only came out two coins ahead, not to mention the little progress I was making toward completing the mission, and the stiffness in my muscles. The constant action was straining my single stamina point.

The drone told me I was clear to move out. It felt strange moving across the open ground, though I had no choice—I had to get closer if I wanted better pictures. Experience had taught me that they only counted from a distance of thirty-five meters or less. And that was great news. If someone wanted to steal my kills, they'd have to look me in the eye while doing it. The problem was that drone pictures didn't yield coins. Not a video, not a picture, nothing. I'd spent a while digging through the store looking for a way to take remote pictures, but there was nothing.

You took the first picture of 32 dead inferior monsters. 32 coins received.

You took the first picture of 13 dead superior monsters. 65 coins received.

You took a picture of 5 interesting inferior monster kills. Bonus received: 5 coins.

You took a picture of 3 interesting superior monster kills. Bonus received: 9 coins.

My jaw dropped slowly as I took the pictures and read the notifications. *And there you have it: the difference between a professional soldier and a student you hire as a gofer.* The bodies I'd already taken pictures of disintegrated into a dark ash. Their lives already over, they'd just been waiting for somebody to stop by and cash in. And that was perfect—you didn't have to worry about burying them. People were eaten; monsters disappeared. There wasn't going to be anything heavier than a few kilograms left on Earth soon enough.

I was about to head out when I noticed another body in the corner of the checkpoint. For some reason, the monster hadn't disappeared after I'd taken the picture. *Could it be alive?* I glanced inside the bullet-riddled space and gasped—the body of one of the guards was lying right there. All that was left of Schwarzenegger's once-stunning copy was a bloody pile. No legs, no arms, guts spilling out, face mangled. The beasts hadn't finished eating the fighter, and I had a new mission. The hero who'd given me so many coins needed a good burial.

His chest rose and fell right back. A low wheeze broke out, and with it shivers down my spine. He was alive! I had no idea how, but the stump of a human was fighting desperately for life. Dashing forward, I stopped short when I saw the syringe next to his head. It was too big to be for regeneration. No, there was an extra attribute right there on the ground. They cost a thousand coins in the store, and I knew the kind of difference they could make. If the single strength point had been so huge for me, another stamina point, for instance, would let me run all the way to the city. A tremor ran through my arm. I was addicted, and my drug was right there in front of me. The soldier was dying anyway. I would be strong enough to kill the monsters with my right arm tied behind my back, strong enough to find and save Squirrel. All I had to do was leave him there. If I healed him, he would definitely ask what happened to his attribute point, and did I need that? *Of course not!* I needed to just pick it up and keep on walking. Keep killing, keep sending Squirrel coins, forget about someone I couldn't save...

I closed my eyes and counted to ten. The delusion passed. I really did pick the syringe up, though I was going to give it to the guard as soon as he regenerated. *I've never been a rat, and I'm not starting now.* Sending twenty coins to the store, I used the regeneration syringe on him without a twinge of regret. His breathing evened immediately. Doing my best to stuff his insides back where they were supposed to be, I picked the guy up and headed back to the villa I'd cleared. That was enough adventures for one day.

As it turned out, I'm not a particularly curious person. And I never would've thought that. The regeneration process had me intrigued, and I wanted to see it happen until the guy's limbs started printing. That did me in. It was an unpleasant sight, and I couldn't eat any of the many delicacies I found in the kitchen the rest of the day.

Everything had been so hectic that I fell fast asleep after sending Squirrel 30 coins. She needed them, and it also told her I was still alive. There was no reason to eat up my battery calling her—it wasn't the time to chat about nothing. A thumbs-up came in reply. She was alive and happy to get the gift.

Sleep crept over me, and even my battles against the hordes of the changed weren't enough to disturb it. Wrapping myself tightly in a blanket, I waited anxiously to see what the next day would bring.

Unfortunately, my morning started off with an unpleasant surprise.

The guard's body had regenerated perfectly. I even felt a pang of jealousy—I was the one with two strength points, and he was the one with the perfect body. When I stepped into the room, he was sitting there staring out the window. I greeted him; he didn't reply. I came closer, and there was no reaction. His gaze was fixed on some point off in the distance. And when I waved a hand in front of his face, there was no response. His expression was blank, he was rocking slightly, and he had no interest in what was going on. Even his phone was lying on the floor.

I picked it up, read a couple lines, and growled

in frustration. *Are you kidding me?*

Player Brighton de Croyt. Status: Insane (unable to restore intellect), level 1. Cash: 3 coins.

Not sure what to do, I plopped down next to him. There weren't many options. I could carry him with me to the city, where he would be a constant liability, or I could forget about him, leaving him there to be eaten by the beasts. Neither option worked for me. But nothing else came to mind. The thought popped into my head that I'd wasted twenty coins on him, but I quickly brushed it aside. There was no way I could have known what would happen. I'd done the right thing.

Pulling out the attribute syringe, I turned it around in my hand, putting off doing what I'd already decided on. Brighton didn't need it. He didn't need anything anymore, including his three coins. I took them, after which I grabbed my phone and added a point to my pistol shooting skill. There was no way around it—I needed to get stronger.

In went the needle...

Pistol shooting +1 (2).
Your body will need 10 minutes to complete the change.
Energy pistol section unlocked in the store.

My fingers twitched, a splitting pain made its way through my head, and my eyes felt like they had sand in them. I dropped to the floor, ready to slip off into unconsciousness, when it all suddenly stopped. My pistol was in my hand. I frowned, not remembering picking it up.

But I forgot all about that when I looked over at Brighton. It was like some functionality had migrated from my phone to my brain—there was a barely visible green glow covering the guard. And when I focused on a part of his body, percentages appeared, from ten to a hundred. The maximum values were all around his head and heart; the lowest were on his limbs. I pointed my pistol at one of his legs, and a red dot as well as a value of 35% appeared. The farther I went up his body, the higher the values grew. I stopped at his head—100%. Everything made sense. I realized what the numbers were, and I knew what I had to do with Brighton.

My trigger finger tightened. A single burst of blue energy shot out of the pistol. Reflexively, I pulled out my phone and took a picture of my first real kill. The monsters didn't count.

Sleep well, Brighton. I'm sorry I tried to wake you.

You took the first picture of a dead player. 10 coins received.

An impenetrable mask fell over my face, only a twitch in my eye giving away my true emotions. *I'll be damned if I go find any other people until I have some real protection.* Rage gripped me, and I was happy to recall that there was an uncleared villa across the road. There was something I needed to do.

You took the first picture of 9 dead inferior monsters. 9 coins received.

You took the first picture of 3 dead superior monsters. 15 coins received.

I only started feeling like myself again when I took the last few pictures. One more building was clear, and I was one step closer to completing my mission. Taking out the monsters was much easier—I studied their weak points ahead of time, which meant I only had to spend a single shot on each. Inferior or superior, they were all the same.

As I hunted the area for hidden monsters, I went down into the basement, where I found an enormous steel door standing open. Switching on a flashlight I found nearby showed me what was inside. On the other side of the door, there were even rows of weapons—pistols, submachine guns, heavy machineguns. The villa owner had an arsenal big enough to wage a small war. Either he'd been quite the enthusiast, or he'd been about to organize a little revolution in the area. And while I didn't know all the ins and outs, and my knowledge of how to use the guns in front of me was primarily based on a few trips to a shooting range, movies, and YouTube videos, it wasn't that hard. I got to the end of the row and found myself staring down the barrel of a heavy machinegun. The name even popped into my head: a Browning M2. A high-caliber American weapon, it wielded fearsome firepower. There were boxes loaded with cartridge belts next to it, and I grinned unpleasantly. If the beasts outside could stand up to that thing, my little pistol wasn't going to have any effect. It looked enormous, though I found to my surprise that I could pick it up. Sure, it was heavy. But it was more "ooph" than "oh damn."

I spent the rest of the day hauling the gun and its ammo boxes up to the roof of the next building over. There was a beautiful tower atop it, perfect for what I was thinking. A few boxes of grenades and a couple Kalashnikovs followed it. They were there to take out the fastest monsters, though the centerpiece of my plan was the M2.

It didn't turn out too difficult to work. Pull the bolt back, open the feedway, slip an ammo belt inside, close the feedway, slide the bolt forward, set it to automatic, and pull the trigger. The only thing that worried me was the kick, though I prepared for that by carrying a few sacks of sand up to the roof. One went behind my back; the others held the stand down against the roof tiles. The whole thing was jerry-rigged, of course, but I knew it would work for a few minutes. Swinging the barrel around toward the champion's lair, I paused. *Go for it or wait for tomorrow?*

After glancing up at the sun, and then the neighboring villas, not to mention another emoji from my sister, I made up my mind. I couldn't keep putting off my problems. It was time to finish up with the village and move on. The only thing I was missing was some music from my phone, but I cleared my head, aimed at the champion, and pulled the trigger.

Let's do this!

It's hard to convey the feeling of absolute power that came with those first few rounds. I'd never shot a gun of that caliber, and so I just wasn't ready for what happened. The oversized rhinoceros was thrown back against a wall and pinned there until the glow around its body died away. I spent an entire belt on the monster before I was able to break through its defenses and turn it into Swiss cheese. Quite a few clicks later, I realized the belt was done. It took just a few seconds to replace it, and then I redirected my attention from the lifeless champion to the onrushing horde. Little fountains of sand and stone kicked up on the road. Giving no thought to saving ammo or taking care of the gun, I kept the trigger firmly pressed. It was a one-time experience—there was no way I was going to lug that thing around with me. Monsters howled from the properties I hadn't yet cleared as the gunfire drew their attention. Another belt, and I was pointing the gun almost straight down. The quick little buggers had already made it to the tower.

The Browning jammed on the eighth belt. A bullet had wedged itself sideways, but I didn't have time to fix it. *Time for grenades.* Press the lever, pull the pin, drop it over the side. Just the way I'd been taught. Once I'd gone through three boxes of them, I picked up a Kalashnikov. The wounded monsters weren't giving up—digging the remains of teeth and limbs into the stone, they crawled toward me. But the weapon turned out to be incredibly ineffective, taking half a clip to kill each of the creatures. And that was only when I was shooting them in the head. Tossing aside the useless gun, I grabbed my pistol. The green numbers popped up. One shot, one kill.

I had to head back to the store twice for new energy blocks. Oddly enough, the high-caliber machine gun only really worked against the champion, proving weak against the faster inferior and superior monsters. The grenades weren't up to the task, either. Losing a limb or two wasn't enough to stop the bloodthirsty beasts.

My arm was starting to shake from the exertion. The red dot bounced around, I started missing, the dead bodies piled around the base of the tower, and my head was buzzing. But then suddenly, it got quiet.

It took the breeze playing around the tower, the leaves rustling, and my vibrating phone to tell me I hadn't gone deaf.

Clear the village updated. 183 inferior and 42 superior monsters killed. Monsters left: 1 champion.

I was stunned. Glancing in the direction of the rhinoceros, I saw it still lying motionless against its wall, the enormous holes in its body visible even from where I was. *It's alive? How?!*

When I tossed the sandbags aside, shell casings poured down the stairs. The door was demolished from both sides, so I had to go through the building. The idiot changed had come straight at me without thinking to go that way.

The champion really was still alive. Bloodshot eyes followed me as I stepped closer, and it even tried to get up and shoot lightning at me. Its broken horn put paid to that idea, however. The holes were big enough to stick a hand through, and I decided to record the moment for posterity. The pictures of the bodies went who-knows-where. But that one I wanted for myself. Turning the camera to selfie mode, I made sure the champion and I were both on the screen before tapping the button to take the picture.

You took a picture of a live champion from less than three meters away. 100 coins received.

You took a selfie with a live champion in the background from less than three meters away. 300 coins received.

***

You're the first player in this location to take a picture of a live champion from less than three meters away. Free attribute point received.

You're the first player in this location to take a selfie with a live champion in the background from less than three meters away. Free attribute point received.

My heart practically stopped when I saw the two small syringes forming in my palm. *That's... That's...*

A hoarse groan and heavy sigh forced me to turn around. The job wasn't done yet.

There wasn't a single spot on the creature's body that gave me 100% damage. I had to fire ten shots into it before my phone started to vibrate.

Clear the village complete.
Would you like to collect your reward?
Level +1 (3).

Of course! A wave of happiness overwhelmed me, and I fell to my knees and burst into tears, thrilled that the whole thing was over. I couldn't hold back the rivulets coursing down my face. I didn't want to, either. My body shook, I felt turned inside-out, and a howl burst out of me. The emotions that had built up over the previous two days demanded to be released, and I did nothing to hold them in. It was only when night fell that I came to my senses, burrowing into the still-warm body of the champion. I might have even gotten some sleep.

A glance at my phone told me that my sister had tried to call several times. Either she was worried, or something had happened. My itch to see what my reward was fought with the urge to find out what was going on with her. The latter won out.

"What happened?" I asked in a whisper as soon as she answered.

"You're alive?" she exclaimed too loudly, and I heard Wart hushing her in the background. "I thought you..."

Squirrel broke down, and someone in a better state to talk took her phone.

"Mark, it's bad. The monsters started dragging the train cars somewhere, and they're going to get to us by morning. If we don't get a weapon, I'm not going to be able to do what you asked me to do."

"I didn't ask you to do anything; I gave you an order," I barked, myself unsure of where that came from. "You'll get your weapon. Two hundred coins.

That's enough for a pistol and three energy blocks, plus some extra for food."

"Send it over." Wart was past thanks, and we both knew that I wasn't just doing him a favor. It was the only way to save my sister.

When I hung up, I thought for a second and sent two hundred and fifty coins, leaving myself two hundred and twelve. Phones only lasted ten hours—not so long—and there were twenty people in the train car. Each of them would need a battery, otherwise they wouldn't be able to survive in our god-forsaken world.

Alone with my pile of bodies, I finally tapped the button to collect my reward. A point on the ground next to me started to glow, growing quickly until it turned into something inconceivable. When it was complete, I swallowed and carefully picked it up. *Mother of god! Where have you been all my life?* Things would have been much easier with that baby.

I caressed my reward, realizing I knew exactly what I was going to spend my three attribute points on.

U-II energy rifle.

Ignores physical and energy armor for opponents up through level 2. Blocks regeneration for opponents up through level 2. Blocks one random ability. Charge lasts 200 shots. 1 upgrade slot. Range: 500 meters. Cost: 8000 coins.

***

Rifle shooting +1 (1).

Your body will need 10 minutes to complete the change.

Energy rifle section unlocked in the store.

Chapter 5

AS SOON AS THE SUN was up behind the crowns of the trees in the area, I got to work running around collecting loot with my phone.

You took the first picture of 152 dead inferior monsters. 152 coins received.

You took the first picture of 35 dead superior monsters. 165 coins received.

You took the first picture of 1 dead champion. 300 coins received.

You made it into the top 100 players in your location (99th place).

That was an unexpected bit of news. Pulling up the list of monsters, only the human ones that time, I scratched my head. I was the only player in the top hundred at level three. Everyone else had already cleared level ten. *How?!* How had they pulled that off in less than three days? *Did they pay for it somehow? Sell a kidney? Where's the "become superman" button?*

Obviously, there was no answer forthcoming. I decided the list didn't matter anyway and was about to leave when the garage caught my eye. Like a bolt of lightning, I remembered what had happened and dashed over. *There's a girl in there!*

But it was just an empty space that greeted me. She'd been eaten. Although...there was no phone, and there wasn't much blood, either. There had been entire pools back by my first villa, completely unlike what I was looking at—just a couple drops and a trail leading away.

A few... And they were a good distance away from each other. It was like the body had been dragged away rather than being eaten on the spot. I tried to think back to when I'd first seen the girl, and I remembered her being young and healthy. The second, the one that had been eaten while I watched, had been older. *That's odd.* Young meat is generally more tender... *Could champions have different tastes? Or were they hauling off the good stuff for someone else?* The inferiors had dragged the food over to their boss...

An unpleasant buzzing from my phone told me that I was on the right track.

New mission: *What's scarier than death?*
Description: You figured out that the monsters are hunting young women and dragging them off somewhere. Find out what the creatures want from

them.

Huh... The name was kind of colorful. Champions were the highest rung in the monster evolution chain that I'd come across in the prerelease, but nobody said there couldn't be anything stronger. The logs said something about a larva appearing in the location. *What if that's the real boss, and champions are just little chumps?*

Somehow, I wasn't feeling all that excited about the mission. The only reason I'd been able to take out that rhinoceros was that I'd happened across the machine gun. And if the difference between larvae and champions corresponded to the difference between superior monsters and champions, I felt bad for the girl. Because I wanted to head in the opposite direction.

I stepped out of the garage and followed the bloody trail with my eyes. The monsters were predictable once again—they headed straight off, crashing right through the fences as they went. As I went over to the hole they'd made and peered through it, I sighed. There was a similar trail running through the corn field. The beasts knew the direction they wanted to go in, and the worst part was that their path led west. Toward the city. And that was where Squirrel was.

Hey, how's she doing, I wonder? I gave her a

call, but there wasn't an answer. It just rang. A clammy feeling gripped my chest. Calling again and again, I got nothing. I began pacing the courtyard, chewing on my lip anxiously. *What happened to them? Why isn't she answering?*

Suddenly, my phone vibrated.

Incoming call from Squirrel Derwin.

"Don't you do that again! When I call, you answer!" I barked.

"She can't answer," I heard Wart wheeze. The man's voice gurgled, almost as if he had water in his mouth. "Nobody can answer anymore."

"What happened?!" I yelled. My head swam. *Not Squirrel!*

"The monsters. They broke into the train car. All the girls were dragged off, the guys were torn apart. I fought them off, but I'm not going to be able to hold out for long. Squirrel... I have her, too. She's breathing, but her chest is shattered. Legs are gone. She won't last long... I'm sorry, man. I did my best... But you only sent enough coins for one pistol..."

"Don't die—I can fix this!" I replied hurriedly. "You're going to get some money now. Go to the store, buy regeneration syringes. They'll completely regenerate you! You hear me? Don't die!"

"I... I..."

71

He coughed as the call dropped, and I sent my sister a hundred coins. That was enough to regenerate so long as Wart didn't pass out before he could use the syringes. *Damn it!*

If he pulled it off, they'd be out of it for eight hours. *No, not if. When he pulls it off. That's the only way. I'm not going to let some monsters kill my sister!*

I never would have thought that time could drag on the way it does when you're really waiting for something. It felt like I spent a few hours pacing the courtyard, but a glance at my watch told me that just around ten minutes had passed since the phone conversation. *No, this is no good, and I need to pass out, too.* And there was a good way to do that: attributes.

One more piece of bad news reared its head when I decided to get pistol shooting or rifle shooting to level three. I couldn't do that while my agility and stamina were as low as they were, and so I had to spend my points where I really didn't want to.

Rifle shooting +1 (2).
Stamina +1 (2).
Agility +1 (2).
Your body will need 3 hours to complete the change.

I wasn't out as long as usual, presumably

thanks to the injection of strength, but it still did a number on me. It was a good thing I'd had the sense to inject myself in a comfortable bed rather than outside. When I came to, I decided to leap out of bed to see if it had worked. Oh, how it had worked. At least, it wasn't exactly what I'd expected—instead of jumping up onto my feet, I flew upward, somersaulted in midair a few times, and slammed my face into the ground, just barely throwing out an arm to protect myself. Getting up, I went over to the door, though even that was a challenge. My movements were jerky, unnatural. Each step sent me hurtling upward. I had to shuffle out of the building.

There was no way I was going to be walking to the city. At that point, it was simpler for me to leap like some kind of kangaroo than stride off like a normal person, so I headed toward another garage to see if I could find myself a ride. And I did, fairly quickly, in the home of the arsenal owner. *I like this guy.*

New device detected.
Would you like to connect your Mytoy 1500 to your phone?

You bet! The enormous four-wheeled toy was the perfect option for the situation I found myself in. Maneuverable, fast, and all-terrain, it was great for going off-road, and it was even electric. The energy blocks from the game fit it perfectly, and just a couple minutes later, I was racing around the village at 40 kilometers an hour.

Once I'd had my fun, I decided to make some purchases. I was going to be hunting monsters, after all.

Optical sight. *Dynamic optical sight that fits all types of energy weapons. Automatically calibrates the distance to the target. Built-in night vision. Cost: 200 coins.*

BRO-I tactical equipment kit. *Tactical outfit made of ultrastrong material capable of withstanding a direct hit from level two monsters. Slots and pockets adjustable to fit the needs of the wearer. Waterproof boots. Can be restored when less than 20% damaged. Does not include BRO-I tactical helmet. Cost: 300 coins.*

I parted with the coins without a second of regret. Easy come, easy go, just a happy memory on the way. While the game was printing out my new clothes, I bought ten batteries, three portions of food, and five energy blocks for my weapons. All of that fit beautifully in the pockets. My feet snug in the boots, I felt like a new man. My pistol found its way into the holster, my rifle was slung over my back, and I wondered if I should buy the helmet. The only problem was that it cost 12,000 coins. *That's more expensive than the suit and rifle put together!*

I had just 66 coins left, but that was fine. Much more than that morning, I was looking like I belonged in the top hundred. But the happy smile on my face was replaced by a look of confusion when I pulled up the list of players in the location. *I'm in eighth place?* And all I'd done was pick up a few attribute points and some clothes.

Surprised by the progress I was making, I sat astride on the ATV, set my phone down in front of me, and sent the drone out ahead. It wasn't easy constantly looking down at the screen as I went, but it was still safer that way.

What were the chances of me getting myself into trouble knowing ahead of time what I was going to be coming up against? Minimal, I thought, but I somehow still pulled it off. The next half-hour was spent driving around cars stopped in the road like monuments to a former life. I had to come to a complete stop soon enough, however. The road was blocked by a fallen tree, and I couldn't even get around it on the shoulder. Feeling my new strength, I got off the ATV and headed toward the obstruction. That's when the attack came. A fire burst in my chest, almost as if something sharp and incredibly hot had been jabbed into me. The blow was so strong that I was thrown back into a ditch, my back plowing a trough in the ground. It was hard to breathe. There was an unpleasant hollow in my chest.

My protection kept the attack from penetrating, but it wasn't able to completely absorb the impact. Regeneration kicked in—my ribs crunched into place, eliciting an agonized scream. Blood bubbled out of my mouth.

"Is he dead?" an evil voice called.

"Go check," replied a second.

"You check! Did you see what he was wearing?"

"How about a grenade? That'll definitely finish him off."

The bright flash blinded me for a few seconds as a wave of shrapnel riddled my body. The chain around my neck heated up before disappearing—my whole supply of protection was gone. *Damn it!* I didn't even have my phone there, so I couldn't jump into the store.

"Ah-ha! Now he's definitely dead. I don't see any numbers. Okay, the ATV's mine! I shot the bastard, so I get the loot. Who's taking the picture?"

"You can tell Gray it's yours," the second snorted. "And you take the picture. Gray got mad at me last time, so I'm giving him a wide berth."

"Fine. Oh, wait, is that a drone? You're kidding!"

"Yeah! And Gray has everything for it, too."

Right then, I jumped to my feet. There were two people on the road, one holding the kind of enormous gun they use to shoot down low-flying tanks. As they were looking up at the drone, they had no chance to react to my sudden appearance.

They had no chance, but they somehow still pulled it off.

The red dot appeared right in the middle of the first fighter's head, and I pulled the trigger just as I was thrown backward, a huge chunk taken out of my shoulder. When I hit the ground, I rolled to avoid the next shot. It still hit my hip, but just barely. Still, it left behind a hole. Throwing out my hand, I summoned my phone and took a look at what was going on from up above. The bandit was crouching over his friend's body and howling.

"No, Pockmark, no! No-o-o! You bi-i-itch! I'm going to tear you to pieces, you bastard!"

That last part was directed at me. Minus twenty coins, plus a force field to protect against ten hits. A grenade came flying at me, and I hit the dirt. This guy was no monster; he knew how to kill people. I realized too late that I should've grabbed a few grenades for the road, too. I'd been figuring that the toughest opponents I'd come up against would be monsters, not even thinking about other people. And I'd been wrong.

Stone and sand sprayed right by my head. The bandit was shooting surprisingly well, to the point that it was like he could see me. He moved slowly, with soft, cat-like strides, not taking his eyes off where I was lying.

That was his downfall.

The electric ATV could accelerate all the way to

twenty or thirty kilometers an hour in a matter of seconds. It wasn't that heavy, but a hit to the back at that speed meant nothing good. And nothing good happened—with a curse, the bandit's body flew over my head and crashed into a tree. I bellowed, trying to ignore the pain from my wounds as I jumped up, knocked his weapon away, and introduced him to my fist. But my fingers just crunched against the force field that appeared to envelop the guy. My hand went numb, but my brain was faster than the pain. It gave the command, and I ripped the chain off the bandit's neck with my swelling hand. His eyes widened in surprise as I buried my forehead in his nose. His body went soft, telling me I'd knocked him out. Pulling myself to my feet, I looked down to see that I'd actually killed him—his skull was shattered. After a couple seconds of convulsions, he went still.

New mission: *Gray's gang*. Description: A gang of criminals was able to break out of prison and form up in the forest. They're terrorizing the safe zones and kidnapping survivors. Take care of them, making the area safe once again. Opponents left: 34.

I flopped down next to the body. As always, there were more questions than answers. What were those safe zones? How had the convicts managed to level-up, and where did they find weapons like that?

The next hour was spent partially regenerating. During that time, I checked out the universal food packets, which turned out to be full of a tasteless goo made of whatever humans need to survive and nothing more. I was really worried about the holes in my costume, but when I decided to examine my wounds, they were gone. The coat and pants were completely restored. The problem was the wounds themselves— the black dots moved too slowly, telling me where I needed to invest my next attribute points. Finally able to walk normally, I headed over to collect my trophies. There weren't many of them, unfortunately.

The two pictures got me 20 coins. But the phones were empty. I grabbed their rifle, not to mention their grenades, resolved not to trust humans again. Really, the necklace I'd torn off the one bandit was the only valuable loot there. Though I did notice something strange: the criminals were both... *Modified?* Their arms were a bit longer than usual, their foreheads both small. Their teeth were sharp. Their bodies were so hairy it looked like they'd gone overboard with testosterone. *What did they juice themselves with?* Sure, they had plenty of agility—they were faster, stronger, and more dangerous than normal people. But the problem was their appearance. I had the sudden urge to check myself out in a mirror. *What if I look like that? No, I don't want to.*

Judging by their tracks, the pair had hidden behind the fallen tree and come from somewhere on the right. I sent the drone soaring above the forest—there was a wisp of smoke trailing above the trees not far away. That could have been anyone, of course, but it was worth a closer look. After all, I had to agree with the game—there was no way I was going to leave opponents like that behind me. The forest had to be cleared.

Riding the ATV a couple hundred meters in, I stopped and threw some spruce branches over it to make sure it wouldn't get stolen while I was otherwise occupied. Then I moved on, keeping the drone behind me and using it to keep my bearings. A half-hour later, I came across an enormous clearing. The pain in my leg and shoulder was brutal. All I could think about was a painkiller, though that thought left my mind as soon as I saw the clearing.

The central figure occupying the picture was a gloriously branched oak tree. I'd always figured trees like that didn't occur in nature, that they were chopped down immediately, but no, there was one right there. And the bandits had set up camp under its crown. They all had tents, and I had the great idea to take one with me. But after scoping in on the camp, I growled quietly. There were cages around the base of the tree. Most of them were empty, though there were two bound women in one.

Once I'd taken up my position, I had to get a picture of the oak. It really looked incredible, the kind of thing you want to remember. I'd figured out where the picture gallery was in my phone. And just as I suspected, the only pictures it saved were the ones that didn't get me anything.

You took a picture of a cache. 10 coins received.

Damn it! Suddenly, I understood why the bastards had such an advantage over everyone. They absolutely had to be taken out. I'd read about caches on the prerelease forums, though I hadn't found one myself. The game randomly generated chests in hard-to-reach places. If you found one, you got a nice reward. Players could only pick up a reward once each, though the cache stayed available to everyone else. And that's why they were dragging people there—the latter got the reward, and the bandits took it away from them.

I flew the drone in closer to get a better look at the field. And there were my first customers, a few bodies at the edge of the field. They were going to die first. Sighting in on them, I growled again when I saw that it was a thug raping a woman. She showed no signs of life, her head just wobbling in time to his thrusts. The scope measured the distance. A 100%

appeared right on the bastard's head. I was about to pull the trigger, but I was stopped by motion in the corner of my eye. The branches parted, and ten superior monsters walked over with a champion at their head. And while the superiors were the same as the ones I'd seen in the village, the champion was far different from the one I'd killed. It looked like a giant, overgrown gorilla fed a diet of nothing but steroids. There were spiked metal plates covering its body.

I grunted nastily—that was even better. *Let the monsters take out the bandits, and I'll clean up whoever's left.* The champion roared, slammed a fist against its chest a few times, and went down on all fours. Checking my sights, I was stunned to see that the thug was still going at it with the woman. *Looking for a good send-off, I guess.*

I could practically see the blood spraying from the shredded rapist, but the gorilla just dashed off toward the tree, ignoring him completely. Its entourage followed. *Wait, what...?* Some guy stepped out of a tent, and that's when everything completely stopped making sense. It wasn't a person. No, it was something hairy, enormous, heavily muscled, and big-eared. His bare torso rippled with strength. There was a force field necklace hanging around his neck, too, only with a blue gem. Mine was red. *The upgraded version, I guess.*

The champion ran over to the camp and stopped. The two hairy creatures stared each other down, and I would have been hard-pressed to say that the champion was the bigger of the two. What happened next was the strangest thing I'd seen so far: negotiations. The gorilla barked something, and Gray (he certainly looked like the head criminal) shook his head. The champion pounded the ground in rage; the bandit was unmoved. Snarling, the gorilla called over one of the superior monsters and dug a paw into the bag attached to its side. Metal flashed, and it was only then that Gray nodded, pointing at the cage with the bound women. With a howl, the monsters dashed over to pull the women out, throw them over their backs, and head off somewhere.

Unbelievable! Gray had managed to come to an agreement with the creatures, and he was over there trading slaves. The gorilla pointed over at the pair at the edge of the clearing. With a guffaw, the bandit nodded, and another of the superior monsters went over to the rapist and pulled him off his victim. There was an indignant cry, but nobody paid any attention— the woman was already being carried off into the forest. Another metal object found its way into Gray's hands.

The champion roared its satisfaction and beat a retreat in the same direction they'd carried the three women off in.

My phone buzzed to remind me about what I was supposed to do.

What's scarier than death? updated. You found out that a group of non-humans is slave-trading, giving the monsters live players in exchange for supplies.

***

You took a picture of a live champion. 20 coins received.

My joy at picking up the coins was dampened considerably by the first message. *A group of non-humans? Those animals aren't from our world? Damn it! Why is the game so negative all the time? Where are the superheroes with their laser vision? Where are the pink ponies pooping out thermonuclear bombs?*

The gang whooped as they gathered around to see what they'd gotten in the trade. A lot of them looked similar to Gray, though there were others who looked more like people, similar to the pair that had ambushed me. I sent the drone after the monsters. *Where are they taking the women? And why?* But seven kilometers later, at the edge of the drone's range, the creatures still hadn't changed direction. They were going in a straight line interrupted only by large obstacles. I sent the drone skyward and noticed a column of smoke on the horizon. The monsters were clearly heading in that direction.

There were two hours left before Squirrel and Wart revived if they were going to revive at all. And that was just enough time to take care of the creatures in front of me. Whoever they were, there was no place for them on Earth—we had our own to take care of. Sighting down the barrel, I was happy to see that they were all gathered in one place. I opened fire.

It was like time stopped. The rifle was deadly— my first shot turned Gray's face into a bloody mess, the bullet having ignored his physical and energy armor. From there, it was like back at the shooting range. I scoped in on one after another, spending less than a second on each shot. The criminals took too long to realize what was going on. By the time they all dropped to the ground, ten of the thirty were not going to be getting back up. I sent the drone in closer to see what was going on, keeping up my fire in the meantime. Even when I couldn't see my targets, the percentages told me how much damage I could score. *That's how they got me back at the road. Good to know.* I shattered heads through stones, roots, and even their supposedly strong defenses. I was an executioner there to punish them for their wrongdoing. And even if they'd been people, they still would have been monsters in human form to me. Our world needed to be rid of them.

Gray's gang complete, all opponents killed, Aspen Safe Zone officially confirmed in the registry.

New title: Bandit Bane.
Would you like to collect your reward?
Level +1 (4).

I glared sullenly at the message. There was no enjoying my victory—all I could think was that I could have saved the three women if I'd gone after the champion and its entourage. But I hadn't, they'd gotten away, and the women were quite possibly no longer in the land of the living.

Chapter 6

STANDING UP, I limped over to the bodies. I'd gotten an attribute syringe for taking out the gang, which was great for the future but less than ideal for the present. What I'd been hoping to get was something on par with the rifle. The game apparently calculated victory difficulties and gave you the reward you deserved— gunning down the gang hadn't been that much of a challenge.

You took the second picture of 34 dead players. 0 coins received.

My body reacted faster than my brain could wrap itself around what I'd just read. By the time I finished the message, I was prostrate on the ground and crawling over to a small ditch. Shoving the body of a bandit out of the way, I laid down in it.

The move made sense—someone had just stolen 340 coins from me. And they might have been smart enough to shoot at me with something dangerous.

"Hey, man, I'm over here! Help!" someone shouted. I aimed the drone in that direction and noticed yet another cage, that one occupied by a bound man with a phone in his hand. He looked to be around thirty. And judging by his bruised and swollen face, he'd never heard of regeneration.

"Who are you?" I yelled back at him.

"Just help me already!" he called, anger creeping into his voice. "What the hell are you waiting for? They took them away! I have to catch them!"

Peeking out of the ditch, I looked around. The bound character was perfectly capable of taking a picture, but I still dove back into my hiding place. Who said it was him?

"Were you the one who took the picture of the gang?"

"Are you kidding me? Get me out of here!" The guy started jerking around, and I stopped paying attention to him. I needed to find the person who had stolen my loot. Apparently, the prisoner realized that, too. "Me, it was me who took the picture! Are you happy? Get me out of here!"

A couple minutes later, I was forced to admit that there wasn't anyone else in the clearing. I went over to the cage, and the battered man looking up at me angrily.

"You stole my coins," I stated evenly.

"What, is taking pictures against your religion or

something? There are the bodies. What are you waiting for?"

"You only get coins for the first picture. And you took it."

"So what? Yes, I did. And I'd do it again if I could—I have to get the girls back. Damn it, are you going to untie me or just stand there like an idiot? What are you doing?! Stop it!"

He screamed the last two phrases at me, wrenching against the ropes holding him back. Instead of running over with open arms to untie him, I stepped into the cage and took his phone.

Player Valdemar Kurkin. Status: Active, level 1. Cash: 340 coins.

"That's my loot," I replied, transferring the coins to my account. He howled and threw himself around hysterically. Judging by what I could make out, he was going to make life hell for me as soon as he got free.

I kind of wanted to see what he could do. Valdemar was bigger than me, though I didn't imagine he was as strong. And so, I cut his bonds and stepped back. That was what he'd been waiting for. Leaping to his feet, he threw himself at me in a headlong attack. But that wasn't going to cut it. Without me needing to react in the least, Valdemar bounced off me and fell spread-eagle at the bottom of the cage. All I felt was a twinge in my bad shoulder.

"Take a picture of the tree—that'll get you ten coins."

I tossed his phone back to him and headed over to Gray's body. Valdemar didn't represent a threat, so I didn't care what he did.

Player Baralin Caracas (Gray). Status: Dead. Cash: 1224 coins.

I spent a few minutes staring at the thug's phone in an attempt to remember where I'd seen that name before. Finally, it hit me, and I pulled up the playing ranking. *Of course!* There had been a level 18 player named Baralin at the top, but he was gone. It suddenly made sense how the bastard had climbed so high that quickly—he'd been working with the monsters. That shed a new light on everyone else in the ranking. I was right there in seventh place, and the players in front of me were between levels 14 and 17. *Who are they? Cut from the same cloth as Gray? And what are they even doing in our world?*

"Hey, man, give me the coins back." Valdemar had gotten to his feet and was heading toward me unsteadily. "I need to head after those girls."

"Who are they to you?" I asked, giving him a light shove that sent him tumbling to the ground.

Valdemar thought for a while before replying.

"My wife and sister. We were out hiking when it started, and then those bastards took us," he said finally with a nod in the direction of the bodies. "They raped the girls, and then they handed them off to the monsters. I can't let them be eaten."

"And how are you planning on killing the champion?" Seeing the confusion on his face, I continued. "The gorilla that took the girls. Regular weapons won't do anything against it, and all 300 coins will get you is a wimpy pistol. You won't be able to take a champion out with it."

"I'll think of something," Valdemar replied with fanatical confidence. "If I can't free them, I'll at least kill them myself, so they aren't eaten alive."

"I don't want to make this any worse for you, but the monsters don't eat women." I looked the man in the eye and saw nothing but otherworldly pain. He'd figured that out long before, he just hadn't been able to admit it to himself. "They're doing something much worse with them."

Valdemar's cheeks quivered, though he maintained control. Suddenly, I felt myself respecting the guy. He had a goal the same way I did, and he was ready to wade in against the world armed with nothing but his fists if need be. It's better to die fighting than to live holed up in a cave.

"They didn't kill them right away, so there's a chance they're still alive," I said against my better instincts. "But you can't fight a larva with your bare hands. We need to get ready."

"We?"

"You're not the only one feeling the way you do. My sister's stuck in the city, down in the metro. The only difference is that she has someone helping her, and your girls don't. You don't count. And neither do I. There are some things we need to do to get ready."

Valdemar's face darkened.

"How long are you planning on that taking? A day, two days, a week? What do you think they'll do to them in that time? They may not live that long."

"Perhaps not," I replied. There was no sense contradicting logic that was entirely sound. "But if they don't, we can't help them. We can, however, get revenge on the bastards who killed them. Are you with me?"

"What are you thinking?" The doubt in his voice didn't escape me.

"I want to collect all the loot and get to the safe zone. There's a village called Aspen around here somewhere."

"Yes, I know where it is—we went through it. It's in that direction."

"In that case, give me a hand. Grab anything that looks like it could be of use. Oh, and yeah, take a picture of the oak."

Just as I'd suspected, all the bandits' coins were

on Gray's phone. The neckless with the blue gem offered protecting from up to fifty critical hits and was worth a hundred coins, judging by the description. I slipped it on and handed mine to Valdemar—I didn't want to accidentally lose an ally. The metal plates protecting the gang leader's body, on the other hand, turned out to be fused to his body. No matter how hard I tried, the best I could do was rip one out along with a chunk of flesh. But the plate instantly disintegrated in my hands. *Damn it...*

I didn't recognize the device the champion had traded for the girls. The description didn't help, either:

Calcium rinesc. *Improves mantorak twitch by 10%. Cost: 200 coins.*

What is that? It could have been a super-sophisticated death machine, or it could have been a blender for all I knew. Collecting all the weapons in a single pile, I sighed unhappily—not a single game item. The bandits had only used regular weapons. But that was when Valdemar shouted happily and waved me over. He'd found a chest in one of the tents full of treasure: a pile of metal objects. Again, there were quite a few strange descriptions, but one thing caught my eye:

Drone modifier. Extender I. *Description:*

Universal device that can be applied to all drone types. Lets you integrate up to four game devices. Cost: 12,000 coins.

I brought the drone down to earth and stuck the extender on it without much thought. My phone started blinking again:

Enter a name.

A name? Um... Mark-1? Sure, let's just go with Mark-1. No sense making it harder than it has to be.

Name set.
Player Mark Derwin now owns the drone Mark-1.
You're the first player in this location to get a flying game device.
Reward: free attribute point.

The syringe appeared in my hand. Although, to be fair, I had no idea what had just happened. *Why is the game so happy that it gave me such a generous reward?* Valdemar handed me something else.

"Here, Mark. It looks like this is for the drone, too."

Modifier for Mark 1. Cartographer 1.

Description: Transforms the drone video into a two-dimensional map. Cost: 400 coins.

***

Local map functionality unlocked.
Synchronized with Mark-1.

The drone shot up into the sky, and I smiled like a happy child—the kind of local map I recognized from my old life spread out below in the viewfinder. *God, how I missed maps and GPS.* Sadly, no old data had been saved, though I at least knew where I was. The phone showed me as a small triangle. But most importantly, I was able to record the coordinates of the cache and send them to anyone who had the money and desire to make the trek into the forest.

I didn't find anything else intelligible among the game items. It hit me that they were probably suited to Gray and his people—they weren't humans, and they probably knew what to do with them. *But you can keep those body plates.* I wouldn't have wanted anything I couldn't take off.

"Have you opened the cache?" I asked Valdemar, who shook his head. "Okay, let's go. Hopefully, there will be something good in there."

We had to climb the tree, which was a challenge with my damaged shoulder. But I pulled it off and hauled Valdemar up behind me. We sat there staring at the gleaming box.

"You first," I said. He nodded, opened the lid, and froze. Swallowing hard, he pulled out a BRO-I outfit with shaking hands. It was the same as the one I was wearing, also sans helmet. He tossed a wary look in my direction, worried I'd try to take his loot, and put it on as he tapped away at his phone.

Then it was my turn to feel my face freeze. Not only was there a small item in the cache; my phone told me about some new changes:

You found a cache.
Level +1 (5).

"What are you going to level-up?" I asked casually as I pulled out the clearly expensive item with the odd description.

Phone modifier. Camera zoom-1. *Description: Phone modifier. Lets you take pictures from 10 meters farther away. Cost: 1,500 coins.*

The device had barely touched my phone when it melted away. Both cameras transformed, bulging away slightly from the phone's body. Turning the lens toward Valdemar, I zoomed in. Yes, it worked beautifully. There was no shaking, no loss in quality. *But what's the point?* And at that price...

"Strength," the man said as a syringe appeared

in his head. "I need to be stronger so I can help the girls."

And before I could stop him, the idiot plunged the needle into his shoulder. I roared in frustration—the first modification took eight hours, and what was I supposed to do that whole time? I couldn't leave him alone.

The only thing I could do was ease Valdemar down to the ground and go get my ATV. It looked like I was going to be spending the night in one of the tents. But as I loaded all the loot onto my transportation and tried to make it fit, I noticed a strange glow. Some items turned radiant when they were held close to the ATV. Deciding to experiment, I moved one around, watching how brightly it glowed to see where it was supposed to go on the vehicle.

Enter a name.

Interesting! I already have Mark-1, so I guess I'll go with Mark-2. Simple and easy.

Name set.

Player Mark Derwin now owns the ATV Mark-2.

You're the first player in this location to get a modified game transport.

Reward: free attribute point.

One syringe later and twelve items down, all attached to different parts of the ATV, my Mark-2 was looking completely different. It had a second seat, powerful springs, bumpers, a gun emplacement, and even a top speed of 90 kilometers an hour. It was the kind of machine you could ride up to a club.

I was overjoyed to see my screen light up with an incoming call. Judging by the display, it was my sister. *It worked!*

"Welcome back to the land of the living!" I said happily, though there was no answer. The smile disappeared from my face. "Squirrel? Are you okay?"

My sister sobbed in the background, and I heard Wart's voice.

"Enough with the games, Mark. If you want your sister back whole and in one piece, you're going to have to pay. And not the pittance you've been sending over."

"Wart, what's the matter?" I asked with a frown.

"You still don't get it? Okay, let me explain. When you're a hair's breadth away from death, you start seeing a lot of things differently. There's no way I'm going to die just because I have to haul your kid sister around with me. She's a liability, to the point where she could mean the end for me. And with that in mind, you're going to make sure she isn't a liability. You hear me?"

"Oh, I hear you," I replied, my voice lowered. "If

you do anything to her, I'll—"

"You'll what?" Wart interrupted, laughing unpleasantly. People in their right minds didn't laugh like that. "You'll come punish me? Go ahead, make my day! We're a hundred meters underground, there are monsters all around us, and you think you can get to me. I'm the only one who can get us out of here! So, shut up and listen to me. Nothing will happen to your little sister so long as you do what I tell you to do."

"What do you want?" I asked after a pause.

"That's better. It's time to help, and not just with the scraps you've been throwing us. You're going to send me 1,000 coins every day from now on. Got it? If I don't get them, I'll hand Squirrel off to the monsters, and you'll never find her again. You have three hours to send me the first payment. If I don't get it, your sister is gone. Oh, and I'll make sure I have some fun with her before I get rid of her."

"You're a dead man," I hissed angrily. The blood was pounding in my temples, and my head was heavy. "You're a walking dead man off your rocker."

"Three hours, Mark," Wart giggled, happy with the result he'd gotten. "Let's see how much you care about your sister. Little, juicy..."

The call dropped, and I screamed in rage and pain. *You bitch! Why?! Why couldn't you just be normal about it?!*

The trunk of the oak was right next to me, and I

buried my fist in it as hard as I could. Bones crunched; I felt nothing. Turning my body, I slammed my other fist home. Again, a crunch, though that time I felt it, more in my shoulder than in my hand. But that didn't stop me. Another turn, another blow. My fist was flattened, and tears flew from my eyes. Another hit. Another. Another...

I turned my fists into bloody messes. And it was only when my head started to spin from the loss of blood that I fell to my knees and burst into tears. I hate it when you can't do anything about what's happening to you and the ones you care about, when bastards like Wart are dictating their own rules.

The emotions passed, leaving nothing but pain behind them. I even started to regret what I'd done. Howling in frustration and smearing blood all over my phone, I sent Squirrel a thousand coins. That was enough to keep her safe for twenty-four hours. Wart wouldn't do anything to her as long as he could keep milking me, after all, and I made up my mind to demand that he let me talk with her the next day. Otherwise, I wasn't going to send him any more coins.

Having made up my mind, I grabbed a syringe and thrust it into my leg. If I wanted to save my sister, I was going to need to be stronger. Much stronger than I was right then.

Pistol shooting +1 (3).

Rifle shooting +1 (3).

Regeneration +3 (5).

Your body will need 3 hours to complete the change.

When I woke up, my wounds had completely healed—my shoulder, my hip, my long-suffering hands, all of me. I wiped the blood from my phone's screen and pulled up my attributes.

Status table			
Name	Mark Derwin		
Coins	640	Level	5
Titles and ranks			
Bandit Bane			
Attributes			
Strength	2	Regeneration	5
Stamina	2		
Agility	2		
Skills			
Pistol shooting			3
Rifle shooting			3

I decided to check out the difference in my rifle shooting immediately. Glancing over at the motionless Valdemar, the thought crossed my mind that he was perfect for the test. And no sooner had I thought that than my hand jerked all on its own. My pistol appeared in it, and it took quite a bit of willpower to keep from shooting. My body was doing the work for me—the process of shooting took almost no time at all. Looking over at the trunk of the oak tree, I decided that it would stand in as my opponent. Again, my hands kicked into action. Five shots hit exactly where I was looking. I didn't even have to aim, as my body took care of everything. *Fantastic!*

It was about the same with the rifle, just for targets farther away. The trees on the edge of the clearing had a rough go of it—my barrel swung from side to side, I shot with the speed of an automatic weapon, and the trigger fluttered feverishly. And I could see perfectly well that not a single burst of energy missed its target. Sure, it was a waste, but I needed to see how my new abilities worked. The only problem was that I was going to have to get all my other attributes to three before I could try out level four for my shooting.

I dragged the groaning Valdemar over to the second seat and made sure he wouldn't fall off, packed up all the equipment I wasn't able to use, and headed off after the drone. It even mapped out the area—Aspen was a bright red spot. I needed to dump Valdemar in the safe zone and make a beeline for the city. *Sorry, buddy, but you're going to have to take care of your problems on your own. You're not the only one with a sister.*

Chapter 7

I DIDN'T LIKE ASPEN from the minute I saw it. And it wasn't the uneven stockade made of prickly bushes with branches that looked like they were alive. It wasn't the massive gate blocking the path, not even the odd machineguns atop it. It wasn't that the asphalt road gave way to a sandy track just a couple meters from the gate. And it wasn't the dozen towers situated around the perimeter of the settlement. I didn't like the people there. Aspen wasn't populated by humans—the locals were the same kind of hairy beasts as Gray and his gang.

When I rode up, the gates opened welcomingly, and my phone lit up from its position set in the ATV's dashboard. The message told me I was in a safe zone and didn't have to worry about monster attacks. There weren't many buildings, just around a dozen. And there were fewer locals—the guard at the gate, a couple people sticking curious heads out of windows, and a statuesque gentleman who greeted us in front of the largest building. He was an exact copy of Gray. Hairy and reminiscent of a mutant gorilla.

"Welcome to Aspen, traveler," he said in a singsong voice. "You and your companion can find shelter here. If you don't mind, let me show you to your rooms—as the first visitors to the village, they're free for you."

He spoke strangely, almost as if it wasn't his native language. It came out a bit pompous, too. Regular people didn't talk that way.

"He'll need a room," I said, pointing at Valdemar. "I'm heading out."

"Please, Mark, Bandit Bane, stay for a couple hours, at least. We'll get you some food and a chance to rest, and we can even discuss buying the pile of goods I see loaded on your Mark-2. Believe me, our conversation will benefit us both."

My stomach grumbled treasonously at the mention of food. In all the commotion, I'd forgotten that I needed to eat, and the mess of amino acids wasn't that appealing.

"A couple hours," I said, giving in and sliding off the ATV. A few of the hairy characters stepped out of the hotel and carried Valdemar inside.

"I'm Olson, owner of the hotel," the statuesque gentleman said. "Pick any room and get yourself cleaned up. When you're ready, we'll talk."

Honestly, I needed it. I was starting to stink. The hot water and enormous bath were perfect, and I was done in completely when they brought me a foamy drink that tasted better than anything I'd ever tried. For the first time since the game had started, I forgot about my problems.

Two hours had passed by the time I came back downstairs, drawn by the delicious smell of roasting meat. I didn't really want to crawl into my dirty, sweaty tactical outfit after my bath, but the game had a pleasant surprise for me. The suit smelled fresh and clean. A universal self-cleaning system was apparently built in.

Olson was waiting for me in the main dining area, where he was playing lazily with the dish in front of him. Gesturing for me to join him, he asked the staff to bring some food. For the next ten minutes, I was lost to the world around me.

"I always enjoy watching hungry people eat," Olson said with a smile when I sat back in my chair. "Are you ready to talk, or do you need more time?"

"Let's jump right in—no need to beat around the bush. I'm in a hurry."

"Okay, jump right in it is." Olson turned serious. "I want to hire you to handle a few missions. You can't make it into the city yet—you're too weak for that. I know about your problem. You have to pay a thousand coins every day, and my missions will help you earn that money while you're getting stronger. In a week's time, you'll be able to survive in the city. Help me, and

I'll help you. What do you say?"

"Who are you?" The relaxed mood was gone. My pistol appeared in my hand, pointing itself at the hairy character. But he didn't even twitch.

"I'm Olson, owner of the hotel," came his simple reply. "I belong to the Shurvan race, though you may know us better as NPCs. Non-player characters. The ones who are here just to do what we were programmed to do. My job is to own the hotel and develop the village, which is exactly what I need you for. There are a lot of things in this area that are keeping us from doing our jobs. And I know everything the game knows about you since I'm part of the game. Does that work for you?"

"What makes you think I won't make it to the city? Are you going to stop me?"

"Nobody's going to stop you. You'll just get eaten on the way. Squirrel Derwin is currently in the metro, a relatively safe area, and she and her companion can survive there if you keep them supplied with coins. Up on the surface, there are barely any people left. Just the changed. You made your cities too big, and it's time to pay the piper."

I didn't understand that last sentence, so Olson explained.

"To go from an inferior monster to a superior, you have to eat one person. For a superior monster to become a champion, you need a hundred victims. Ten thousand bodies later, you have a larva that can control vast swathes of territory. How many larvae do you think there are in a city with thirty million people living in and around it? I'm afraid we're just hours away from a general appearing, and you can forget about the city when that happens. You can forget about everyone living within fifty kilometers of it, too. If you head in that direction, you'll die before you're ever able to help your sister. I don't want to push you, which is why I'd like to offer this option: one of my missions is closer to the city, so it'll give you a chance to go see everything for yourself. You'll see what your world has become. Then you'll come back here and get to work on yourself. Do you want to get rid of all that junk I saw on your Mark-2? You helped the village earn its official status, so I'll give you my best price— 70% of the value. And remember that I'll always buy anything you can't use yourself."

"You don't strike me as an NPC. You can think for yourself."

"Still, it's true. I belong to this village, this hotel. When the safe zone disappears, so will I. That's the fate that awaits all worlds that can't beat the game."

"Beat the game? So, there's an end?" I asked in surprise.

"Of course. You can't have a game without a way to win, though nobody knows what the end is like. My world lasted half a year before it disappeared. And now

I'm here, on Earth, doing my job. When you lose, and you will lose, you'll also become a function. Something like the bandits you destroyed. That's the fate that awaits all players—the game doesn't like wasting resources. And with that, you're out of questions. I told you everything I was supposed to, so now you have to choose. Do you want to get rid of the junk I saw on your Mark-2?"

Olson had already mentioned that. He really was behaving like a program—well-written and highly advanced, but a program with a built-in set of responses, nonetheless.

I couldn't get him to talk after that. He ignored my questions, just offering to buy my junk. Finally, I agreed, as I really didn't know what else to do with it. And adding a hefty 2,393 coins to my account was definitely a plus. That bought Squirrel two days, just enough time for me to find her. Needless to say, I was skeptical about the monsters Olson had mentioned in the city, unwilling to believe him until I saw them with my own two eyes.

"What's your mission about?" I asked as I was getting ready to leave.

"Nothing too difficult for a player with level five regeneration. There's a nuclear power plant ten kilometers from here, and a few champions are over there destroying the reactor with their retinues. There's already a radiation leak. I'm afraid the beasts don't know there could be an explosion, and my function can't let that happen. I need you to deal with the monsters and neutralize the leak—you have to toss this item into the active area."

I stared at Olson in shock as he held out a small metal sphere. As a student in the physics and mathematics department at my university, I knew very well how reactors work, and I could imagine what would happen to the person who tried to "neutralize the leak" with their bare hands. Olson could tell what I was thinking.

"Again, there's nothing impossible in the mission for a player with level five regeneration. You'll be fine. Believe me, there aren't enough players at your level to risk throwing one of them away."

"I'm not doing that," I replied firmly, though a message appeared on my screen regardless:

New mission: *Shut down the reactor.* *Description: Take out the monsters destroying the nuclear reactor and liquidate the leak of radioactive fuel (place the blocker in the active zone). Opponents left: 3 champions, 182 superior monsters.*

"Nobody's going to make you do anything." Olson still foisted the blocker off on me. "But if you decide to take my offer and then get more missions, you'll have to... What is that?"

A strange expression flashed across the hotel owner's face. I felt a powerful shock and slowly turned in the direction Olson was looking. Swallowing and wishing I were wrong, I saw something I recognized all too well on the horizon. The familiar mushroom cloud of a nuclear explosion. And it was right where the city was. A silence fell over Aspen. Not a minute later, the remains of the blast hit us. I was afraid the electronics in the drone and ATV would be fried, but everything turned out fine—the game protected its devices, my phone included. Olson glanced over at me oddly and began speaking with respect in his voice.

"You humans are strange creatures. Perhaps, you'll be able to hold out longer than other races—I've never heard of anyone else prepared to sacrifice their own. Forty-four explosions around the planet... All cities with more than a million people living in them reduced to ruins. Mark, I'm afraid you're going to have to change your plans. The city is gone."

I wanted to howl, but an emptiness inside me held me back. It sucked in all my emotions, ripping me away from reality. What was there left if everything I'd been fighting for was gone?

It was a while before I did anything about my vibrating phone. There was nothing I wanted to read less than information about another mission or something else like that. But the device wouldn't leave me alone. About to toss it away in a fit of anger, the screen caught my eye at the last second.

Incoming call from Squirrel Derwin.

My hands shook, and I just about missed the *Accept* button.

"Mark," came my sister's barely audible voice. "Mark, it's you..."

"Where are you? Are you okay? Where's Wart?" I rattled off.

"I just called... I was able to... I'm sorry... Goodbye, Mark..."

Squirrel fell silent, only her heavy breathing telling me that she was still alive.

"Squirrel, what's going on? Squirrel?! Answer me! Don't you even think about leaving me!"

"I can help," Olson said suddenly. I could barely keep from pouncing on him and driving his head into the ground. He was part of the game, and I wanted to destroy everything that had anything to do with it.

"Just a thousand coins, and you'll get Squirrel Derwin's current status. Her condition, her injuries, and an analysis of her surroundings. Do you agree?"

"Yes!" I shot back. My phone dinged, and disappointing news flashed on the screen. Squirrel was buried under debris somewhere in the depths of the metro with enough oxygen to last another hour. She'd only survived thanks to a force field, though it wasn't enough to block the radiation. My sister had taken a dose large enough that she had just a 10% chance of living long enough to die when her oxygen ran out. It was a matter of minutes.

"Can we save her?" I asked Olson, looking at him hopefully. In that moment, I would have made a pact with the devil himself if it meant saving my sister. The game character thought for a moment before nodding.

"She can deploy an autonomous life-support module, give herself a regeneration shot, and wait for you to arrive. It's just that..."

"What?" I shouted as soon as Olson fell silent. "Out with it!"

"Autonomous modules cost 50,000 coins. Neither of you have that much money."

"You need a player for your function. Save Squirrel, and I'll handle all your damn missions!" I said, hearing the gurgling coming from the other end of the line. Squirrel's time was running out.

"I can give you a loan, but you'll have to repay 100,000 coins. And if you die before you pay it off or can't pay it off within a year, your sister will die, and you'll be my slave when you respawn. If you agree, I'll need your consent to control your sister remotely. The game only permits that in extreme cases, and only when the person being controlled is unconscious. Squirrel can't do anything for herself anymore."

"It's a deal," I said hurriedly. Olson held out his hand for my phone. After tapping away at the screen, he spoke into it with an icy voice.

"Squirrel Derwin, I'm informing you that with the consent of your brother I am temporarily taking control of your arm. Don't resist."

The wheezing coming from the speaker turned into groans, which gave way to howls. My sister was in so much pain that it even broke through her unconsciousness. Something metallic scraped, I heard rocks falling, and Olson handed me the phone. The call dropped.

"The restoration will take eight hours, after which she will be put into a medically induced coma. Once a day, she'll be woken so you can talk. The module is thirty meters underground with enough resources to last a year. And now, Mark, Bandit Bane, you have things to do. The monsters are at the nuclear plant. Take care of that mission, and then come back for the next one. You have quite a bit of work ahead of you."

Olson headed into the hotel, leaving me alone with my thoughts. I couldn't get that mushroom cloud out of my mind—the military wasn't willing to hand Earth to the monsters, and they were prepared to annihilate their own people to keep that from happening. And the worst part was that I agreed with them. We had to stop the animals. All of them.

Including Olson. *I'll take care of him later, once I pay off my debt.*

I checked my phone. Needless to say, it knew about the changes.

You took out a loan in the amount of 50,000 coins at a 100% annual interest rate. You need to repay 100,000 coins within 365 days.

The nuclear plant was in for an unpleasant surprise. I found a fairly comfortable position in a tall tree with a view of most of the area, though I froze when I scoped in on the closest monster. The red dot was right between its eyes, but the game just gave me a value of 50% potential damage. I scanned the creature's body. Only one other area gave me 50%: its heart. Other than that, it didn't get any higher than 10%. And that was strange—I wouldn't have missed news about another monster upgrade. But the beasts were clearly stronger than the usual ones I'd been up against. *Could it be because they're close to the radiation?*

I had to wait a few minutes until some of the monsters moved on about their business before I was ready to risk it. Aiming for the head, I pulled the trigger twice. There wasn't even time for the monster to squeal—its body dropped lifelessly to the ground. But I didn't notice, as I had already moved on to the next target. My upgraded agility and level three rifle shooting worked wonders; the monsters dropped like flies. It was like shooting fish in a barrel. After taking out the last superior, I sent the drone in. There weren't any of the creatures left on that level. I was going to have to lure them—

A sharp pain shot through my body, and I felt myself fall into a fit of convulsions. Clutching a branch, I lost touch with the world around me for a few moments. The only thought in my head was how completely and utterly painful it was. My chest was pinched, my temples felt like they were about to explode, and suddenly everything was over. A noisy exhale, a release of my cramping fingers, and I dropped toward the ground. Landing hit me hard, but I didn't lose consciousness. It felt sharpened, actually. I was able to notice a movement off to the side, and I strained my tendons to leap in the other direction. A thick bolt of lightning slammed into the ground right where I had just been. It just barely caught me, and another tremor ran through my body. My heart quivered a plea to stop tormenting it. The thought crossing my mind that I couldn't stay in one place, I jumped behind the tree. That kept me safe from my opponent, who I was finally able to catch a glimpse of.

A champion. This one was humanoid, walking upright with both arms and looking something like Gray. It was just bigger and scarier. Yet another lightning bolt was forming between its hands. It hit me that having mages in the game wrecked the balance, though that thought only occurred to me in midair. I was already off performing an evasive somersault. The ground behind me exploded, and I whipped out my pistol. *Good thing I got it up to level three!* I didn't even have to aim—a couple of charges hit the champion right between the eyes. Sadly, they didn't make a difference. The humanoid's defenses held up.

And the pistol itself wasn't long-lived. From the side, a direction I wasn't paying attention to, a fireball came flying at me. Yes, the same kind of fireball you read about in fantasy novels. Pain exploded in my arm, nothing but ash and memory left of my right hand. I howled and flipped backward. Another fireball and a bolt of lightning flew backward, and I saw my second opponent, an exact copy of the first mage. *Two damn champions! How?! I was going to kill you one at a time and at range!*

The only thing I could do was beat a heroic retreat. The champions looked too big to run quickly, so I dashed off as fast as I could, trying to put as many trees between us as possible. Dodging back and forth to make it hard to aim, I was able to avoid any more hits for a little while. The fireballs and bolts of lightning flew by on either side. In fact, I was starting to think that I was going to get away, though it hit me that I'd managed in just one battle to lose everything

I'd worked so hard to gain. At the edge of the forest were my Mark-2, rifle, and inflated ego. In front of me appeared a deep ravine, and I slowed to think about what I should do. That was a devastating mistake—a second later, a fireball smashed into my back, throwing me forward over the edge of the ravine. Branches flew by, there was a moment of weightlessness, I heard a dull impact, and the pandemonium around me suddenly came to a halt as I smashed into the ground. It was incredibly hard to breathe, but I maintained consciousness. I squinted with difficulty. Wanting to curse, I couldn't—there was a gaping hole seared through my chest. My body started working on its own, summoning my phone, logging into the store, buying a regeneration syringe, sticking myself with it. That all took less than five seconds. And it was a good thing my arm could still move, as I couldn't feel the rest of my body.

Small rocks and branches rained down on me as the champions started down the ravine. I fell into a panic knowing that I was about to pass out and become easy prey. My chest yearned to take a breath, but it was so hard. Only the traces of oxygen kept hold of my conscious. I threw my hand out and grabbed a root. Pulling myself toward it, I did my best to crawl away from the mages. *Sure, they're going to find me. There's no question about that.* But without the ability to fight back, I was going to at least make it as hard for them as I could. If they wanted to kill me, they'd have to climb down to where I was.

Another fireball flashed by. Burning branches dropped onto me. My body, however, didn't even react to the new burns—it was beyond feeling anything. I pulled myself forward a few more times using branches and roots until my hand grasped at nothingness. *A hole, damn it!* Lightning flashed after the fireball. It shook me, but not too badly. A nearby tree took the brunt of the blow. With a creak, it started to topple over. The champions couldn't see me, though they could sense that I was still alive. That was why they were taking pot shots. And I couldn't blame them, seeing as how even one lucky hit would send me off to my eternal rest. I didn't have any energy left to keep going, so I pushed off with a charred stump and toppled into the hole. Something crunched underneath me. There was a pitiful howl. Feeling that I was about to lose consciousness, I pulled myself off whatever the soft thing I'd landed on was with one final effort. It got dark for some reason, almost as if someone had turned off a light, though I knew I was still awake.

My phone appeared in my hand. Using the light from the screen, I looked around the dark space before holding it closer to my face with a shaking hand. It was difficult to read the text:

Congratulations!

You're the first player in this location to discover the dungeon *Gray Lair*.

Free...

I didn't read far enough to see what was free. The regeneration shot finally reached my brain, and the merciful darkness took the pain away.

Chapter 8

MY HEAD WAS SPLITTING, though there really wasn't a good reason. I was alive and well once again. All there was left to remind me of the battle I'd just fought were the gaping holes in my coat—the BRO-I suit wasn't able to regenerate that kind of damage. Without a weapon, without protection, and without any kind of cavalry ready to ride to my aid, the situation was dire. Champion mages awaited outside the dungeon; even stronger ones were inside. And my force field was useless against lightning and fire, just strong enough to stand up to physical attacks.

Olson may have been right about how they'd eat me in the city.

It was my phone that kept me from really being depressed. It continued blinking merrily, driving away the surrounding darkness. I checked to see what I'd gotten for finding the dungeon.

Free attribute point available.
Level +1 (6).

Yet another syringe capable of turning a human into a beast. Once it had materialized, I spent some time just staring at it, trying to figure out where to invest my two points. The attributes I had at that point were useless against anyone who could shoot fire or lightning. And I knew there were going to be bastards in the damn game who could use ice or poison. I needed to even the scales.

But what was there that would give me a better shot at surviving?

I spent the better part of an hour paging through and reading about the different attributes, finally figuring out which one was best. Resilience, or the player body's ability to resist non-energy and non-physical damage. I'd been wrong—fire, lightning, poison, and ice were but a small portion of the long list of tools the monsters had at their disposal. Decay, necrotic energy, air, soil...it went on and on.

Resilience +1 (1).
Strength +1 (3).
Your body will need 3 hours to complete the change.

I picked up resilience so I had at least a shred of a chance to survive after the dungeon. Strength was for dealing with what I was going to face inside it. Without my pistol and rifle, I did have 1,373 coins and access to the store, which I immediately made use of.

A hundred went toward a pistol, ninety toward three energy blocks, and another three hundred bought me a new BRO-I. I'd realized that it actually didn't offer that much protection, though I was a mere 14,000 coins short of a BRO-II. *A pittance.*

I didn't have my drone, either, so I was going to have to explore the dungeon the old-fashioned way. The bait was me.

The first monster came at me on the other side of the first bend. Finally, it was an inferior who looked different from the rest. This character was reminiscent of a rat, just a meter tall and with tumor-like growths all over its body. The rat squealed and tried to bury its long teeth in me, though there was a reason I'd gotten my strength up to level three. Dodging the first attack, I slammed my fist into the creature's head. There was a crunch, and it fell into convulsions. I followed that up with a kick that broke its neck. There was no need to let it regenerate.

Monsters in dungeons are generated by the game and do not give you coins.

I'd assumed that would be the case, but it was worth checking. And that was why the inferior monsters down there differed from their friends in the outside world—they were digital. Less than real.

Although, if you asked me, none of the changed monsters were real anymore.

Fist-fighting turned out pretty well. Thanks to my agility, I only took a couple bites, and they were blocked by my force field. I didn't even need my pistol until I got to the first real challenge: a big cave where several dozen of the creatures had gathered. There were rats, spiders, and even a few wolves. I ended up having to spend my precious energy on the latter. Somehow, I doubted I'd be able to take them out with my bare hands—they were up to my chest.

I came across caches with player bonuses twice, both with energy blocks in my case. And once I'd cleared that final area, I stared at my phone in surprise.

Congratulations!
You destroyed the first round of monsters.
The dungeon has been updated, monster levels bumped up twice (current level: 3).

The body of the last rat I'd killed flickered and disappeared. A couple seconds later, a drawn-out howl reached me from the corridor, joined instantly by another dozen. I listened closely, trying to figure out who I was going to have to fight. And that's when a quiet rustle broke out. My body again reacted faster than my brain, delivering a backhanded blow as I ducked to the side. The strike turned out juicy, powerful, and incredibly painful. My arm went numb, white frost covering it up to the elbow. As I started shaking it, trying to get rid of the thousands of needles it felt like were piercing my skin, I looked over at my opponent. It was a big wolf with a frosty white muzzle that spoke to its age. Wandering around in immortality isn't easy when your brains are on the outside. I held my good arm out to the monster, looking to stroke its fur, though I jerked it back—even half-dead, the wolf managed to attack me with cold. A slender icicle shot out of its fur to jab my finger painfully. Once again, my defensive shield was useless. I was sure that if it hadn't been for the resilience I'd just picked up, I'd be a frozen statue, the wolves sitting around a table with napkins tied around their necks, forks in their paws, and food in front of them. *Me, I mean.* My regeneration handled the cold fine—a minute later, all that was left of my wounds was a distant memory. On the other hand, I noticed that the wolf was starting to move, its brains sucking back inside its head. That was no good. And so, I buried two shots between the eyes, though the pistol only did 30% damage to level three monsters.

Beating the dungeon was looking much more challenging, and I definitely missed the rats. Picking up a few stones, I tossed them into the tunnel. Quick footfalls broke out. Two wolves dashed in, tongues lolling out happily. And I couldn't blame them—a little fun, and then a nice meal. What more could a monster want?

But they weren't expecting to see me. At least, they weren't expecting to feel me crash down on their backs, my boots driving right into their skulls. The wolves' passive defense kicked in, a few icicles piercing me, but that really didn't help them much. I was heavier, stronger, and faster. No sooner had I driven their heads into the rocky floor, than I jumped off and finished the deed with two quick shots. A minute to regenerate, and the next stone went flying into the tunnel, attracting the attention of my next victim.

There was only one problem: the big open cave. The wolves had set up their main lair there, and they were entirely unwilling to let themselves be lured out one by one. But that just gave me a chance to show off the intellectual superiority humans wield over the artificial. Using just the tiniest of cracks, I clambered up a wall to get all the way to the ceiling, using everything I could to cling to the rock, teeth included. Then, I pulled a hand away and opened fire. The third level for pistol shooting just had one limitation: to guarantee a hit, you had to see your target. And that was tricky. From what I could tell, wolves were dashing up from all over the dungeon, all anxious to give me one of their patented snarls. Four shots per body, twenty bodies per energy block, five energy blocks, and that was the end of the entire pack. When I got down to the ground, it was covered in the frozen wolves. The icy, fanged creatures hadn't been able to get at me with their claws, their howling, or their icicles, which had a range of three meters. All they could do was leap futilely as they made themselves better targets.

Although, I had to admit that if it hadn't been for the height of the cave and the opportunity to climb the wall, I would have been in trouble. The kind of trouble I might not have been able to shoot my way out of.

Congratulations!
You destroyed the second round of monsters.
The dungeon has been updated, monster levels bumped up twice (current level: 5).

As I read the message on my phone, I sprinted off headlong into some dead-end tunnel. Life hadn't prepared me for that. The game was on the ball, and my next opponents were humanoid. Standing upright, bald, with the faces of overgrown snakes and disproportionately long arms that held equally long spears. For whatever reason, I had no doubt that the spears could shoot something—if not energy, then definitely something sharp. Each humanoid had a chain with a red gem around their neck, a force field protecting them from up to ten hits. Their clothes told me that they were all part of the same military division or perhaps club. Their armor was identical. Shrinking back behind a rock, I watched with interest as their patrols paced the tunnels. There were three of them in each patrol, spears always held at the ready. I glanced down at my miserly little pistol. There was no way the plaything was going to stand up to level five monsters.

Heading over to the store, I sighed. All I could buy with my 883 coins was a coffin, and a simple one at that. The prices for level two weapons started at 8,000 coins. The plasma grenades I also found there must have been handmade and secretly imported from one of the other game worlds under the escort of half the space fleet. That was the only way I could explain why they cost 2,000 coins apiece. *Not for ten; apiece!*

I ended up buying just one thing.

Machete. *A melee weapon that ignores energy armor and slows regeneration. Cost: 480 coins.*

Spinning the enormous blade around in my hands, I got a feel for the balance and felt like some kind of maniac. While all the sane creatures were running around with energy weapons, I was there holding my cold steel. A patrol marched by. Letting it go past, I decided to just go with the flow and forget about the future. I leaped out of cover and threw myself at the trio.

The machete came down on the neck of the

humanoid to the right. Its head almost came off, but only almost. The blade got stuck, and I was forced to let it go as the other two started turning slowly. Grabbing them by the heads, I smacked them together as hard as I could. Their force fields stood up to the blow; their heads didn't. It was something like what happens when you put a helmet on and bring a sledgehammer crashing down on it. Sure, the helmet will be fine. But will you? The monsters confirmed my logic as they sank to the ground, dark blood trickling from their noses and ears, their consciousness flying off to wherever beasts like that were made. Thrilled by the easy win, I grabbed one of their spears, though the smile quickly faded from my lips. The weapon disintegrated on the spot. Furious, I ripped my machete out of the humanoid's neck and finished what I'd started. I couldn't take any of their weapons, their clothes, or their force field necklaces. The game was doing an excellent job making sure I beat the dungeon with nothing but what I had with me.

After dragging the bodies off into a dark corner, I settled down to wait for the next patrol. The strategy was in place; the only thing left to do was avoid screwing it up. And I did. Nine patrols were sent to their digital heaven without ever knowing what hit them. Finally, they stopped showing up, and I went out to hunt myself, finding one or two of the humanoids off doing whatever in each of the dead-end tunnels.

Half an hour later, I was covered in black blood from head to toe from the unpleasant slaughter, though there wasn't a single one left. Only the large open area where'd I'd taken out the wolves was left untouched. There were at least twenty of them in there.

The humanoids had proven smarter than the wolves—none of them bit when I tossed a pebble into the cave. In fact, the opposite occurred. Spears bristling, they formed a tight circle in the middle of the area. And at the center was a powerful warrior with an unusual-looking spear. While the others all had metal-tipped weapons, his featured a black tip that looked like an animal bone. The hair on the back of my neck stood up when I saw it. Everything inside me recoiled, and I knew I had to avoid making its acquaintance at all costs. Otherwise, it was going to be a quick end to the game for me.

It took ten minutes for their wariness to pass. With constant glances cast at the tunnels leading to the cave, they all went back to what they were doing. Some sharpened their spears, others cooked, still more were making artwork on the walls. It was the usual life in the wild that they showed in all the movies. At least, until you caught a glimpse of their outfits and weapons.

I didn't have a timer, so I just spent a couple hours sitting hidden close to one of the entrances. But that did nothing for me—nobody was in any hurry to leave. They were all busy with what they were doing. *Yeah...* They really were game creations, not at all living creatures. They each had their function, all of which were inside the cave. I had to doubt they even knew there was a world outside their little space.

And so, I took a risk. There was no point shooting—I only had two energy blocks left, and I wanted to save them for the final round of monsters. That just left melee tactics. Gripping my machete tighter, I dashed into the cave, where the nearest trio was drawing on the cave wall. They were so engrossed in their artwork that they paid me no attention whatsoever. Or perhaps they were just relying on their defenses. Either way, three quick strikes later, there were three corpses on the ground.

That's when the real fight began.

The strike to the back was equal parts unexpected and powerful. I was thrown against the wall, which was slick with oil paint. And as I slid down it, a couple more direct hits were landed by whoever the heavyweight boxer behind me was. That was the only explanation I could come up with for the force behind each of its punches. I was finally able to turn around, which was when my eyes widened in horror— there was a spear hurtling right at my face. Neither my upgraded agility nor the sense of danger could throw me out of its path. The weapon wasn't able to break through my defense, though it sent my head crashing back against the stone wall. Stars flashed in my eyes.

As I tried to clear my head, I grabbed the nearest body and held it up as a shield. That helped, though the hits kept coming. The group was trying to hit me with their spears. One landed right next to my hand, though I couldn't do anything with it—it disintegrated as soon as I touched it. *Damn it!*

There was just one thing left: a grenade. And I had practically unhooked one from my belt when I caught a glimpse of the long arm of the humanoid I was hiding behind. Like some Scandinavian, it had died with its weapon clutched in its hand and hadn't even dropped it when it gave up the ghost. Whether it made it to its Valhalla or not, I didn't care. The thought that crossed my mind was what would happen if I took its hand instead of grabbing the spear directly. I gave that a try. With one arm wrapped around the body, I used my other hand to keep its fist closed around its spear. It probably looked terrifying—the other monsters stopped hurling their own spears at me. I took one step, then another, saw the character in front of me hesitate, and threw my hand forward. The tip of the spear hit the humanoid's chest, though the force field activated. The blow was stopped. But that didn't worry me—it was what I'd been expecting. In just a few seconds, I'd landed another nine strikes, and the eleventh pierced the monster. *One down!*

And that's when all hell broke loose. Sure, they stopped throwing their spears at me, though instead the whole group bull rushed me at once, trying to stick me like a pin cushion. *Had enough watching, yeah?* I bobbed and weaved as if I were dancing on a frying pan, though the number of jabs they were landing still had me worried—the humanoids knew how to handle their spears. Throwing the corpse I was holding at the largest concentration of them, I jumped in behind it. My machete whirled its jig of death as they dropped one by one. I spun, leaped, dodged, and threw monsters in front of each other, not forgetting to get my own strikes in. There had been forty-five hits left in my force field. A couple minutes of chaos later, they were all gone. And when an agonizing pain shot through my side, I yelled and jerked the spear deeper into me until it came out the other side. My opponent hadn't been expecting that, and he staggered forward a couple steps until I made an extra hole in his body. Only then did he let go of the spear to clutch at his own wound, the weapon disintegrating right inside me. I spat blood. *I'm going to need a few more regeneration points.*

Slashing the nearest opponent with a backhand to cut their number by another one, I turned and sighed heavily. All I wanted to do was lie down and get away from it all. I tried to take a deep breath, but it didn't work. It's hard to breathe at all when the long shaft of a spear is jutting out of your chest, the black spearhead already poking out your back. It was equally unpleasant to stare into the jubilant eyes of the last remaining humanoid. I pulled the same trick, yanking the spear into myself. And while my back burned, the job was done—the bastard wasn't expecting that, either. He fell to my blade.

Collapsing to my knees, I couldn't get back up. But the worst part was when I grasped the spear to make it melt away, and it didn't. There it was, still sticking out of me. Roaring noiselessly—the sound would have spent valuable air—I gradually pulled the foreign object back out of me. Suddenly, I noticed my hands, and I would have screamed in horror if I could have. My skin was peeling back in black strips to lay bare the muscles underneath. Then the muscles themselves started blackening. An agonizing pain ripped through my body, and I toppled face-down onto the ground. The last thing I heard before I dropped was the sound of the spearhead clanging against the stone. The black monstrosity was out of my body.

Darkness fell.

I felt the pain before even returning to consciousness. It came first, and following it, the world took shape to include a champion in the form of a giant wolf. The creature had settled itself comfortably next to me and was eating my legs. The right one was already gone, the left just about. Oddly enough, that's not where the pain was coming from. It was my chest that hurt, though I was able to breathe again. Noticing that I was starting to move, the giant wolf placed a paw on me, holding me down. I thought about blowing myself up along with the creature, but that would have meant a trip to the store on my phone to buy a grenade. My right arm reached for my holster. The wolf roared in response, and that was the end of my arm—it turned to ash on the spot. The beast could apparently breathe fire.

Again, there was no pain. When you think about it, it was just a few lost limbs. Who hasn't been through that? My left arm was pinned by the monster, so I couldn't move it either. Although... My palm was lying on a round stick, and my heart suddenly started beating faster. *The spear!* I gradually pulled the tip closer to me using nothing but my fingertips. Fire seared my arm as soon as I touched it, and that pain I did feel. I was glad I did, in fact. The wolf stopped gnawing on me to see what was going on under its stomach, and I used that reprieve to the best of my ability. With all the strength I had left, I tensed my wrist and thrust the spearhead upward, breaking the long shaft. My hand sprang free to bury the tip in the champion's belly. It howled, raked me with its paw, and left me once again to wash away into unconsciousness.

Pain brought me back. The only difference was

that the fire in my chest had been joined by hell sweeping through my arm. Pulling my eyes open with difficulty, I jerked my hand a couple times to summon my phone. My heart practically stopped when it smacked horrifically against my aching arm. Fighting for consciousness, I pulled up my current status, interested to see what had happened to me.

Cannot restore right arm. Regeneration level 15 required.

Cannot restore legs. Regeneration level 15 required.

Cannot restore wounds inflicted by a necrospear. Regeneration level 15 required.

A necrospear... Are you kidding me? Who put something like that in the game? I could see what the damn thing had done to me, saved as I was yet again by my regeneration, as well as what it had done to the motionless skeleton of the champion lying near me. The dark pool of stinking liquid around it had once been flesh, and I would have vomited if there had been anything in my stomach.

I was torn between regeneration and grabbing my reward. Although, no, it wasn't much of a choice. Just reading my status told me that I was no longer in fighting condition. Sure, there wasn't anyone growling at me, trying to kill me, or standing over me and telling me to fight, but I was still tired of being a cripple. I headed over to the store and bought myself a regeneration syringe.

The only problem was that I couldn't use it. No matter how many times I stuck myself, no matter how hard I pressed on the plunger, it wouldn't move a millimeter. My phone vibrated mockingly, and I cursed when I read the message:

Regeneration kits cannot be used in dungeons.

You bitches! I hate you all! I'm going to find and annihilate whoever thought up this game if it's the last thing I do. And everyone else!

I was flooded with emotion, but at least it dulled the pain. There was no point yelling. I had to drag myself out of the dungeon and stick myself with the needle. That was the only way. But I wasn't going to go through all that without collecting my reward, so I checked out the message:

Congratulations!

You destroyed the third round of monsters.
The dungeon has been updated, monster levels bumped up twice (current level: 7).
Final round. Single combat.

I'd apparently gotten that one while I was lying unconscious. *Damn, level seven! How?* I had to wonder how I was supposed to kill that thing if it hadn't been for the spear.

Congratulations!
You won the single combat.
Gray Lair cleared.
Level +3 (9).
New title: Lone Wolf.
***
You beat a dungeon in a group of less than 4 people. Reward level increased by 1.
You beat a dungeon alone. Reward level increased by 1.
***
Would you like to collect your reward?

My heart skipped a beat. When I'd beaten the dungeon in the prerelease, I'd gotten five items, one for each potential participant.

And if the rules of the game were the same, I was going to be in for a windfall.

With each new item that materialized in front of me, my eyes glowed brighter. *This is going to be fun!*

Attribute syringe (5 pcs). *Description: Player booster, lets you increase a current value or unlock a* *new attribute. Cost: 2,000 coins.*

BRO-III tactical equipment kit. *Description: Tactical outfit made of ultrastrong material capable of withstanding a direct hit from level four monsters. Slots and pockets adjustable to fit the needs of the wearer. Waterproof boots. Can be restored when less than 50% damaged. Does not include BRO-III tactical helmet. Cost: 34,000 coins.*

BRO-III tactical helmet. *Description: Tactical helmet made of ultrastrong material capable of withstanding a direct hit from level four monsters. Integrates with phone map, integrates with owner's weapon. Along with the equipment kit, forms a hermetic suit with a supply of oxygen that lasts for 30 minutes. Cost: 50,000 coins.*

KORT-III automatic attack pistol. *Description: Ignores physical and energy armor for opponents through level four. Blocks regeneration. Blocks 1 random ability. Magazine includes 400 rounds. 3 improvement slots. Range: 50 meters. Cost: 40,000 coins.*

Modifier for Mark-1: Scanner-III. *Description: Lets your drone spot warm-blooded opponents within a radius of 500 meters. Integrates with BRO-III tactical helmet. Cost: 20,000 coins.*

Virtual storage-III. *Description: Bonus reward, phone expansion. Lets you store up to 20 game items. Item materialization takes 60 seconds. Cost: None, is a mission reward.*

And not a single coin.

The virtual storage turned out to be another button on my phone. Opening it up, I saw the list of items I could store there. I wasn't up for changing right then, and so I dropped in everything but the pistol and the regeneration syringe. My chest tightened when everything disappeared, but I had to believe I'd be getting it back. The necrospearhead went in, as well. My phone identified it as a "broken piece requiring repairs," so I decided to show it to Olson and see how much he'd give me for it. I imagined it would be in the ballpark of twenty or thirty grand, which would go a long way toward paying off my debt.

Crawling along on my elbows, I headed toward the exit. There were a couple champions outside, and I had quite a few questions for them.

Chapter 9

THE ENTRANCE TO THE DUNGEON was hidden among the roots of an enormous tree. To be fair, all that was left of the tree was a charred stump—my escape had apparently gotten on the champions' nerves, and they'd taken their frustration out on the surroundings.

Out under the open sky, there wasn't a problem shooting myself up. The plunger for the syringe slipped downward, and the game got to work regenerating me. But while I could have given in and slipped into unconsciousness, I stayed awake. My pistol swung warily from side to side. Quiet didn't mean safe.

You took a picture of a dungeon. 10 coins received.

Finally, my finances got at least a tiny boost. Checking to see if my devices were available, I found that both Mark-1 and Mark-2 were lying on the ground awaiting instructions. Nobody'd tried to grab them; nobody cared. The drone still had 30% of its charge left, so I sent it hurtling up into the clouds. A fanged maw flashed across the screen, but it snapped shut too late to do any damage. Mark-1 was back under my control.

The champions had returned to the nuclear power plant. I couldn't tell what they were doing—both were hard at work tearing a hole in one of the walls. Too late, I patted my pockets and found that I still had the blocker with me. My stomach returning to its normal position, and I sent the drone in a large circle that brought it back to me. It was time to get ready to go.

The new equipment I'd picked up was great. As soon as the helmet settled into place on my head, my face was hit by a rush of cool air. That felt great, and I realized I'd gotten used to weather above thirty degrees Celsius. All available information popped up immediately on the protective glass. It was fantastic— all the messages I'd had to pull my phone up to see were right there in front of me. They were controlled using my eyes, something it definitely took me a little while to get used to. On the other hand, I finally realized why the helmet came with such a hefty price tag. It was way fancier than the outfit, syncing seamlessly with the phone. And when the drone shot up into the sky, a map appeared on the glass to my right. Not distracting in the least, it was actually a huge help. I showed up as a small triangle; potential opponents were red dots. Two of them were right by the entrance to the dungeon, so I brought the drone lower to find a pair of superior monsters. *Bastards!* The champions couldn't hang around forever, so they'd left an ambush in place in case I showed back up. The beasts snarled at the drone, though they didn't attack, keeping their eyes fixed on the path. From what I could tell, that was the only way back up.

Damn, this is great! I flew out over the nuclear plant. The monsters inside didn't show up on the scanner, though everyone outside appeared as red dots. *Perfect!* I wasn't going to have to deal with any more surprises.

While I still had time left, I decided to do something nice for my devices. That had always been a weakness of mine—helping devices. I had to charge them every ten hours, phone, drone, and ATV alike. That annoyed me sometimes, and I was always worried they'd run out at the worst possible moment. I'd found the solution long before, I just hadn't had a chance to utilize it before then.

Multicharge. *Description: 20 full charges lasting 10 hours each. Cost: 20 coins.*

The price was the same as a single-use charge, it just lasted much longer. Four multicharges left me with only 273 coins left, though I felt better about my devices. I also decided to pick up a pair of regeneration syringes just in case. One dropped into a chest pocket; the other was sent to the virtual storage. I was tired of playing the hero.

Three hours later, I was regretting my decision to stay conscious. Lying there motionless was driving me crazy. It even got to the point that I yelled over at the monsters lying in ambush, trying to goad them into getting to work. But they were impervious to my pleas. With each passing hour, my mood grew darker, until finally the helmet screen told me that my arms and legs had been completely regenerated. I set off to hunt. There was no point even changing—it was just two unresponsive monsters. Would it really have been such a problem for them to run over and die a couple hours before?

Ten coins later, five for each of the two, I felt a little calmer. My head was clearer, too. Climbing into my new armor, I bought myself ten energy blocks for my weapons, which left me almost broke. But I had something else: attributes and a good idea of how to use them. Three were from leveling-up, five were a reward for beating the dungeon. *It's over, you damn mages. You should have killed me when you had the chance.*

Resilience +3 (4).
Stamina +1 (3).

Agility +1 (3).
Pistol shooting +1 (4).
Rifle shooting +1 (4).
Melee weapons +1 (1).

I was liking myself more and more. The only thing bugging me was that using the machete hadn't given me that melee weapons skill, forcing me to unlock it myself. But at least I'd found out where to stick my blade to really make things unpleasant for my opponents. I would have made a great proctologist.

Status table			
Name	Mark Derwin		
Coins	13	Level	9
Titles and ranks			
Bandit Bane, Lone Wolf			
Attributes			
Strength	3	Regeneration	5
Stamina	3	Resilience	4
Agility	3		
Skills			
Pistol shooting			4
Rifle shooting			4
Melee weapons			1

Excited to see how well I was doing, I pulled up the list of top players in my location. But I was surprised to find that I was nowhere in the top hundred. An entire mob of high-ranking players had appeared out of nowhere, some guy with a name I couldn't pronounce in 99th place at level 24. A Surtun was in first—Level 42. Of course, there were no answers to my *how?*, *where?*, or *what the hell?* to be found anywhere, so I quickly closed the list and decided not to check it again unless I had to. While I'd been lying around, everyone else out there had been hard at work.

It was time to catch up.

I found my Mark-2 and rifle where I'd left them. The ATV was under a tree; the rifle was in some dirt surrounded by charred branches. It hit me that with so many players in the location, one of them might try to steal my Mark-2, and so I decided to give the virtual storage a workout. Tapping the *Items available for archive* button, I practically jumped for joy. Both of my devices had made the list. Mark-1 and Mark-2. The ATV was sent right off to my phone, and I watched with interest as it melted away in front of me. The game had accepted it as its own. That made things much easier— I didn't have to worry about my loot and property all the time. I could just send them off into virtual reality.

Rubbing my hands together, I was getting ready to begin the hunt when I unexpectedly froze. The game had thrown me another curveball:

Monster levels increased by 1 (current level: 3).

A general appeared in your current hexagon.

I watched as the champions transformed before my very eyes. They stepped away from the wall and paused, an additional glow appearing. Sure, there weren't many outward changes—most of the revisions were apparently on the inside. *Their magic is probably stronger now.* The superior monsters around them got bigger, somewhat reminiscent of hairless grizzlies. I'd seen a picture of a sick bear at some point. The monsters in front of me looked just like that, only with protective spikes all over their bodies as well as fangs and claws the size of my machete.

That was all well and good, but it didn't get me any closer to completing my mission. I headed back up the tree and pulled out my rifle. So well had my helmet integrated with my scope, that I didn't even have to look into the viewfinder. The crosshairs showed up right in front of me. Scoping in on the first monster, I started scanning it to see what damage percentages I could do. *Ha!* My level four rifle shooting had completely canceled out the creature's new level, and I was back to two shots for each kill. And that's what I did. My first target dropped, and the crowd of red dots came dashing in my direction. *Perfect!* Shot after shot was spent on them, though I made sure I kept track of the imaginative champions. It was obvious how they'd ambushed me the first time—while the main wave of superior monsters came at me from the front, they made their way around the sides. And pretty quickly, too, I had to admit.

That time, however, I wasn't going to just sit there, and so I waited for them to pop out behind a tree before suddenly reorienting my attack. The hairless bears were welcome to come at me—I had more important things to worry about. Burying three rounds in the head of the first champion before it could figure out what was going on, I watched as it threw up its arms and cast a green glow around itself. But it was too late. My fourth shot smacked right into its heart for 25% damage. The body dropped to the ground, and my Mark-1 pulled it from its list of targets. The second red dot froze where it was, hidden in a small gully that got in the way of my shots. With just 2% damage values showing up, I decided against wasting valuable energy. Everything in the damned changed world cost money, and coins didn't grow on trees. Instead, I switched back to the superior monsters while the champion decided what to do next. The beasts had closed the distance and were licking their chops in anticipation of fresh meat.

Only ten of them made it all the way to the tree, which gave me a chance to try out my KORT-III pistol. And, well... One shot, one corpse. It was a killing machine.

The mage was the last red dot in the area

surrounding the nuclear station. For a long time, he stayed motionless in one spot, which made me nervous. *He's either calling for backup or getting a surprise ready for me.* I knew a champion who'd just leveled-up wasn't about to give up without a fight, and so I climbed out of the tree and laid down in the grass a good ten meters away. From my new vantage point, I couldn't see the monster at all, so I had to orient myself around the drone. I sent it closer, knowing I was taking a big risk. I needed to see what the mage was cooking up.

A couple seconds later, I found out. The tree exploded in a flash of bright color, and the mage appeared right above the perch I'd been shooting from. Without losing a moment, he dropped his arms and turned the branch to ash. The fire pouring from his palms was so powerful that even the giant's roots caught fire.

The problem was that there was nobody home on the branch—the teleportation, which is what I was positive had just happened, was a failure. The mage realized that, too, and he only had time to look up before three bursts of energy from my automatic pistol dug a hole the size of my fist in his forehead.

You took the first picture of 142 dead superior monsters. 710 coins received.
You took the first picture of 2 dead

champions. 600 coins received.

There we go! It was just a shame I hadn't been able to take a selfie with them in the background. The extra coins would have been nice, though I'd made out pretty well as it was. And the fact that the champions had left me a couple presents made it even better.

Fire modifier. *Description: Adds fire energy to every tenth shot, burning the target. Cost: 30,000 coins.*
Lightning modifier. *Description: Adds electric energy to every tenth shot, paralyzing the target for 2 seconds. Cost: 30,000 coins.*

There was no need to think about whether to stick them on my guns or not. Both the pistol and the rifle had expansion slots, so I went with fire for the latter and lightning for the former.

A champion and forty superior monsters were all I had left to deal with. I was getting ready to head into the building when the drone caught something interesting: there were three red dots moving in from the direction of the road. Immediately jumping behind the building closest to me, I realized what was going on. The way they were moving and the direction they were coming from could only mean one thing. *They're...*

"Grust, look what he pulled off! Are you sure

you want to find him?" came the first voice. It sounded young, maybe fifteen years old.

"Shut up and keep your eyes open," the second shot back. *Grust, I guess.* He was older, and apparently had plenty of testosterone. Enough macho to go around.

"Bro, what did you expect? Olson wouldn't offer us ten thousand coins for nothing, and especially not ten thousand each!" The third voice belonged to a woman. And a rough one at that. I didn't like her kind. Sending the drone forward a bit, I caught a glimpse of the scene: three well-dressed fighters. One of them really was younger, maybe a touch older than Squirrel. They all had rifles, and they looked like game weapons to me. A couple Kalashnikovs were there, too. Holstered pistols. Daggers. One of the BRO kits. Helmets, but from our world. Plenty of grenades, and an ability to communicate with gestures, something I really didn't like. That wasn't something you just learned in everyday life.

When they noticed the drone, I pulled it up onto a roof to keep it safe. The trio dashed into that building, apparently deciding I was hidden there. *Move out*, the command was barked, after which the door was kicked in and a grenade was tossed inside. A flashbang, it turned out. My helmet adjusted automatically, darkening the picture. The three fighters dove inside, and I heard shots—there were presumably monsters in there.

"He isn't here!" yelled the kid when he appeared on the roof ten minutes later. I checked the mission description and grunted. The trio had cleared forty level 3 superior monsters, and they hadn't lost anyone. *Tough cookies.*

"And the drone?" Grust asked, poking his head out of a second-floor window.

"Nope. All clear!"

And of course, it was clear. As soon as they'd stepped inside, I'd moved my Mark-1 to my virtual storage. The last thing I needed was for the newcomers to shoot it up.

"Okay, though the monsters were still alive, so he hasn't been here, yet," the woman said as she walked out of the building and looked around. "Where could he be?"

"By the reactor," Grust said. "Olson gave him a mission to stop the leak, so he probably headed that way."

"There's fuel leaking? You didn't say that! There's no way I'm going over there," the kid replied, his tone nervous. "There has to be all kinds of radiation!"

"Shut up and get down here! We'll meet up below—it may take us a while to finish this job."

Yeah-h... I tried to think of what to do next. I understood what Olson's motives were—as a representative of the game, he'd seen what I'd been able to pull off in the dungeon, not to mention the reward I'd picked up, and he knew I'd make for a great slave. And so, he sent a trio of advanced thugs after me. Taking a quick peek, I found that Grust was in the top thirty and at level 32. I knew what I had to do with Olson, of course. Once I'd paid off my debt, he was getting gunned down. But the three characters in front of me... *Kill them just in case?* That thought definitely ran through my head. In fact, that was my plan for a good three minutes until the kid showed up and I saw Squirrel in him. It wasn't their fault they were out to stay alive no matter the cost, even if they had to kill another player.

Hm, I'm going soft. It wasn't going to be long before I even developed a bit of empathy. It was time to fix that, and I opened fire as soon as they left the administrative building and started looking over the reactor. Grust was my first target—out of the three, he was clearly the most dangerous. Two shots to the legs, a pair at each arm, and a few in the stomach for the finishing touch. *That should be enough to incapacitate him.* The woman was next. She reacted quickly and dropped to the ground, though I was faster. Then, the kid dropped, hit in both arms and a shoulder. I didn't have time to finish him off, though there was no need to hide any longer. Jumping out of cover, I dashed toward the three, slipping my rifle over my shoulder and pulling out my pistol as I ran. A few tough smacks landed on my chest as the little bugger was fast enough to hit me with a burst from his Kalashnikov. But my force field handled that, and a second later there was a scream of pain as both his shoulders were pulverized. I spared no expense. Finally getting to where they were, I repeated my execution, giving all of them a shot to each extremity, their elbows, and their shoulders. They needed to be alive, if incapacitated.

The kid wailed in pain and rolled around on the ground, though the man and woman laid there silently, their eyes fixed on me with a look of hate. They didn't even curse. Without saying a word, I picked up their phones to get to know them a bit better.

Player Grust Kilvan. Status: Active, level 32. Cash: 9441 coins.

Player Milady Tzirt. Status: Active, level 23. Cash: 6975 coins.

Player Little Tzirt. Status: Active, level 23. Cash: 5772 coins.

Nice work! They had plenty of money on them, too. Without a single twinge of conscience, I took three thousand coins from each of them. They'd been looking to kill me, so they had to know what they were risking. But that wasn't the end of my machinations. Picking up Grust's phone, I bought three regeneration syringes.

"Milady, you're first." My helmet hid my unpleasant smile, though the tone of my voice told the woman that she was in for trouble. When I started unbuckling her pants, the air filled with curses and threats. And they were actually from the kid—the woman let the striptease happen in silence. From the boy's fiery speech, I could only really tell that bastards like me shouldn't touch his sister. Grust said nothing, just looking away. When I finished with the belt, I pulled her pants down to her knees and reached for my machete. One quick blow left Milady's right leg detached from her body. The kid suddenly fell silent, though that's when Milady finally broke her silence. And it wasn't that she thought she was about to be raped; it was the incredible pain. But I wasn't about to stop there, and my next swing bereft her of her second leg, turning her into a stub of a human. I could have let her suffer, but I'm no maniac. She shut up and drifted away into unconsciousness when the regeneration syringe emptied into her shoulder. Standing up, I went over to the kid. He realized immediately what was about to happen and started yowling piteously, throwing his head back and forth. Begging me not to do it, he jerked around, making it hard for me to get his pants off. But there was no changing my mind. A couple quick swings, and another player was sent off into the darkness.

"That's some nice regeneration. Up to ten already?" I asked when I crouched down next to Grust. Just to make sure nothing went sideways, he got another round of shots to the joints. Incredibly, he'd almost healed himself in the time I spent working on Milady and her kid brother.

"Twelve," came the answer. "I want to max it out."

"What's the maximum? Fifteen?" I asked, and he nodded. Finally, I was getting some information about the game. Grust spoke up suddenly.

"Thanks for not ruining our equipment. We're going to need it. Did you take all our coins?"

"Three thousand each. Call it payment for services rendered."

"Services? Sending us off for eight hours is a service?"

"What are you worried about? There aren't any monsters here, and players definitely won't be showing up. Relax, regenerate, and get back to what you're doing. But hey, do you happen to need a cache and a dungeon?"

I could tell what his answer was by the way his eyes lit up.

"Well, three thousand is payment for the coordinates. If the three of you beat the dungeon, you'll get a second-level reward. The five items will be worth much more than three thousand coins."

"What do you care? You know we're going to keep hunting you, don't you?"

"You haven't figured it out, yet? You're human, and Olson isn't. The point of the game is to get rid of us all, so they turn us on each other when the monsters aren't up to the task. I'm not a fan of that—I'm going to fight to the end. There really aren't many of us left, and we have to get stronger. When they level the monsters up in a week, your little pea shooters aren't going to do the trick. You have to get better. And Olson, with his damn functions, can't stand that. Which is fine—I'll head back to Aspen and have a chat with him. Oh, by the way, can I ask you a question? Where did you three come from?"

"The city." Grust gazed at me for a while, though he answered eventually. "Three hours before the nuclear blast, there was a siren and a warning for everyone left alive. The groups all headed this way. Some ended up in this location, others in the next one over."

"And locations are...?" I was finally getting the chance to fill in some gaps in what I knew.

"Areas fifty kilometers by fifty kilometers, part of a hexagon with a radius of a thousand kilometers. All of Earth was divided up into them."

"Got it... That makes sense. Do want to hear about the rounds in the dungeon and how to beat them? Or will you be okay on your own?"

Once again, there was a pause.

"You're an odd duck... We're here to kill you, and you're giving us the chance to get stronger. You can't know that we won't come back to get our revenge tomorrow..."

"Get better, and then get your revenge. Anyway, there are three rounds, one after the other..."

I went through the particulars of the dungeon and how to beat the monsters with him, just with one small adjustment: I told him I killed the champion with grenades. For some reason, it just felt like I shouldn't tell him about the spear. I decided they'd figure out what to do if a humanoid showed up with one—they'd been around the block a couple times. And if it didn't... I didn't want them to know what I had. Weapons like that had no place in our world.

"There are two champions dead in the clearing. Make sure you take a picture of them, since you should get something for the second picture. And that's about it. Which would you like me to start with?"

"Doesn't matter to me. I'll regenerate in four hours—remember that," Grust said. "I hope you're done by then. These two will want their revenge."

With an already practiced hand, I dropped his pants to make sure I didn't ruin them and strip him of his protection, cut off his legs, and stuck him with a regeneration syringe. His eyes closed, and I set off to finish the damn mission. But as soon as I got close to the active area, I realized that I might end up stuck there for a little while.

The control rods had been ripped off the reactor—they were lying over by a wall. A notification about heightened temperatures and radiation levels flashed in front of me, though the game let me know that my level four resilience and level five regeneration were more than enough to handle it. I would have been in trouble if it weren't for them.

Something odd-looking was hovering over the reactor, something reminiscent of a gigantic jellyfish. Its transparent flagella were buried in the reactor, and there was something toxic and green running up them. In fact, the jellyfish was already half full of the stuff as it continued sucking it out of the reactor. *What is that, nuclear fuel? Oh, damn.*

I quickly pulled out the blocker, pressed the single button, and tossed it right into the center of the active area. The metal sphere disappeared out of sight, the building suddenly quivering. Steam poured out of all the cracks before giving way to a yellow foam. Jerking, the jellyfish quickly pulled its flagella back up into itself, clacking jaws appearing on the end of each of them. *They have some nasty bastards in this game!* Foam continued pouring out of the reactor until it filled the entire active area, and that's when the radiation and temperature warnings went from yellowish-red to yellowish-green. Still dangerous, but no longer critical.

The champion didn't pay me the least bit of attention. Drifting slowly through the air like a real jellyfish in the ocean, it eased its way over to the wall. I quickly put two and two together when I noticed the hole the two mages had been making right there. The jellyfish banged against the wall a couple times, somehow believing it was still there, and then froze. A strange guess flashed across my mind: *it's a harvester!* Enormous, powerful, and incredibly resilient, it was a harvester, and not some battle machine. Taking a few steps forward until I was right next to it, I...

You took a picture of a live champion from less than three meters away. 100 coins received.

You took a selfie with a live champion in the background from less than three meters away. 300 coins received.

Score! I reached for my pistol to complete the mission, but my humanity woke up at just the wrong time. *Although, no, that's definitely greed.* I was missing out on some extra bonuses.

It took no time at all to haul the three bodies over. Setting them up with the creature in the background, I took pictures with their phones. The quality, the positioning, the fact that we were all in the picture, none of it mattered. All I cared about was the result, and I was going to collect my 400 coins from each phone.

You took a group selfie with a live champion in the background from less than three meters away. 1,200 coins received (300 for each person in the picture).

With undisguised amazement, I checked Grust's phone—he'd gotten 1,600 coins. Taking the same picture with the other three, I got the same result, only I didn't get any extra coins. *Hm...* I finished up and carried the bodies back outside, figuring that they didn't need to be in there with the radiation, and paused for a couple minutes. Three times 1,600 was 4,800 coins. I wasn't giving them out for free, but taking them for myself... *That's getting too close to the line between payment for services and theft. Okay, got it.* The idea was mine, so I took half, leaving the other half for the owners of the bodies. And I also knew they'd check their logs and find another way to earn coins. Information has a price, too.

My account was 2,400 coins richer when I headed back into the reactor. It was time to wrap up the mission.

You took the first picture of a dead champion. 300 coins received.
Shut down the reactor complete.

Level +1 (10).

***

You ruined the plans of a larva and destroyed a source of energy for its farm. Because of that, an attack group was dispatched (100 superior monsters, 10 champions).

New title: Monster Scourge.

***

You're the first player in your hexagon to get that title.

Level +5 (15).

***

You're the first player in your hexagon to have an attack group dispatched to hunt you. Get ready to fight!

Level +5 (20).

5 free attribute points received.

It hit me that they weren't going to let me back into Aspen. Olson wouldn't want a guest with the problems I would bring with me, and monsters howled off in the distance as if reading my mind. A countdown appeared in front of me.

There was one hour left until the hunt began.

Chapter 10

TAKING ON THE MONSTERS out in the open would have
been suicide. Of course, sitting in one spot, even if that
spot was the roof, was also suicide, but I didn't have
much of a choice. Grabbing the bodies of the
regenerating players and their clothing, I dashed into
the building. Milady and the kid were just starting to
regrow their knees; Grust was all the way to his feet.
He probably just needs another hour.

The timer ticked down inexorably toward zero.
As the howling of the monsters grew louder, I got the
distinct impression that the trees off in the distance
were rocking back and forth, almost as if the body of
some enormous beast were brushing past them. The
Mark-1 whined into the sky. Within a radius of 500
meters, there were only three red dots, and all of them
were right next to me. I took a sad look at the sixteen
attribute syringes I had ready to stab myself with. Even
+1 to my shooting would have done wonders as I took
on the monsters, but that would have meant spending
three hours unconscious. If I'd had the chance, I would

have taken it without thinking. But in that moment, with just thirty minutes before the battle was set to begin, I knew the game wasn't going to cut me any slack.

Red dots started to appear at the edge of the drone's scanning range. One, two, a dozen. I couldn't see them with the trees in the way, so I decided to send my Mark-1 in closer.

But that was when I noticed some dots appearing on the opposite side. Leaping over to the other end of the roof, I peered over toward the trees. The monsters were getting smart. It definitely wasn't the idiot animals who'd come dashing over for me to gun down the first couple days in the game.

A minute later, my chest was feeling tight. Red dots were scattered all around the perimeter, and that's when I got a new message:

You aren't alone.
The attack group now has 400 superior monsters and 40 champions.

"Mark, what's our status?" I heard Grust call over. Still without one of his feet, he was pulling on his pants and checking his phone. His face told me what he thought of what he saw there.

"Royally screwed," I replied frankly.

"I can see that... But we'll be fine. What's your

rifle shooting level?"

"Three."

"I'm at five, though my rifle isn't great."

"Here." Without a second thought, I tossed Grust my U-II. He was going to shoot twice as fast and more accurately than me, and we needed all the help we could get.

"Nice optics," the fighter said, looking the gun over. "But what are you going to use?"

"For starters, I'll take yours, and then I'll switch to my pistol." I glanced nervously back and forth between our different flanks. The horde of superior monsters had encircled us, though they weren't getting any closer.

"You're looking around like you can see them," Grust said.

"And you... Oh, damn it. Here, let me check something."

I dug into the map and display settings. A few taps later, and there was the *Share* button. Feeling like a genius, I tapped it, only to start in shock at the empty list. I asked Grust for his phone and held it against my own. Nothing.

"Do we need to make a group?" he asked. For some reason, I had no doubt he'd served in the army. "Here, give it to me."

It was Grust's turn to play with our phones. I was soon treated to a notification in my helmet:

You were added to a group: *Together to the End.*

It worked, and the map refreshed. Grust gave a satisfied snort, looked over at me approvingly, and set his eye against the rifle scope.

"They're hiding behind the trees." The guy was definitely able to hide his fear, his voice unwavering. "I'll take this side, you take that one—we each get half the roof."

"They're above us!" I shouted, pointing upward. Judging by the map, thirty red dots were hurtling in our direction. They'd just crossed the edge of the forest. I'd sighted down the rifle, but nobody was on the ground. And it was only when I looked up, figuring that my Mark-1 wouldn't be mistaken, that I saw the bad guys. They were flying so high that the drone could barely catch them with its scanner.

"Too far up." Grust aimed his rifle away. "They're going to dive at us."

"Yep, leave them to me. What kind of force field do you have?"

"Level three, a hundred hits." He brandished a chain with a green gem. *Good call.* I pulled up the store and bought myself two of them, slipping one over my head. The other was saved for later. Stepping toward our respective sides, we hid the still-unconscious Milady and Little in the attic.

The timer showed a minute left until the start of the battle.

First-level rifles weren't capable of penetrating energy shields. And while superior monsters didn't have them, they were going to be a problem when it came to taking on champions. And that's exactly what happened: there was a third-class monster in the group circling above us.

As soon as the timer finished ticking off the last few seconds, the red dots swept toward us in unison. I took a few deep breaths and tugged on the trigger, firing back at the beasts racing in our direction. My three shots per second were enough to take one out. Still, a good ten of them landed on the roof. My last six shots all slammed into the enormous harpy in command of the squad, only they didn't do any good. Not a single burst of energy made it through the creature's protective shield.

Once they'd landed, the harpies tried to toss us off the roof, but that just meant it was our turn to show off our agility. Grust didn't even stop shooting. All he did was move to the side, slapping one of the monsters so hard as he went that it dropped lifelessly over the edge.

The champion landed heavily and let out a piercing cry. My partner grabbed his ears, though my helmet kept me safe. The monster, on the other hand, had nothing to protect it from my level three automatic pistol. It shredded the creature's shield as well as its head. And with that, the roof was clear.

"You good?" I yelled nervously.

"Focus!" Grust barked angrily as he scoped back in. Our opponents had left the forest and were crossing the empty space. I was only able to take out a few before tossing the rifle aside in favor of my KORT-III, the 50-meter range more than enough.

A hundred superior monsters and ten champions were sent on to their ever after without even getting to the building—I was on fire. None of them could get close without eating a burst from my gun, ten shots enough to kill a champion. Just as before, one or two accurate headshots were enough for superior monsters. Acid came flying back at me in return, lightning flashed, fireballs spun by, and there was even some kind of blackish-gray blot, all of which I dodged easily. I did have to leave my corner, however. After yet another fireball slammed into it, there was nothing left to stand on. Still, I was starting to think that the attack group really wouldn't have been too much for me to take on my own, though that was when I heard a croaked cry behind me.

"Mark!"

I spun around and was taken aback. Milady and Little had crawled out from shelter, but instead of helping Grust, they'd grabbed him by the arms and legs. Monsters were hopping up onto the roof. After firing a burst into them, I leaped over to Milady and shoved her away. She rolled over to the edge of the roof. As soon as she got there, however, black claws reached up to pull her down below. I fired over in that direction, but I was too late—practically my first miss. And while Grust was busy with Little, I took up his position. Things weren't as sunshiny there as they were on my side, as the monsters were already clambering up the walls under the cover of the champions' magic.

"What's wrong with you?!" Grust yelled, giving Little a backhanded blow. The latter was sent flying, though he hopped onto all fours and came crawling back. A cold feeling gripped my stomach—the kid's eyes had rolled backward, and his irises were a monstrous blue color. As I cleared the wall, I took a few bolts of lightning to the chest. My resilience was enough to handle the damage, though I was still sent flying backward. And that's when Little crashed into Grust's chest. The fighter stood tall, only slipping toward the edge of the roof. By the time I cleared my head, pulled myself to my feet, and aimed my pistol, Grust had been visible to whoever was down below for a couple seconds. Just a couple seconds, but that was enough. The pair stopped fighting. Turning toward me, they both flashed blue eyes.

Damn it! What's that, mind control? The monsters continued climbing up onto the roof, though they were already the least of my problems—the two players were much faster. Grust showed me what kind of strength you get at level 32 by landing a blow so hard I smashed through the attic door and crashed into the opposite wall. I just about lost my will to fight. But my pistol rattled to a stop next to me, which woke me up. As soon as Grust appeared in the opening, I buried a few shots in him without a shadow of regret. He was sent flying. But no sooner was he gone, than in his place appeared superior monsters. All I could do was lie there and keep firing, gradually filling the doorway with their bodies. A minute later, it was blocked. I could take a break from the threat on the roof.

An unexpected silence fell, though I could hear infrequent, if palpable blows. The roof shook. I realized a champion had appeared above me. Aiming my pistol once again at the door, I suddenly heard a strange voice in my head.

Give up. Throw your weapon away. Give up. Throw your weapon away. Give up...

It kept repeating its refrain over and over, and my eyes widened in surprise. Against my will, my hand unclenched, the pistol falling to the floor. And I couldn't pick it back up again no matter how hard I tried.

Give up. Take your helmet off. Give up. Take your helmet off. Give up...

Again, my hands obeyed the order. I yelled, unable to withstand the mental pressure. Hot air hit my face, not to mention ash and the revolting stink of dead monsters. The creatures clogging the doorway started to shake as if someone had decided to rip them away all at once. There wasn't a doubt in my mind—as soon as the champion looked at me, I was going to suffer the same fate as Grust.

Give up. Wait for me. Give up. Wait for me. Give up...

The creature could sense my worry, and it gave me yet another order. I panicked. It's one thing to take monsters on with guns or fists; it's another to try to stand up to that kind of pressure.

Bingo!

The thought crossed my mind with the speed of a racing turtle. *Stand up to it!* My phone leaped into my hand, and I quickly pulled up the settings. While I'd been looking for resilience, I'd come across a different attribute that was exactly what I needed right then. The syringe buried itself in my body, and I distributed the points the way I needed them.

Willpower +6 (6).
Regeneration +10 (15).

I ended up distributing all sixteen of my free attribute points, dumping them in willpower and regeneration. The first was what would let me hold up under the monsters' mental attacks. And bumping the second to level 15 was a move to keep me alive even if the monsters ate off all my limbs. Presumably, they wanted me for something, and not to kill me right there, which meant there was a shadow of a chance I could find a way out of the pickle. Just before the bodies of the monsters burst out of the doorway, I pulled up my virtual storage and dumped everything in there—the drone, my pistol, my helmet, both rifles on the roof, and even my armor. That left me lying there in my underwear. Two piercingly blue eyes appeared, and my consciousness exploded into a thousand pieces.

There was just one thought in my head: *the master will be thrilled to eat you himself!*

I was shaken violently awake exactly three hours later. Thrown across the back of a monster as it dashed forward, I had neither arms nor legs, just as I'd feared. The beasts had gnawed them off before taking me prisoner. Looking over, I saw Grust and Little. Their eyes were still blue, and they were sitting astride their monsters as if on horseback. Immediately, I looked down to make sure I didn't meet their glance accidentally. *It worked!* I'd broken the champion's mental control. Just as I'd thought, it was lower than level 6, meaning my new will was too much for it. All I had to do was wait.

171

I was shaken again, my stubs banged against the monster's body, and I lost consciousness before I could even wonder what was in store for me.

The next time I woke up, I was on solid ground. It was wet. Dark. There was a thick chain holding my body to the ground, though my captors had missed a trick: my legs and arms were back, whole and in one piece. The regeneration had been a success.

Ripping myself free wasn't nearly as easy as I'd been expecting—the chain was made of tough steel that refused to bend or break. I ended up pulling the hooks free from the ground. My level three strength showed itself off in all its glory, and I was soon standing on two legs. Holding out my hand, I waited quite a while until I heard a scrape and a dull impact. My phone smacked into my palm. Activating the pistol, a rifle, my helmet, and my outfit took four minutes, and the monsters missed yet another trick by giving me the time I needed. By the time the bone-crunching scream burst out from above me, and I heard claws clattering against stone, I was ready.

The ten superior monsters that came at me were destroyed in a matter of seconds, not even enough time for them to roar. I pulled out my phone and saw a disappointing message:

Monsters in attack groups are generated by the game and do not give you coins.

It was just like in the dungeon. Suddenly, it hit me why I was still alive, and not digesting in the master's stomach. The generated monsters were supposed to turn me over to real, honest-to-goodness, flesh-and-bone former people. And that was why I'd been dragged into the basement and chained up. They needed to have the other monsters join them, since that was their entire functionality. *Excellent! Bring on the real ones!* I was definitely up for some kills that would actually give me coins.

I heard another howl, and the next squad came at me. They were met on the stairs. In the enclosed space, I was a god among men, especially with the firepower my pistol commanded.

The stairs led me up to a wide, poorly lit hallway, and I ducked instinctively. Three bolts of lightning flashed by. The hair on my neck stood up. The stone wall behind me exploded, sending pieces smacking into me, though that wasn't enough to postpone the monsters' demise—my pistol fired quickly. The shots hurt. Stepping over the motionless bodies, I left the hallway and found myself in a large room. It looked like the remains of the attack group had gathered there for a last stand.

There was a hulking mass in charge of the formation. It continually changed from one shape to another, though two things remained the same: its enormous blue eyes and its giant head. Like some kind of snake trying to hypnotize its victim, the creature danced bewitchingly in front of me, slowly making its way closer step by step. Its troops followed meekly behind it. Misinterpreting my confusion, the monster moved faster, pressed harder, and almost had me hearing the voice. *Give in, you little weakling.* I shook my head to clear myself of the delusion and tossed my new purchase into the center of the group, myself diving into a corner. I'd long wanted to find out what those plasma grenades were all about. There had to be a reason they cost 2,000 coins.

The fiery storm of pure plasma that burst through the hallway answered my question. Even through my BRO-III costume, and despite my level four resistance, I felt the heat. It didn't last long—just a few seconds. And when I peered out from behind the corner, all that was left of the superior monsters were smoking remains. Half the champions were having a rough go of it, too, flailing charred limbs as they convulsed. On the other hand, some of them didn't have a problem at all. They appeared to be the ones who could use fire themselves, though they were no match for my KORT-III. Dodging the fireballs that came flying at me, I worked my way down from largest to smallest. The ones convulsing on the ground were saved for last.

When the last monster twitched and fell silent, a long-awaited message appeared on my screen:

Congratulations!
You destroyed an attack group.
Level +5 (25).
5 free attribute points received.
New title: Stone Wall.

A side door flew off its hinges, and Grust and Little appeared. Judging by the fact that they were coming from the direction of the same basement where I'd been held, they were less guests and more prisoners.

"Where's Milady?" The first question my partner had was about his soldier. *Respect.* I decided to just be frank with him.

"Dead. I saw the monsters pulled her off the roof."

"She's alive," Grust shot back. "And we have to find her. Little!"

The boy stopped giving me a withering look long enough to close his eyes, a minute later pointing in a direction off to the side.

"She's that way—I can sense her! She's hurt, but she's alive."

"Let's go!" Grust barked, though Little just pointed at me.

"With him? After everything he did?!"

"With him. He's one of us now, period. If you have a problem with that, you can tell me later. You have your orders!"

"Yes, sir," Little replied unhappily. *Wow, so it's like that, is it?*

"It sucks that your drone is back at the nuclear plant. We could really use it," Grust said as soon as we walked out of the building. It was a country estate that had once belonged to one of the former rulers of our world. There were a lot of them scattered around.

I said nothing, just tapping the button to materialize my Mark-1. It was fun watching the expression of shock that came over the pair's face as they tried to wrap their head around what was going on. Even impassive Grust, who I didn't think could show emotion, was impressed.

"You'll have to tell me what that's all about later," he said as he looked down at his phone. It was simpler for me—the map popped up in my helmet.

There were quite a few red dots in the area, and they were split into two groups. The first was on the other side of the building—there were about thirty of them. The rest, of which there were quite a few, were coming at us from the front. Without taking long to think, I sent the drone flying out ahead. A detachment of fifty superior monsters and ten champions dashed after it.

"Same as before," I said, tossing Grust my rifle and pulling out my pistol. I didn't have time to materialize my second rifle, so I asked the kid to head back into the building.

"Right, like I—"

"Back inside!" Grust barked as he looked for a good spot to shoot from. The kid was back through the door an instant later. Leaving the fighter alone, I ran toward the onrushing monsters. I couldn't let them get past me—Grust had no protection whatsoever.

Shots flew past me as if fired from a machinegun. Our crowd of guests had appeared on the road, and Grust was only too happy to open fire. Once I'd gotten far enough, I stopped. The champions went with their tried and true strategy, as well, flanking around the sides. Four were to the right, four to the left, and two straight ahead to hold our attention. I very much hoped that Grust would check his map and see what I was looking at. Just in case, I pointed to the left, where the enormous beasts were making their way through the bushes, and dashed off to the right. There were mages in that direction—the lightning bolt I took to the chest told me as much. I was sent flying backward, and the champions off to the left decided to finish off the wounded animal. How were they supposed to know that a player could survive a direct hit from a bolt of lightning? The champions were at level three; my resilience was already at level four. There was no damage besides the holes in my outfit, and they were already closing. When the large, tiger-like champions burst out of the underbrush, they were met by a wall of fire from my automatic pistol. Four for Mark; zero for the champions. Grust saw what was going on and focused on the four on the other side. That left me with the middle group. The small fry were quickly gunned down, though the two champions took some doing. The acid they hit me with was unpleasant enough that I wanted to avoid a second run-in at any cost. It ate through my outfit and down to the bone. Furious, I took the nearest one's head off with several rounds, after which I practically ran into the second one. Of course, a couple shots were enough to tear its chest inside out, though what really stopped me was the fact that the lightning that came with my tenth shot turned the thing into a quivering mass. It didn't look like the poor guy had any resistance to electricity. But it wasn't enough to kill it—the marker on my map told me that it was still alive.

Turning, I waved for Grust to come over.

"We need to figure this communication thing out. Maybe buy some walkie-talkies."

"Learn the gestures," Grust said as he took aim at the champion. I stopped him.

"Easy there. We're taking it with us."

"To Aspen?" Grust replied in surprise. "What for?"

"Going to make some money. Taking a selfie with a live champion in the background gives you four hundred coins, another three hundred for each if it's a group shot. What, you didn't read your logs?"

"When? We started fighting the minute I woke up. And then it was just darkness until now."

"There's a lot in there—check it out. Okay, we have to tie this thing up."

I had to give it to him. The guy knew exactly what to do, making his way carefully over to the hulk. After all, it isn't every day you find yourself in front of a terrifying monster at level three dressed in nothing but your underwear. And he definitely knew what to do with the tough ropes we found in the house. The owner had apparently enjoyed mountain-climbing, as we even found a couple carabiners. And when we called Little over, we each picked up a tidy 1,300 coins. Everyone was thrilled. Who wouldn't have been with a sum like that?

"Just one question. How are we going to get it to Aspen?" Little asked as he looked over our handiwork.

"I'll show you later. You two didn't forget about the second group, did you?" I asked. "We only took out half the monsters. Oh, and where's my share?"

Little had taken the picture of the bodies with his phone, eventually splitting the total evenly between us. That was convenient enough for me. Of course, everyone could go around taking pictures of the dead champions to pick up an additional ten coins each, and I spent a couple minutes doing just that even though it was chump change compared to my 1,100 share. You can't have too much money.

Grust helped Little set up his phone, after which I hooked him up to the drone. The kid gasped. And when I pulled up the video and flew over to the second group of red dots, we all gasped together. They were all women. Their legs and arms gone, they were lying in tubs full of a strange green liquid...and they were all pregnant. A canopy was over each, with life support masks and feeding tubes attached to their faces. Everything was autonomous—there were no monsters to be seen. But that wasn't the scariest part.

"We're going to be here a while," Grust said. "Mark, will you chip in for regeneration?"

I nodded, my eyes fixed on the screen. All thirty of the women were pregnant. The enormous stomachs poking out of the baths made that clear, and one of them was Milady.

No sooner had the last injection emptied into the last body, than our phones went crazy. It was a good thing nobody saw my face in that moment, at least not if it was as confused as Grust's or as shocked as Little's.

You destroyed 1 of the larva's 3 farms in this location.

Title: Monster Scourge changed to Monster Annihilator.

***

A larva designated *Together to the End* a personal enemy. From now on, all the monsters in this location will do double damage to you. You will receive twice as many coins for each monster killed.

***

You attracted the attention of the general in this hexagon.

A destroyer was sent to hunt you.

***

You're the first player in this hexagon to receive that title.

Level +5 (30).

***

You're the first player in this hexagon to become the personal enemy of a larva.

Level +5 (35).

5 free attribute points received.

You can collect any level three item in the store for free.

***

You're the first player a destroyer was sent to hunt.

Level +5 (40).

5 free attribute points received.

You can collect any level three item in the store for free.

Book 1: ⋂o ⋔istakes

There were quite a few notifications, but I was too distracted to really enjoy them. All my thoughts were there next to the tubs.

"We have to find them all," Grust said with a heavy voice. "Mark?"

"I'm with you. Together to the end."

Chapter 11

I SPENT A LONG TIME carefully thinking through how I wanted to spend my thirty-five attribute points. Whoever that destroyer was, the name alone told me it was a beast to be reckoned with. And that meant I needed to boost my main attributes and skills. After pausing for a second, I ended up adding device control. A wave came over me, and it was so strong that I thought for a second my head was going to explode from the pain and pressure. But when it was over, I could control the drone and my ATV without my phone. Just like that. I could turn the camera, flying at the same time, dive and bank... I could do so much that it took me thirty minutes to get used to my new abilities. They were worth it, though. Even my phone connected to my head. There was a projection in front of me constantly, even without my helmet, and that saved me so much time. For instance, I could duck into the store just by thinking about it. Grust didn't have anything to say—he was too busy adding attributes himself. Finally, the system told us that we'd both made it into the list of top ten players in the location. Grust was third; I was ninth.

Status table		
Name	Mark Derwin	
Coins	14 510	Level	40
Titles and ranks		
Title: Monster Annihilator		
Ranks: Bandit Bane, Lone Wolf, Stone Wall		
Attributes		
Strength	7	Regeneration	15
Stamina	7	Resilience	7
Agility	7	Willpower	7
Skills		
Pistol shooting		8
Rifle shooting		8
Melee weapons		8
Device control		4

I contemplated for a long time what to take from the system as my bonus. On the one hand, I needed a better rifle. But on the other, I was doing fine with my upgraded abilities. I ended up going with two devices I really needed.

V-3 vibroknife. Description: *Ignores physical and energy armor through level 4. Blocks regeneration through level 4. Blocks 1 random ability. Rendered inert by magnetic fields. Cost: 40,000 coins.*

II-3 universal force field. *Description: Protects from physical and energy weapons through level 3, up* *to 200 hits. Restores 1 hit every 5 minutes. Cost: 100,000 coins.*

Finally! The main problem for all of us players was that good protection against physical damage did nothing against energy weapons. The cheapest pistol, the one you could buy for 100 coins, could take out the most advanced, imposing attacker. Sure, some of the damage would be absorbed by their protective outfit, but that just reduced the damage. I'd had my eye on that universal force field for quite a while. The price had scared me off, but I jumped at the chance to pick it up and keep myself safe from stray bullets.

Grust grabbed himself a rifle and a BRO-III outfit. And Little... Well, he surprised me. Although, it could have just been the way they did things in their group, something I wasn't aware of. The kid took the same helmet I had as well as a universal force field. It was a good choice, and I was with him all the way, at least until he picked them up as soon as they'd materialized and handed them to Grust. There were no questions, no mute appeals to me for help. He just up and did it on his own.

I didn't get involved. *They probably know what they're doing.*

I jumped a mile when a message popped up in my head, finding myself suddenly on the ground. *Damn, that's going to take some getting used to!*

Conversation with Squirrel Derwin available. Would you like to wake her?

Finally! Yes, of course I would! Just thinking about tapping the accept button was enough for me to hear the ringing. That device control really was something. A few long rings later, I heard Squirrel's sleepy voice.

"Mark?"

"Hi!" A smile crept involuntarily over my face. It was great to hear a familiar voice. "How are you?"

"Good, I think... Why can't I see anything? Where am I?"

"In a life support module. What's the last thing you remember?"

"Some bastard trying to take my clothes off," my sister replied, her voice darkening. "Then everything started shaking and crumbling, and... Oh! I called you! Yeah, I remember now!"

"That's the only reason you're alive. You got in touch, and I was able to save you."

"You killed that thing? Did you make it suffer?"

"That's not how I saved you. You're still in the city, underground... Wait, what's that?"

I could hear a clear scraping sound coming through the speaker, something like a stone being dragged across metal.

"What do you mean, I'm underground?" My

sister's tone took on a sense of panic. "Is that why I can't move? I'm still stuck? Mark, where's the light? I need some light! Why can't I see anything?! Am I blind? Get me out of here!"

Squirrel was yelling by the time she got to the end—a panic attack. I knew she had a phobia about getting buried alive, as she'd watched too many horror movies and had even had to deal with nightmares for a long time. And her fears were coming true. She was all alone, there under a thick layer of earth. And that awful sound... She complete lost it, unable to even hear what I was trying to tell her. I listened as she thrashed against the capsule, convulsing and making me worry she'd hurt herself. Ultimately, I didn't have a choice.

"Put her back to sleep!"

The frantic motion stopped instantly, replaced by a heavy breathing and that teeth-rattling scrape of stone on metal. I didn't like it, and I couldn't figure out what it was. Either someone was dragging the capsule off somewhere, or they were trying to break into it. I wasn't a fan of either option.

"Mark, I need you," came Grust's strained voice in my speakers. Our helmets had synced up easily, and we no longer needed to communicate with gestures. We'd still exchanged contact information in case we needed to call each other.

"Where are you?"

"By the tubs. Send Little to guard the prisoner."

The women were all in fine form, their limbs regenerated, only their stomachs were still distended. In fact, they were bigger. The tubs were too small to hold them, and so Grust had pulled them out onto the ground. *Yes, the kid doesn't need to see thirty naked bodies about to—*

"They're going to give birth," I said, my voice unfamiliar.

"All thirty of them," Grust replied. "And it's a good fifteen kilometers to Aspen."

"Why didn't they wake up? Shouldn't they have?"

"You're asking me? This is the first time I'm seeing anything like this. I have chills, and it's not good that their stomachs are growing so quickly. Have you ever helped anyone through childbirth?"

"No." I was surprised by the unexpected question.

"Me, neither. But we're going to have to. That half is yours; this half is mine. I hope the chicks know what to do."

When the women started to groan, still without regaining consciousness, I panicked. It was only Grust's threatening yell that snapped me out of it. Right then, for the first time in my life, I saw someone give birth. At least, I stood there, held out my hands, and caught something slippery, black, limbless, and very unlike a human child. A curse came from Grust's direction—he was looking at the same thing. We spread a piece of cloth out on the ground and started piling on top of it the little creatures that came crawling out of the women. They were like dolls, only with something beating inside. A couple seconds in the sun, and one of the dolls opened up to reveal a strange creature that was fleshy, hairy, and long-eared. I'd already seen something like it. Gray, Olson. Shurvans. The children didn't cry or look for warmth. Instead, they just laid there and looked at us with their entirely intelligent eyes. Chills ran down my spine, and I almost vomited. It was a terrifying sight.

What's scarier than death? complete. You figured out why the monsters are kidnapping women of childbearing age.
Level +1 (41).

"Incubators," Grust growled, slamming a fist into the ground as hard as he could. "Damn incubators! That's what they're doing to Earth."

I went over to the closest girl. She was young, about twenty. Cute, but not overly so. The only problem was that she was motionless and unconscious, her eyes rolled back—I pulled them open to check. Her phone gone, there was no way to see what her status was.

But just then, she groaned and curled up. The other women followed her lead, only to relax a couple seconds later. And that's when my heart skipped a beat—their stomachs were beginning to grow right in front of me. Another round. Eight or nine hours later, they were going to give birth again.

"They're not going to wake up again, are they?" It was difficult to look at Grust. I'd never seen him like that—gloomy, dark, agonized, twenty years older.

"No. I've seen this before, and their minds can't come back even though their bodies are healthy."

"Mark, I need you to leave."

"Grust, I—"

"Leave, I said!" he screamed. "Get out of here! I loved her, and I have to do this myself."

I made my way over to Little on stiff legs, jumping every time I heard a shot. Finding two shovels in a shed, I returned to where Grust was. The powerful man was on his knees sobbing next to Milady. A neat hole in her forehead told me she wouldn't be giving birth anymore.

Silently, I stuck my shovel into the earth and started digging a hole. Grust joined me a minute later. Without saying a word to each other, we tossed the bodies in and covered them with earth. Then, we placed an enormous slab on top, so heavy that we had to carry it together. Grust scratched an inscription on it.

Here lie thirty keepers of the hearth. Respect their memory, traveler.

"I'll tell Little myself," Grust said without looking at me. "What's Olson's problem with you? He wouldn't just hand out an order to hunt you for no reason."

"I owe him." There was no sense hiding the truth, and so I told him about my sister, how I'd saved her, and what I thought about my potential future as a slave.

"A hundred thousand coins is a lot."

"I already have ten, and the rest will come. If we can get the champion to Aspen, it'll be a piece of cake."

But that wasn't going to happen. Out on the porch, we were met by a scowling Little.

"I didn't do anything! Honestly! That thing died on its own!" he said adamantly, hiding his eyes. But the ten deep holes in the monster's head told me a very different story.

"Why?" Grust asked.

"They killed my sister! The animals! I hate them all." No matter what kind of a brave face Little tried to put on, he was still a kid, and he broke down crying.

"You're right to hate them." Grust embraced him. "You just have to be smart about how you do it. Did you take a picture?"

"What?" Little asked, sniffing.

"Did you take a picture of the monster? Did you

get your coins? How are you going to avenge your sister's death if you're just going to be miserable? You have to take the picture. That's an order!"

"Yes, sir..."

I would have given anything to not be in Little's shoes. It's a horrible thing when children have to grow up too quickly, especially for a reason like that one. My phone received 220 coins, my share from the dead monster and the second picture. The drone soared up into the sky to show that there wasn't a single living soul within a radius of five hundred meters.

"Where to now?" Little asked.

"We're off to find the next farm. You have something else to do, and that's another order," Grust said in a voice that didn't brook objections when he saw the boy about to give one. "You have an important mission: you need to beat a dungeon. Alone. Mark, walk him through it."

I was on the same page as Grust. Little needed to get stronger, and there wasn't anywhere better than a dungeon for him to pick up new equipment. With his level 32 and a good weapon, the dungeon was going to be a piece of cake, even with the final boss. And he'd pick up a tidy bonus.

"And when you're done, you sit inside until I call you. Got it? Okay, get to work."

"Yes, sir!" Little grabbed his rifle and dashed off. The entrance to the dungeon was twenty kilometers away, which meant it would take him about an hour and a half to get there.

"The area around Aspen is almost clear," Grust said as he watched the kid go. "Milady made me promise that if anything happened to her, I'd take care of him. And whoever that destroyer is, it won't go into the dungeon. Mark, do you know where the next farm is?"

"I have an idea, and we can stop by the cache at the same time." I thought back to Valdemar and his women. It was a shame—he'd lost two at once. At least, their deaths wouldn't be a waste, as I remembered the direction they'd been dragged off in.

"Let's go. Ready for a run?"

"There's a better way." A minute later, my Mark-2 showed up next to us. Grust just grunted, and I spent the next five minutes telling him about my virtual storage and how to get one as we made our way around deep holes.

"We're here," I said thirty minutes later when we pulled up next to the oak. Grust clambered up and pulled a zoom lens out of the cache, the same one I had.

"Useless piece of junk," I said sadly. I'd been hoping he'd get something better. "I haven't a single chance to use it in the time I've been playing."

"Hey, I leveled-up," my partner replied as he updated his phone. "Where to now?"

The monsters had left a wide path behind them—it looked like they'd been back. We were able to drive about thirty meters, but that's when the underbrush really got thick, and we had to continue on foot. But it was only a couple kilometers later when the drone alerted us to a bunch of red dots. Only they weren't where we were expecting them. They were off to the side.

"Check it out," Grust said, stopping. Keeping the drone close to the tops of the trees so it would go unnoticed, I flew in closer. There was a small, rickety house that looked like a forester's lodge. Around it were thirty-two people going about their business. Some were lying on the ground, others were cleaning their weapons, still more were playing a game. And they weren't just players; they were a force to be reckoned with. Two off roaders were equipped with machineguns, and there were a few ATVs, though they weren't as nice as mine. Even motorcycles. There were wheels for everyone, and their equipment looked great. In charge was an enormous, bald-headed warrior with the body of Hercules and an unpleasant look to him—a low forehead, deep-set eyes, and a deformed skull. While everyone else was relaxing, he was hard at work jumping from one pillar set in the ground to another. He was even summersaulting between them. The guy's agility was amazing. And what immediately grabbed my attention was that all the fighters in the group had monster body parts. Tails, fangs, claws, a little of everything.

"You can pull the drone back—I know them." A nastiness crept into Grust's voice. "Wax and his gang. Crazy thugs. I came across them in the city, barely got away. They don't care about anyone, killing whoever they come across. Monster or player, it doesn't matter."

I pulled up the ranking and sighed. Wax was easy to find—it would have been hard not to notice the first line and the number 73 next to his name. *Yes, that's a beast right there.* I was about to say that we should head back when I notice something strange. There were a few more red dots in the vehicles, all very close together. *But I thought they were empty!* I pointed them out to my partner, and he asked me to bank left a little.

"No good, there's a guard there, and he'll see it." I turned the camera to show a nearby fighter. He was looking in the wrong direction, which was why he hadn't seen us. But suddenly, from the opposite side, there was a whistle, and another group of red dots joined the main one. Grust cursed when he saw who it was—a champion in the form of a mage and his entourage. I was used to the game characters working with each other, and the conclusion was obvious. Wax wasn't a player.

"How is that even possible?" Grust asked in shock when I told him about Gray and his gang. How he'd been number one until I took him out. Wax looked like the same kind of guy.

"Sure looks like you're right," my partner said when he saw that the mage was in no hurry to attack. The bald giant finished his workout and went over to meet it. Again, there was a curse from Grust. The pair hugged like old friends.

Finally, I saw what had been hidden in the cars, as the fighters pulled out four bound girls. But that time the game really had a surprise for me: I recognized two of them. It was the same unlucky pair I'd come across right before I'd wiped out Gray's gang. *Valdemar's sister and wife? But they already traded them! How are they alive?*

The mage smiled as it looked over the victims, after which it dumped a few items in front of Wax. Again, they hugged, that time in parting, and the monsters beat a course parallel to ours, dragging their prey with them. The fighters forgot about their prisoners and crowded around to see what they'd gotten. As I found out later, not far from the clearing, Grust and I had come to the same conclusion. Wax and his gang had to be put down.

But the monsters were first.

They were moving at the same speed we were, as they were loaded down with their prisoners. And the drone kept a close eye on them over the next hour as we dashed through underbrush and gullies. Finally, just when my legs were starting to give out, we ran up to yet another abandoned village.

"Look at that thing!" Grust burst out. I was right there with him—I'd never seen a beast like that one. There was an enormous, many-armed monster keeping watch over the village, which we assumed was the next farm. The only way I could think of to describe it was an octopus fused with a centipede that looked like a nimble cheetah. The flexible body was the size of a truck, it had long feelers, and it moved around terrifyingly on its numerous legs. And it was patrolling the perimeter as though expecting someone.

"The larva?" I asked as I peered through my scope. The most damage my rifle could do was 0.02%.

"Who the hell knows? But it's nasty, going to be tough to take it out. I just get 0.03% if I hit the eyes. Ready?"

"Hold on."

The monster's feelers shot forward to grab the prey from the superior monsters, and two girls were discarded onto the ground. It was Valdemar's pair. The other two were slung over its back, and the creature swept off into the forest, trees crashing to the ground under it. Not that far from us, actually. Unable to resist, I zoomed in as far as I could and took a picture. I wanted to see what it was.

You took a picture of a live larva from less

than 3 meters away. 10000 coins received.

And there it was, the main monster in our location. Grust grunted next to me, looking thoughtfully at his phone. He'd gotten the same message as me. *Finally, that zoom came in handy.*

The mage and its entourage watched the larva go before grinning happily, turning to look at the two women as they tried to crawl away.

"They're going to eat them."

"No, they're not." Grunt dropped to a knee. "Cover them!"

Our two rifles spoke in unison. The mage didn't have time to twitch before his head was riddled full of holes, and the superior monsters were next. They rushed toward us in search of revenge for their leader. A prolonged howl broke out, and the village was overwhelmed with motion. Monsters came pouring out of every nook and cranny, the scanner turning the area into one big red blotch. At some point, I had to toss aside my rifle and grab my automatic pistol. Grust worked on the bigger targets with his U-III, while I took out the small fry before they could get to us. The last red dot died away, and we were left with just fifty around the main building. The drone headed that way to reveal fifty tubs and their blood-curdling contents. And judging by the fact that they weren't swollen with child, the larva had just collected the harvest and run off to the next farm.

You took the first picture of 39 dead inferior monsters. 78 coins received.

You took the first picture of 264 dead superior monsters. 2640 coins received.

You took the first picture of 18 dead champions. 10800 coins received.

"Your share." I sent Grust his coins.

"Nice chunk of change," he said as he headed toward the tubs. "Find some shovels and see how the girls are."

You destroyed 2 of the larva's 3 farms in this location.

There was no long text that time—the game had gotten used to our achievements. It was just kind of ho-hum, apparently. *The larva will make itself another farm.*

The women were okay, or as okay as pregnant women can be. Both Laura, Valdemar's sister, and Ella, his wife, were three months pregnant. With regular, human babies. The monsters saw them as receptacles, only those two were already full, which was why the larva had tossed them aside both times. When they saw us, the girls broke down in hysterics.

They think we're Wax's people. We had to take off our helmets and explain that we were regular people, and I even mentioned Valdemar. Sadly, I didn't know where he was, but hearing a familiar name helped. The two did what women do in their case: they burst into bitter tears, sticking close to us. Although, there was a second round of hysterics waiting when the two saw the contents of the tubs and realized the fate that had been awaiting them.

"It's twenty kilometers to Aspen as the crow flies," I said, pulling up my map as soon as an enormous rock we found nearby took its place as a tombstone. Grust was busy scratching away at a message to our descendants. "The larva went off in the opposite direction, so the third farm is somewhere over there."

"We can't just leave them." Grust sighed heavily and looked over at the women, who had fallen silent. They knew their fate was being decided. "But we can't just go through Wax's territory with them, either."

"And going around isn't an option. That would take a couple days, and the larva would open a new farm in that time."

An oppressive silence fell. Each of us was occupied with their own thoughts, trying to decide what was best to do, and that's when a barely audible sound broke through the air. It sounded like a tree branch snapping. A few seconds later, I realized that it didn't just sound like a tree branch snapping. That's exactly what it was.

"Everyone into the building!" I yelled, the first to dive behind the protection offered by the stone walls. "There should be a basement somewhere!"

"Find it!" Grust quickly got his bearings, grabbed the women by the waist, picked them up, and barreled after me. The sound hadn't come from the direction the larva had run off in, so I doubted the creature had doubled back to attack us from the flank.

I ripped the door off the hinges and found a staircase leading downward.

"Stay down there!" Grust shoved the women down the steps and closed the door. Then, he turned to me, his voice serious.

"Let's head outside. You think it's the destroyer?"

"Yeah." The drone soared high into the sky to offer a picture of the village. We could see flashes of gunfire, tracers, and even some explosions. The destroyer was on its way past Wax's lodge. For a second, it paused before resuming its progress toward us. I could only imagine that the gang had been wiped out. *That's something, at least.*

Finally, the drone gave us a good picture. There was something heading toward us that was metal, enormous, and equipped with all kinds of sharp disks. A red dot appeared on the scanner, and that was the last thing the drone saw in its short life. Lightning flashed. There was an explosion.

Mark-1 destroyed and removed from your equipment list.

The final trees were swept aside, and I was treated to a vision of the bastard that destroyed my drone. Up on a metal platform levitating above the ground, there was a creature that looked like an old iron. It was just as massive, sharp-nosed, and metal. The destroyer was outfitted from top to bottom with cannons, dischargers, buzz saws, and arms that were in the process of throwing branches aside. My rifle wouldn't give me anything more than 0.01% no matter how much time I spent scanning the war machine. And it really was a machine, either a robot, or something controlled remotely. The perfect killer. Pausing to look around, the destroyer made its way toward us as if it knew exactly where we were hiding.

"Fire!" Grust barked, and our rifles jumped into action.

Chapter 12

IT WAS A GOOD THING Grust and I weren't standing next to each other. No sooner had we opened fire and sent ten or twelve charges at the thing, than a shot from a high-caliber energy cannon came flying back the other direction. My protection kept my body intact, though it did nothing for my rifle. It was practically taken apart at the seams. The machine fired away with two weapons on the sides, adding its frontal cannons to the mix.

I peeled myself off the wall the shock wave had imprinted me on, collapsed to my knees, and shook my head. It had been a heavy hit. Throwing the piece of trash in my hand to the side, I pulled out my vibroknife. There was no giving up. Suddenly, a shadow flashed by. Grust, dodging nimbly from side to side, dashed toward the monster, shooting with his pistol as he went. He'd drawn the same conclusion I had: we couldn't take the thing on in a firefight. We had to get in closer.

Yelling a battle cry, Grust leaped toward the

destroyer, sidestepped the grabbers, and jumped on board, his knife cutting deeply into one of the emitters. I hopped to my feet, intending to join him, but that just meant I got to see his final seconds. A powerful energy wave travelled up the beast's body. With it, a smoking hunk of meat flew off to the side, all that was left of Grust.

From there, it was all instinct, no strategy. Forgetting everything else, I dashed toward my partner, pulling out my regeneration syringe as I went. *Good thing I decided to keep one on me!* Gravel kicked up around me. The earth shook. I was thrown back and forth a few times, though my protection held. With one final leap, I got to Grust, buried the syringe in him, grabbed his hot body, and, like some hammer-thrower, hurled him onto the roof of the neighboring building. Then, I summersaulted to the side in the same motion and galloped off. I needed to pull the monster away from the village.

The destroyer set off after me without a second thought. Neither tree nor rut slowed it down as it rammed through the forest just like a powerful iron smoothing out a wrinkled shirt with steam and its own power. I jumped to the side yet again, though that time I caught a shot in the back from the cannon. The world around me darkened for just a moment. Somehow, however, my protection held up. My P-III was stronger than that monster, and that brought me back to life.

It wasn't a superpower. It was just a level three monster I could take. Sure, it was a strong, powerful machine. But it was still just a machine, a device that obeyed the laws and logic of the game. *And what do I have?*

Yes, access to the store and coins to spend!

Skill upgrades only took ten minutes, nothing like attributes and their three-hour schedules. Attribute syringes cost 2,000 coins, and I had one free point ready from the last time I'd leveled-up. That left buying time my biggest problem. I continued dodging shot after shot, running at top speed, and stabbing myself with the attribute syringes as they appeared in my hand. *Screw the cash, I need to live!* Four syringes later, I started my upgrade:

Device control +4 (8).

A gully appeared in front of me, a happy sight indeed—everything else aside, the destroyer was a massive hulk. It was going to have a hard time getting down the incline. And that would buy me a few minutes. A jump to the left, another to the right, one more to the left, running the whole time, and I dove over the edge, rolling down the steep side. I didn't even take time to stop and reflect when I slammed into a tree. My next purchase, two thermonuclear grenades, had appeared in my hand, and I hit the button and tossed the first up to where the destroyer was about to appear the second it materialized. Off I ran, deeper into the gully. I needed eight more minutes.

The detonation shook the ground—I'd never seen a grenade like that go off in an open area. Unable to help it, I looked back at my opponent to see that if it had hurt him, it was only somewhere deep down inside. But the heavy bastard at least stopped at the edge of the gully the way I expected. From there, it began riddling the whole area with the entire extent of its firepower, turning enormous trees into kindling in a matter of seconds. Earth showered down, kicked up by explosions that sent sparks flying everywhere. And from my position in the middle of the chaos, I activated my second grenade and hurled it at the destroyer. My strength and agility held up their end of the bargain. Cutting its way through the barrage of fire, the explosive landed on the machine and exploded.

My helmet adjusted to the brightness, and I saw a little sun appear next to the destroyer and rip off its cannons and a few emitters. But no sooner did it begin to fade, than the beast regrew its weaponry. It was so fast, in fact, that I wouldn't have noticed if it hadn't been for the dimmed light. My stomach fell, and I just wanted the battle to be over. There was no point fighting a monster like that—it regenerated itself faster than I could hurt it. I could have thrown as many grenades as I wanted, but they wouldn't have made a dent.

At least, it wasn't as simple as it had at first appeared. The return fire didn't pick up immediately, as the monstrosity apparently needed time to recalibrate and refit. I even counted how long it took: thirty seconds. A flicker of hope appeared where there had only been emptiness a moment before. Yes, I still needed more time, but I had an idea of what to do.

Run. That's what I need to do!

Without allowing myself any cover fire, I sprinted off. Finally, the beast noticed me and began shooting. I was forced once again to dodge from side to side, eventually—and for this I owed the guy my thanks—catching a shot to the back. It hurtled me high into the air, and the destroyer didn't let me down. Right at the top of my arc, it buried a powerful impulse in me. My protection kicked in, and I was thrown forward, far out of the gully. Sure, it was a risky move, but that was the fastest way to put some distance between us.

Having the head start was great. The destroyer headed after me via the gully, hurtling over it with the speed of a crazed turtle. It was fast, just not as fast as it could go over flat terrain. That gave me the chance to open the distance between us to a hundred meters as I traced a circle around the village. Grust was recovering there, and I couldn't let myself get too far away. Yes, recovering—the syringe had emptied itself into him without any questions.

For the ten minutes I needed to adapt to my new skills, I ran in a straight line. The destroyer kept up its fire, though it was clearly getting lazy about it. The monster knew its stamina was better than mine. There was no hurry. Sooner or later, I would collapse to the ground exhausted, and that's when it would grind me into powder. It was a destroyer, after all.

Activating a grenade, I stopped suddenly and retraced my steps. The cannon and machine guns opened up, and I had to make like a drunk rabbit to ensure I didn't rejoin my parents earlier than I'd planned.

When I was about thirty meters away from the death machine, I hurled the grenade and ducked, a few rounds flying over my head.

There was an explosion and I jumped onto the monster before the fire died away. My body was singed even through the BRO-III outfit, and my boots melted on the scorched metal, but my resilience kept me from screaming in pain. There was only a vague idea of what to do in my head. Still, I tossed off my gloves and laid my bare palms on the machine.

A message appeared in my head, right next to the image of the phone:

Controllable devices discovered.
Would you like to take control?

Yes, hurry!

Hijacking control block... Unsuccessful.
Hijacking protection block... Unsuccessful.
Hijacking attack block... Unsuccessful.
Hijacking platform... Successful.
Would you like to connect to the PL-III levitating platform?

Yes! There, in the spot my drone had once been, a new flying device appeared, and I sent it spiraling without much thought. It nosed forward, the platform spun upward, and the destroyer's entire mass was sent ahead. Right at me.

It was probably the highest a human had ever jumped. There was no space to the side, ahead, or behind me—the destroyer and its cannons were everywhere. Plus, every fiber of my being told me that it was about to fire off the same charge that had knocked out Grust. And that's why I leaped straight into the air. With all the strength I could muster. The toppling destroyer's tail end whipped by under my feet, and the game took away my new toy:

PL-III destroyed and removed from your equipment list.

That damn iron took out my device! I landed next

to the remains of what had once been the PL-III, my next jump taking me farther away from the destroyer. It was clearly enraged. From its position on its side, the creature fired away with everything it had, turning the area around it into a veritable hell. It was only at the bottom where the platform had once been that there weren't any weapons. In fact, a small, rectangular hatch had been uncovered. Having never learned the lesson that heroes don't live long, and instead of running off to find a deep hole to hide in, I ran toward the death-dealing guns of my opponent. Of course, I took a few hits, but my protection held up long enough for me to make it to the underside. My vibroknife cut through the latches like warm butter. Throwing the hatch aside, I found a mass of wires and mechanisms that I would never have been able to make heads or tails of.

But I didn't need to.

My cash reserves dropped by another two thousand, and a plasma grenade went flying into the guts of the destroyer. I jumped to the side, there was an explosion, and the world around me suddenly froze. Only the sound of the trees shuddering told me that I hadn't lost my hearing.

You eliminated destroyer ST-4.
Title: Monster Annihilator changed to Destroyer.

***

You became the first player on Earth to eliminate a destroyer.

Level +20 (61).

10 free attribute points available.

Level 4 items unlocked in the store.

You can collect any 4 level four items in the store for free.

***

The general in your hexagon is unhappy with you and sent the bosses from two neighboring locations to reinforce the larva.

You're the first player in your hexagon to worry the general. From now on, all the monsters in your hexagon will do triple damage to you. You will receive three times as many coins for each monster killed.

Level +5 (66).

5 free attribute points received.

You can collect any level four item in the store for free.

***

You're now the top player in your location.

Access to the list of top players in your hexagon unlocked.

Book 1: No Mistakes

***

You took the first picture of a dead larva-level creature. 60000 coins received.

I picked up quite a few bonuses, though I was in no hurry to go around jumping for joy. Placing my hands on the machine's body, I listened to my inner voice. *Come on!*

Controllable devices available for extraction.
Hijacking control block... Successful, 8 level three devices available.
Hijacking defense block... Successful, 3 level three devices available.
Hijacking attack block... Successful, 4 level three devices available.
Extract devices from the body?

I agreed, and the enormous hulk melted away, leaving a bunch of parts behind. There were cannon, shields, some pins, springs... Most of the items had names I didn't recognize, so I gathered them into a pile and swept them into my packed virtual storage. And with that, I limped off toward the village. The platform, drone, and weaponry could wait for later. Grust was first.

From what I could remember, that was the first time since the game had begun that I felt a surge of happiness. I got to the roof and saw the shining eyes of my partner. His body wasn't back yet, and it looked like that might take the whole eight hours, but Grust was alive! And that was most important. His singed mouth spread into a painful grin. *He's even trying to smile!* It was only then that I noticed his helmet had been blown completely off, not to mention the rest of his clothes.

Picking him up, I leaped down to the ground. There was a quiet groan, though I was only too happy to hear it—he was only feeling pain because he was still alive. I carried him into the house, placed him on a bed, called the girls over to take care of him, and activated my Mark-2 so I could head back for the drone and the platform. They were my loot, too. And there was no way I was leaving them behind.

The drone was a mess. The destroyer's shell had left an enormous hole that went clear through it, demolishing the motors, the scanner, and everything else. Basically, it wasn't a drone anymore, and the game offered to break it down into its components. I agreed with a wry smile. All that came out was the Cartographer-I, everything else disintegrating into dust.

Things were better with the platform. Only the nose was banged up, and so I picked up quite a few more parts—thirty-two, in fact. Again, they had the unfamiliar names, though there wasn't any more space for them in my storage. I brought my ATV over to load them onto a tarp and haul them to the village. But that's when almost all the parts started glowing, which surprised me. The platform and the ATV were completely different machines, after all. Still, I started sticking the parts onto the Mark-2, turning it into an awesome hybrid. And when I ran out of parts from the platform, I waited fifteen minutes for the parts I'd gotten from the destroyer to materialize. Ten of them fit. Stepping to the side, I looked my creation over, even feeling a kind of pride deep down. *Where was that destroyer earlier?*

Mark-2. *Description: Modified flying transport built for Mark Derwin. Maximum altitude: 5 meters. Maximum flight speed: 120 km/h. Number of seats: 4. Maximum load: 250 kilograms. Weapons: 2 frontal ray guns (PL-III). Protection: universal force field (P-III). Cost: 25000000 coins.*

It was still technically an ATV. At least, it had four wheels. The only difference was that they'd taken on a completely different function: they were now jets or magnets that held the Mark-2 in the air. I couldn't figure out how they worked, though they were rotated horizontally to the ground. There was even a field around them that you could actually see. And the Mark-2 itself was hovering. The device didn't have a steering wheel, as it was controlled exclusively using my device control ability. Two seats were up front; two were in the back. There were no seatbelts, which made falling out a risk. The front seats were equipped with machineguns, though they didn't have much range of motion, meaning that the only direction you could really fire was straight ahead.

I climbed onto the Mark-2 and eased it gently forward, getting used to the controls. It was smooth and clean. The branches and earth beneath me didn't present a problem, though my breath caught in my throat when I sent the machine upward. It pressed me instantly into my seat. Scared I might fall out, I brought it back down and set off along the path the destroyer had cleared. But I sent it forward too quickly. Braking just as suddenly, I almost fell out the front when the Mark-2 stopped instantly. Sure, I'd given the command, but I hadn't been expecting that kind of response.

Finally, after kind of getting used to it, I headed toward Wax's lodge. The destroyer had made its way past the gang with barely any resistance. That meant there was loot lying around, and I wanted to get my hands on it. Also, Wax was still in the list of the location's top players. He was in second place.

Without the drone, I felt like I'd been bereft of my hands, and I had to keep stopping every hundred meters to look around. The lodge and equipment had been destroyed completely. Only fragments were littered around. There were also scorched bodies, which elicited a mutter from me. I wasn't going to be getting any loot from them. After three trips around and nothing dangerous to be seen, I stopped next to the vehicles.

6 devices available for extraction.

I didn't hesitate to go through the remains and carry what I came away with over to the Mark-2. It gained a protective roof, a railing, a skylight, and even seatbelts. I was a set of doors away from a beauty of a machine. The pile of equipment melted away, and I heard a light groan—Wax had been lying under all of it. He was hurt bad. His leg was bent at an unnatural angle, he had ribs jutting out of his chest, and his arms were crushed, but he was still alive. And I knew it wouldn't take him long to regenerate completely. Someone at that level definitely had strong regeneration.

"The destroyer couldn't pull it off?" the player asked with a nasty laugh when he realized who was standing next to him. He jerked, but I reacted in time. Just barely, too—an activated plasma grenade appeared in his hand. I leaped forward, ripped it out of his weak grip, and hurled it off to the side. A wave of fire swept through the clearing, wiping out everything the destroyer had left behind. I didn't give Wax a second chance. Taking his phone, I shot his arms off at the elbows just to make sure. *You won't be throwing anything now.*

"You don't have long to live, anyway—the game doesn't like high-level players," Wax said, spitting blood. "If it's not a destroyer, it'll be three larvae. And you can't even run forever on your Mark-2. Earth is doomed no matter what you do. We're all going to be its slaves!"

There was an unpleasant sensation in my chest, almost as if an electric current was running through me. Wax really was part of the game, working for it by supplying the monsters with women, killing off unneeded and overly developed players. Humans saw him not as a monster, but as someone similar to themselves. And they were wrong. Wax was the real monster, not the toothy beasts everyone was fighting.

"Anything interesting you'd like to tell me about before you die? Caches, dungeons? Where to find them?"

Wax snorted and coughed up blood, but he made a mistake. There was just one eloquent glance cast at the phone I was holding. A look away that was slightly too quick. He was trying hard to look natural, too hard, in fact. Ripping off his shield, I slashed down with my vibroknife. His head rolled away from his body, and there was a change at the top of the list of best players in the location. Grust took over the newly vacated number two slot.

You took the first picture of 34 dead players. 1020 coins received.

From there, it was a matter of looting everything I could find. I pawed through all the bodies, dug around in all the corners of the clearing, peered into every crevice, and found all the items and phones that were lying around. While there were 34 bodies, unfortunately, I was only able to find three phones. The destroyer had apparently done a number on the rest.

Player Wax. Status: Dead. Cash: 32970 coins.

Just like with Gray's gang, Wax was the only one with any money. I piled all the weapons, shields, equipment, and parts onto the Mark-2, pausing for a couple seconds. There was 113,000 coins in my account, which was enough for me to pay off my debt, though I put that idea aside immediately. Half of what I'd just gotten belonged to Grust. I would have been the worst of assholes if I'd run off with his share, though I could still head over to Olson and sell off what I had. That would add up to a couple hundred thousand, I figured. But Wax's phone was the top priority.

Would you like to hack into this player's phone?

Oh, cool, I didn't know that was possible! I'd been planning on just poking around, but then that message popped up. *Of course I want to!*

Hacking contact list... Unsuccessful.
Hacking list of store purchases... Unsuccessful.
Hacking map... Successful! Would you like to download the map?

With my heart pounding, I agreed and pulled up my updated map. Wax had really done a good job exploring the area. He'd been in the city, not to mention our location and the next one over. *That's a lot for one week!* Right away, I could tell that he had some kind of skill that improved his map, as each area had a name and a legend. Mine was just a two-dimensional picture. I found the oak tree with the cache I knew about, noticed that it was marked with a green triangle, and swallowed nervously when I zoomed out. There were several triangles in our location. The same was true of dungeons—Wax and his people had found two of them in each of the three locations. And that told me how he'd leveled-up so quickly. The game had been helping him. *You bastards, I hate you all! Idiot cheaters! It wouldn't be so easy if you had to do it the same way as everyone else.*

When I got back, Grust was already outside. He was weak and limping, but level fifteen regeneration worked miracles, especially when you coupled it with a shot. My new toy earned an admiring look, and he climbed up and sighed in relief. Walking had been difficult. Digging around in the loot and not finding anything worthwhile for himself, he glanced over at the women before looking back at the pile of weapons. I understood his wordless suggestion and nodded. Of course, it was a good idea to share, especially since the pair didn't have anything from the game.

"Tell me everything." Grust wasn't about to turn down 47,000 coins, though he asked why it was that much. I told him about the battle, how my meeting with Wax went, about creating my Mark-2. Of course, I wondered if Grust would demand that I turn over a share of the parts I'd spend on the vehicle, but he was all praise.

"Good decision—this thing is great. It's just a shame about the drone. Have you checked into getting a replacement? It really helped having it around."

"No, I haven't checked the store at all yet. I just know that a regular drone won't work. To make one game-based, you need an integration kit, and they cost around a hundred grand."

"I can chip in," Grust replied, though he realized what was going on when he saw my reaction. "No, you're right. You have to pay off your debt first. If you don't have enough, just let me know, and I'll help with the rest. But don't forget to check out the store. There's a lot of great new stuff in there—I had no idea what to pick as my bonuses."

I was intrigued, though my brain just wasn't making sense of anything anymore. It was exhausted. The crazed race with the destroyer had taken its toll.

"Let's head to Aspen." Grust looked over at the women, who were digging through the pile of weapons. "We need to leave them there and think about where to go next. If the larvae are half as strong as that destroyer, we won't be able to take on three of them. Especially with them doing triple damage."

"True... Although... You know, I have an idea."

"Excellent, you can tell me all about it." He settled into his seat and fastened his seatbelt. "I love bedtime stories!"

Chapter 13

OLSON'S PAINED EXPRESSION told me that I was on the right track. As part of the game, he knew very well what Grust and I had managed to pull off, and he wasn't thrilled to see us. But his functionality played right into my hands. The head of Aspen couldn't not buy my game items off me no matter how much he would have liked to throw me out of the village.

I ended up collecting a hundred and twenty grand. Grust was up-front, telling me that everything was mine, and that put me in the clear. The most expensive part turned out to be the engine boost, a copy of the one on my Mark-2. Olson didn't say a word when I repaid my debt. He just sighed heavily, and an announcement rippled through Aspen.

Mission to destroy Mark Derwin rescinded.

Your debt has been fully repaid.

Aspen itself had transformed since the last time I'd seen it. While there had been twenty unsightly buildings surrounded by a simple ring of shrubbery the first time, the village had grown since, with a fence even popping up. Our success with the larvae was doing wonders for it. Of course, the guy in charge wasn't as thrilled.

And when I heard what exactly he wasn't thrilled with, I was surprised, to say the least.

"We agreed that you were going to do what I asked you to do, not go off taking care of things that don't matter," Olson muttered. "I can't grow the village while there are monsters all over the place. And if it doesn't grow, we can't bring in new people. You saw for yourself—there are tons of refugees coming here from all the other locations, but there isn't room. No food, no protection, no nothing. The monsters attack every day and carry off two or three players. And there aren't many to begin with. But instead of taking care of your own, you're off galivanting around the location."

I could partly understand Olson's point. There really were a lot of people around Aspen, and all different kinds, too. Men, women, and children. But not all of them were allowed into the safe zone. The free quota had been exhausted, the last ten rooms costing a thousand coins each. And who had that kind of money if they weren't able to fight? So, the players just huddled together, paying the monsters their hideous tribute every night.

"What do you need?" I asked begrudgingly. My

current state made fighting regular monsters a piece of cake.

"You can't do anything yourself. You need a team. People. Anyway, the village needs resources. Lots of resources. Wood, stone, sand. And all that's far away, so someone has to take care of delivery and protection. Let's say I provide the workers—who will defend them? The game will start generating monsters to keep the village small as soon as they head out. If you're looking to take care of the people out there, you need to protect them."

Surprisingly, I heard Olson out even though I was seething inside. *That bastard!* He'd found the perfect way to sideline me, knowing as he did my attitude toward my fellow humans.

But there was one thing his functionality had missed: I had connections.

"Get the workers together. You'll have your protection."

New mission: *Help Aspen grow*. *Description: Protect the players gathering the materials needed to grow the village. Objectives: 20 tons of lumber, 20 tons of building stone, 30 tons of building sand. The resource points are marked on your map.*

As soon as we stepped out of the hotel, Grust called Little over. The kid had beaten the dungeon, getting himself up to level 32. *Not bad for fifteen years old.*

"There's a mission for you, and people's lives depend on it," Grust said to our first protector as I went off to find the next one. As the first inhabitant, Valdemar had been given one of the best houses, his right on the square. He hadn't come to terms with the loss of his loved ones, so he was in the throes of despair when I showed up and foisted the two pregnant girls on him. It was time for the guy to work off his little piece of heaven.

"I thought so." Grust wasn't the least bit surprised when I showed up with the two women in addition to Valdemar. The pair had rifles slung behind them, their faces stony. Everyone wanted to level-up, earn coins, and get some revenge on the monsters.

The first group of resource gatherers set off twenty minutes later, and I finally had time to take a shower, relax, and figure out what I wanted to do about my bonuses. There was a reason Grust had said he'd had a problem picking them out. When I saw what the fourth list included, I sat back. The problem was that everything at level four had requirements. Just take the rifle.

U-IV energy rifle. *Description: Ignores physical, energy, and impulse armor through level five. Blocks regeneration. Blocks 2 random abilities. Magazine holds*

1200 rounds. Requirements: Rifle shooting (11), agility (10), strength (10), camouflage (9), monster knowledge (9). Cost: 250000 coins.

Sure, judging by the description, a player with a weapon like that represented a huge threat even to larvae, but what did I need camouflage for? And level nine, to be exact. I wasn't out there to spy or play the sniper. I just wanted to kill monsters at range.

And it was like that for everything in the list—right next to the hefty requirements for my main attributes were equally hefty requirements for secondary attributes nobody needed. Sure, I could have gotten myself to the attribute and skill level I needed for the rifle. But if I had, I would have turned myself into a long-range specialist. And experience had shown me that the game generally didn't give you ideal combat situations. It was hard to survive alone as a specialist.

As always, Grust helped me out.

"I say we stick with the way we've been doing things. You stay out front and take care of all the little stuff; I hang back and deal with the bigger targets. I'll take a rifle, a helmet, armor, and protection. Plus, we'll both spend one bonus on a drone and scanner—we're blind without it. What do you think?"

There wasn't anything to reply other than to agree wholeheartedly. If we wanted to execute our plan we were going to have to work together, and specializing as part of a group wasn't so bad.

DR-IV universal drone. *Description: Fourth-generation flying device. Range: 150 kilometers. Flight speed: 150 km/h. Maximum altitude: 5 kilometers. 12 integration slots. High-resolution camera built in. Cartographer-IV built in. P-IV universal protection built in (up to 300 hits). Requirements: Device control (10), device repair (9), agility (9), cartographer (9), Cost: 500000 coins.*

Yes, it was an expensive toy, and it required a lot that it didn't have, but it was worth it. From the outside, it didn't at all resemble the drone I was used to—there weren't any propellers or other breakable parts. It just looked like a fat pillow 70 cm by 70 cm, and it hovered noiselessly and at the ready in front of me. The name the game gave it was no good, so I changed it to Mark-1. That was easy enough. Grust handed me an expansion part, and the drone got a bit fatter.

Modifier for Mark-1: Scanner-IV. *Description: Enables the drone to identify the location of all enemies within a radius of 2000 meters in open space, and within a radius of 300 meters when they are inside buildings. Integrates with cartography. Requirements:*

Device control (10), device repair (9), cartographer (9), perception (9), detection (6). Cost: 350000 coins.

I had 40 free attribute points, and before moving on to my weaponry, I had to upgrade myself. There was a red exclamation point in the part of my brain that handled device control. No matter how much I might have wanted to, I wasn't able to control the drone right then.

Strength +2 (9).
Agility +3 (10).
Stamina +2 (9).
Device control +2 (10).
Device repair +9 (9).
Cartographer +9 (9).
Perception +9 (9).
Detection +6 (6).

Damn it! I actually had to buy two syringes before I could control the drone, and they were attribute syringes, too. The game also forced me to spend one of my bonuses on something required to get the device repair skill.

Repair kit-IV. *Description: A universal set of materials and tools required to repair devices. Required for the device repair skill. Cost: 250000 coins.*

I would never in a million years have bought something like that if I'd had the choice. The drone blinked green, and I had control. My phone and helmet synced right then, too. I was in a daze—everything connected to the game was highlighted and labeled. For example, I didn't even need to log into the player ranking to see Grust's level, as it showed up on my screen next to him. Perception, a new way of seeing the world around me, was great. I flew the drone out of the room and up into the sky. It seemed staggeringly fast, much more so than my old Mark-1. Although, I couldn't figure out what made it fly. The thing didn't have motors, propellers, or nozzles. But it still flew!

Aspen spread out below me, and I felt a surge of joy when the name appeared. It was just like on Wax's map. Deciding to make sure of that, I flew over to the dungeon I hadn't yet beaten, feeling intuitively how my cartographer, perception, and detection all worked. The monsters on the way were all marked. They even had their level indicated, not to mention their classification: inferior, superior, and a couple champions settled in villages. The dungeon itself was illustrated beautifully along with how to get into it. Grust whistled next to me as he got his helmet set up—he was seeing what I was seeing.

Things got trickier from there because I had to choose another three items. My eyes widened—I wanted everything, only I didn't have the cash to buy the mountain of attribute needles I would have needed. Ultimately, I decided to stick with my level three helmet and armor. I picked up something else, instead.

KORT-IV automatic pistol. *Description: Ignores physical, energy, and impulse armor through level five. Blocks regeneration. Blocks 2 random abilities. Magazine holes 1000 rounds. 5 expansion slots. Range: 200 meters. Requirements: Pistol shooting (11), agility (10), strength (10), monster knowledge (9). Cost: 200000 coins.*

Modifier for KORT-IV: Lightning-IV. *Description: Adds slight electric damage to each round. Offers a small chance of blocking nerve endings and immobilizing opponents. Requirements: Pistol shooting (11), agility (10), monster knowledge (9), perception (9). Cost: 150000 coins.*

Modifier for Mark-1: Machine pistol-IV. *Description: Ignores physical, energy, and impulse armor through level 5. Blocks regeneration. Blocks 2 random abilities. Magazine holds 1500 rounds. Range: 200 meters. Requirements: Pistol shooting (11), agility (10), device control (10), monster knowledge (9), perception (9). Cost: 500000 coins.*

That gave the drone some offensive firepower,

too. Of course, I did have to head over to the store and pick up fourteen attribute syringes, but I was really starting to appreciate myself once that expense was out of the way.

Status table			
Name	Mark Derwin		
Coins	54 445	Level	66
Titles and ranks			
Title: Destroyer			
Ranks: Bandit Bane, Lone Wolf, Stone Wall			
Attributes			
Strength	10	Regeneration	15
Stamina	10	Resilience	7
Agility	10	Willpower	7
Perception	9	Cartographer	9
Skills			
Pistol shooting			11
Rifle shooting			8
Melee weapons			8
Device control			10
Device repair			9
Detection			6
Monster knowledge			9

Three hours later, my Mark-2 set a course for the dungeon I found back at the beginning of the game. If it had taken Little just three hours to beat it, I knew Grust, cyborg that he was, definitely wouldn't need much time. And that's exactly what happened. Half an hour later, my partner emerged, glowing with happiness, to hand me a U-III rifle equipped with a scope. When I asked him why, he just muttered something about owing me and how he had to. Anyway, I wasn't going to say no. My old weapon had been sent off to the great beyond.

While Grust was taking care of the dungeon, I got busy exploring the neighboring locations. Their larvae were coming over to help ours, and that meant their farms would be left unattended. Sure, level three champions were a serious problem, generally speaking. But not for us. Once I'd mapped out the heaviest concentrations of monsters and gotten my partner back, we headed off for the first one.

But we didn't get there. As I sent the drone off to the side, looking to expand my map and maybe even find a couple caches or dungeons, it suddenly froze. And right in the middle of the sky, too. It couldn't go any further. Not only that, but the area on the other side of the invisible boundary wasn't showing up, which was strange. I flew around the spot, constantly banging up against the invisible field. A black, perfectly round circle half a kilometer wide eventually appeared on my map. Grust agreed that we needed to see what was going on, and we found ourselves at the edge of an enormous field after half an hour of making our way through the underbrush. It was empty. The drone hung in the air, telling me in all the ways its little game brain knew that it was hitting up against a wall of fog. But we were standing right there. Nothing was standing in its way. The only thing I noticed was that my head was aching slightly.

I sent the ATV forward and just about knocked my teeth out on my helmet when the Mark-2 slammed suddenly into the invisible barrier. Grust cursed next to me.

"What the hell was that?"

"Good question." I gave the order to drive forward, but the vehicle just whined piteously. While the engines were doing their best to push us ahead, it just wasn't happening. The drone camera showed a thick gray fog.

"Let me check it out." Grust got out of the vehicle and went over to the invisible barrier. Holding out a hand, he called over in surprise. "I can't get through! There's really some kind of force field here."

It was actually a thick wall of air. Nothing glowed to tell us there was a field, and it didn't do any damage. It was just an impenetrable transparent wall and an even field a kilometer wide. *What the hell?*

Frustrated that nothing was working, I kicked at the dirt. A few larger stones rolled away and...

Suddenly, they were inside the field. As if it wasn't there. Only they disappeared, and Grust and I exchanged glances as we bent over to pick up more stones. I found a small stick, too. All of it flew inside without a problem, as did the stick up until the hand I was holding it with hit the invisible wall. I pulled it back out, expecting to see its charred remains. But it was whole and intact.

And that was fascinating. The field didn't let human or game items through? Or was it just game items? My partner and I, after all, were covered from head to toe in protective outfits.

I quickly decided what to do. As I pulled off a glove and my protective necklace, Grust came over to stand next to me with a regeneration syringe, ready to wrench me out of the field's sticky grasp at any moment. But when I reached for the spot where the field began, I felt nothing. A finger slipped easily inside as if there was no barrier whatsoever. In went my whole hand. It only stopped when it hit my sleeve, though it was something seeing my arm turned into a nub. Nothing hurt, though. It didn't feel hot, nor was there any pressure. I pulled my hand back out and looked it over. Nothing. There weren't any burn marks, it didn't hurt, nothing at all.

"We need a rope. A regular one, not from the game," I said. I really wanted to see what was on the other side, though I wasn't going in without an insurance policy. My map showed a village with fifty superior monsters and two champions not far away. It presumably had everything we needed for our exploration.

Grust was brutal with his new weapon, taking out most of the beasts before we'd even really gotten to the village. And when the remainder formed up to fight back, the drone went into action. I wanted to see what it could do. Of course, I left the champions to Grust. One of them threw lightning bolts, and I wasn't about to risk my expensive toy. It didn't have a problem with the small fry, however.

You took the first picture of 53 dead superior monsters. 780 coins received.

You took the first picture of 2 dead champions. 1800 coins received.

Once we'd looted everything we could find, I started to feel the urge to just go around farming coins. That would have been great for everyone—us, the location, and humanity as a whole. The fewer of the animals we left there, the fewer there would be to reach level four. *After we take out those larvae, we'll definitely have to get to work.* But first on our to-do list was figuring out what was going on with that mysterious field.

We found a rope in one of the sheds and headed back. Honestly, I was worried that the field would disappear, that it would turn out to be some kind of unique anomaly, but it was right there waiting for us when we arrived. The rope went in and out without a problem. Grust started getting undressed. Once he'd tied one end around his waist, he handed the other to me and nodded at the Mark-2.

"You can control that thing, and I can't, so I should be the one to go in. Hold on to this and try not to let go. If I tug twice, get me out of there. Okay?"

"Okay," I said with a nod, tying the rope to my Mark-2 just in case. It would be strong enough to pull Grust out and couldn't get dragged in after him.

Stripping down completely, Grust paused for a few seconds as if unsure if he wanted to go through with it. But then, he took a deep breath and a step forward. The field swallowed him up instantly, and only the rope hanging in midair told me that he hadn't stepped away from the edge. A minute went by. Grust still hadn't moved, and I was starting to get worried. But just as I was about to pull him out, he appeared on his own. His face bore an expression of shock.

"We need to head back to the village, find some regular clothes. Pull your helmet off and stick your head in—you'll see for yourself."

I followed his instructions and peered into the protective field. *Wow...* Life hadn't prepared me for something like that—there was no field to be seen. Instead, there was a strange construction, some kind of mechanism. It wheezed, croaked, whistled, and looked anything but ultramodern, more like it had been pulled straight from the Industrial Age. I'd seen things like it in museums. Enormous pipes jutted out of the ground, and, judging by the unpleasant sucking sound, they were pulling something out of it. And there were guards all around the thing, too. Dozens of hairy Shurvan creatures stood shoulder-to-shoulder with regular superior monsters. *So, this thing was built by the game, and not humans? But why can't we get inside when we're wearing anything from the game, if that's the case?*

"Those bastards are pumping something out of the ground." Grust's serious voice greeted me when I finally returned to our regular reality. "Monsters, levels, and everything else is just bells and whistles there to distract us from what's important. Those animals need Earth for its resources, and as soon as they drain them, they'll get rid of all of us. They won't need us anymore. What a bright future, huh, Mark?"

Grust's train of thought made a lot of sense. It looked like we'd been invaded, like the invaders needed something from us and our planet. And the game was just a cover.

"What do you need clothes for?"

"I want to know what they're mining. I saw a couple of hunting rifles in the village—I'll bet we can use them inside."

"That's dangerous. Our abilities might not work in there."

"They might not, you're right. But what does it matter when we die, if it's now or in a couple months once the mines run dry? And what if we're able to stop

them, buy ourselves a couple days? Or even months...
I'm prepared to take that risk. What about you?"

"I'm with you." There wasn't a second's
hesitation—I knew he was right. "But let's take our
time about it, spend a couple hours. Back where I
initiated, there's a little house with a nice basement. I
think you'll be a fan. Do you know what an M-2 is?"

Grust nodded in surprise and climbed into the
vehicle without a word, not bothering even to get
dressed. If we were able to clear that one jammed
round, taking out the hairy beasts and their monster
friends would be much easier.

Chapter 14

AFTER DEACTIVATING THE ATV and the drone and dumping them into my storage along with my equipment, I buried my phone. Just like everything else that came from the game, it couldn't go through the invisible curtain. With one hand, I picked up the wheelbarrow in front of me loaded with cartridge belts and a bunch of smaller weapons, holding the M-2 Grust had fixed in the other, and took a step forward. Everything went smoothly. The picky shield accepted our weaponry and let us through. My partner was next to me, another wheelbarrow with him. The only difference was that he was holding an anti-tank rifle instead of a machine gun. I wasn't even going to ask what the previous owner had needed it for.

We were noticed right away. The hairy creatures started hopping around, while the monsters howled and pawed impatiently at the ground. But that worked for us. The more time they gave us to get set up, the easier it was going to be. We placed the M-2 on the ground, and I stuck three spikes into the supports to stabilize it. Happily, our upgraded bodies remained the same. We were advanced, agile, strong. Apparently not part of the game, our very organisms had been modified, mutated. I didn't want to think of myself as a mutant, but that was the only thing that came to mind. And with the regeneration thrown in, I was Wolverine in the flesh.

"Let's do this," Grust said with a grin as he opened fire. Holes appeared in the container holding whatever was being extracted from the earth. If anyone thought we were there to kill the beasts, they were gravely mistaken. Our goal was simple and noble: take out that damn device.

"Let's do this," I replied. Raw power surged through my hands once again. But there was bad news to start off with, as the monsters turned out to have protection. There was a plus side, too, however: the bullets' impact threw the creatures back against the contraption, and it was easier to deal with them there. Something seared through my shoulder—they were returning fire. Keeping the trigger squeezed, I turned my aim on the upper platform, making a nice line of perforated metal as I went. The hairy creatures went flying. Then, I turned back to the monsters, as they'd regained their footing and were coming at me. The bodies were once again thrown back at the contraption, though that time a few of them didn't get back up. Their protection had been exhausted. A quick belt change later, and I continued my execution. The pipes and walls took more punishment than the bodies. But suddenly, something erupted in a deafening explosion, and fire belched skyward. One of Grust's shots had landed home. A gloating smile flitted across my face. And with that, the creatures lost all their protection, and the entire force field dropped, too. The monsters howled; the hairy bastards panicked and tried to dodge the bullets. But none of that mattered. The incredible killing power of the M-2 gave no quarter. I stretched out an arm, my phone slapped against my hand, and I immediately materialized my drone. I needed to know who was left. One more explosion, and the big contraption started keeling over like an old steamboat, creaking and smoking. By the time the drone soared into the sky, it was all over. Grust took out the last three monsters.

For the next ten minutes, we stood right where we were, waiting for our protection and weapons to materialize. I sent the drone in a wide circle to see if there were any monsters in the vicinity. There was a strong feeling in my gut that the game would throw everything but the kitchen sink at us, and I was exactly right. I was almost speechless when I saw how many monsters were sprinting toward us to get their revenge for the fallen hulk. There were around three thousand inferior monsters, more than six thousand superior monsters, and four hundred champions. If there had been a larva nearby, I was positive it would have been in with them, too, but we were lucky. The location boss was off hanging out with our old friend. We had enough on our hands without it, though. I couldn't imagine how fast we were going to have to squeeze our triggers to gun them all down in time.

Grust grinned when he saw the horde coming at us, and he pointed over at the contraption.

"It'll be easier up there. Ah, this is going to be a good battle!"

"We're not dead, yet." I quickly stepped into my costume, snapped my helmet shut, and ran off. My automatic pistol was going to have to materialize on the go. "Hurry, they're going to be here in one minute!"

We weren't going to give up that easily, and I set the drone on a few squads of superior monsters. *Let the thing have some fun!* A leap took me up onto the overturned hulk, and I looked around for a good vantage point. There was one right by an old brace that was sticking up there like a big old spike. Grust climbed up, made himself comfortable, and peered into his scope. There were three grenades lying on his lap. An excellent argument when you're dealing with a crowd, I thought, and picked up three for myself. A thick silence fell. Soon, the rustling of trees broke it, though the monsters were running without their usual howling. And that seemed strange to me. I aimed at a tree and took a shot. At least, I wanted to take a shot—

my rifle just clicked. I heard the same clicks above me, and they were followed by a string of curses from Grust. Game weapons didn't work around the broken-down mechanism. An unpleasant thought hit me like a bolt of lightning, and I pulled out my vibroknife. It was just your usual cleaver. Dragging it across my arm, I saw blood spurt. I had no protection.

"We have to get out of here!" I barely had time to say before the trees around the clearing unleashed an endless horde of monsters. A grenade went flying, but it just bounced harmlessly on the ground. *Damn it! What didn't we check our weapons ahead of time?!*

"Go!" Grust leaped down onto the ground. But there wasn't anywhere to go—the monsters had the field surrounded. A few moments to regroup, and they came rushing at the fallen piece of machinery.

Machinery...exactly!

"Grust, I need time," I bellowed as I pulled off my gloves and helmet. They were just getting in the way. My partner said nothing, just throwing up his fists. I placed my hands on the piece of alien hardware and listened to my senses. Device control wasn't a game skill; it was an integral part of my body. Something modified that couldn't be destroyed next to a deep wound cut into the heart of the planet.

Earth noa concentration plant. Status: Damaged.

Would you like to see the list of available equipment?

Yes, and hurry! I started paging through the descriptions of assemblies and components with the speed of a computer, sensing as I did the opponents coming up behind me. My eye caught the words I was looking for, and I opened the description:

Protective field. Status: Valtron generator damaged. Would you like to fix it?

The enormous tank and its multiple antennae started to glow. That's what Grust had hit right before the monsters' protection fell away, and so I jumped over to it. Not exactly sure what to do, I ripped my repair kit off my belt and held it up against the hole.

Valtron generator supply circuits repairs.
Protective field available. Would you like to activate it?

"Mark!" my partner yelled with warning in his voice, and a monster buried its teeth in my shoulder.

"Activate!" I yelled before I was torn away from the contraption and tossed into the onrushing crowd of monsters like some kind of kitten. They all snarled at the unexpected gift, and the last thing I remembered before I lost consciousness was that I couldn't move for some reason. The monster had apparently hit something vitally important. *You've got to be kidding me... And I could have done so much more in the world...*

Darkness fell.

My consciousness returned slowly. The sticky claws of complete indifference fought to the end, unwilling to let me return to the hostile world. The first thing I saw was the red sky—the protective dome played with color however it wanted to. That was followed by sound, which came in the form of wheezing. Lots of wheezing. Some of it was coming from me, as breathing was difficult. Some was coming from my partner. I recognized his voice. But the majority wasn't human, as it was the kind of wheezing you only heard from monsters.

Feeling my strength return, I got up and... Only no, I continued lying on the ground, unable to move. Nothing was wrong with my body; it was just that I was trapped in my motionless armor. The dome switched off game items, turning my level three outfit into a reinforced concrete trap. I couldn't move or catch my breath. A wave of understanding washed over me, and I looked over to see Grust not far away. He couldn't even get his helmet off. *Wait, he's choking!* That gave me impetus, and I was able to overcome the resistance coming mostly from myself long enough to bend an arm at the elbow and place a palm on my chest.

BRO-III tactical outfit. Status: blocked.

Disassemble! Destroy! Annihilate!

My device control ability worked exactly the way it was supposed to, and I filled my lungs with air when the armor disintegrated. Glancing around quickly to see a field packed with motionless monsters, I ran over to my partner, broke the clips holding his helmet on his head, and ripped it off. He gulped down oxygen, his face blue. The crazed look on his face took a while to pass, and I was even starting to worry that he'd lost his mind when the look finally did pass. After catching his breath, he cursed eloquently. I felt better—crazy people can't curse like that.

"What the hell did you do?" That was the only intelligible question I could pick out.

"I saved us." Holding out a hand to summon my phone, I wasn't surprised when nothing happened. The device was lying dead on the ground. My entire body nearly cramped in horror that my equipment would be trapped forever inside it, and I forgot about Grust and dashed over. It really wasn't working. Even my device control couldn't do anything to break inside it. Hopping across monster bodies, I made it over to the edge of the dome. There was an enormous crowd outside. Tossing my phone at the feet of the closest monster, I felt an incredible sense of relief when I saw the screen turn on. It just didn't work under the dome. Suddenly, I realized that I could still feel the drone. Having destroyed the squad it had been sent after, my Mark-1 was hovering motionless in the air above the forest.

When I concentrated on my phone, I could sense it, too. I pulled up the video feed from the drone and sent it flying around our area. *Yeah...* Only about a quarter of the monsters had made it under the dome. Most of them were waiting for us outside the invisible barrier. We were going to have to leave sooner or later, and they would be there when we did. I glanced down. The monsters wheezing on the field couldn't move or make a noise. They couldn't do anything, really, pinned to the ground as they were. Just to see what would happen, I slammed my fist against the skull of the nearest one. Its wheezing stopped; its body softened. It's hard to keep going when your brains are spread out across the grass, after all. My hand went numb, but my regeneration had it back in no time. *No, that's no good.* Kicking bodies aside, I made my way over to our wheelbarrows loaded with weapons. A Kalashnikov was the first thing I saw. *Perfect!* There was a whole mountain of bullets for it, too. Pulling back the bolt, I set it to single shot and smiled evilly. I knew how Grust and I were going to survive. At least, as long as we had enough ammunition.

I didn't free Grust, knowing that I was going to have to repair his helmet as it was. Instead, I made sure he was breathing and feeling okay before getting on with my execution. There were thirty rounds in each clip. One shot per monster, no matter the type. Inferior, superior, and champion alike, they all died just as quickly without their protection. But to make my way around the whole field, it took me two hours and fifty clips. One look outside the dome was enough to tell me that I didn't have enough rounds. *I might be wrong, but it looks like there's even more of them out there than there were before.*

I had to do something about that, though I needed to get my partner free first. I pulled him over to the contraption in the center of the field.

"You're going to have thirty seconds to get undressed before I reactivate the force field. I'm counting on you—don't let me down!"

Grust muttered something unintelligible, though I could tell from the look in his eye that he would be fine.

"Go!" I yelled as I placed a hand on the contraption to remove the protection. The monsters howled happily and dashed in, only caring about their chance to get at the two pieces of fresh meat in the center. I was able to quell my instincts long enough to only activate the field when the monsters were a leap away. A few flew over my head, crashing into the remains of the machinery, though they were already frozen when they hit it. Grust looked down sadly at his armor, which had once again turned into a concrete tomb.

"What's next?" he asked, noticing that I was ripping a long spike off the machine. My powerful body was strong enough to have the piece of sharp metal bouncing in my hands before too long.

"Just follow me," I said, waving him over and dropping my improvised spear into the head of the nearest monster. The result was fantastic—the spike held, and a hole appeared in the monster that rendered continued living untenable. There was a loud, unpleasant squelch as I pulled my weapon out. It soon found a new home in the head of the next monster, however. Grust picked the game up quickly and was soon heading off in the opposite direction, leaving a bloody trail behind him.

Things went much faster that time around. It only took us a little more than half an hour to work our way through the second wave, not to mention the third, the fourth, and even the fifth. The sixth was the last. There were finally no more monsters to kill.

Collapsing on the ground, I didn't even care that I was sitting in a pool of dark blood. I just didn't have any more energy. My hands were shaking, my head was buzzing, my palms were caked with blood, and even my regeneration wasn't keeping up. There had been so many of the monsters. So many. But they were all dead.

Grust sat down beside me. He didn't look a bit better than I did, just as dirty and bedraggled.

"Did you figure out what that thing is?" He nodded in the direction of the listing contraption.

"An Earth noa concentrator. Don't look at me like that—I don't know what that means, either."

"Can you take it apart?"

"You want me to hit you?"

"Are you so sure we're not going to have a new wave of monsters in a couple minutes? We won't have time for this thing if that happens. Come on, let's go, we can rest when we're dead."

That's some damn motivation! Against my will, I stood up and collapsed against the machine. Grust said something, so I had to reassure him—it didn't matter what position I was in so long as my palms were touching the damn thing.

Earth noa concentration plant. Status: Damaged.

The names in the list of main components didn't mean anything to me. *What the hell is a restupitor, a calciner, and a bartinost?* Either I was a bad mechanic, or there wasn't anything like that in our world, and the game just transliterated the names from the original language. Most of the items in the list were damaged. I figured my device repair skill wouldn't be up to the task, though I wasn't really interested in getting the devilish contraption up and running again, anyway. The fact that it was protected so fervently by the monsters meant that it had to go.

That part was easy—I knew from personal experience how to demolish different mechanisms. My BRO-III suit was proof of that. The problem was that I had to go through each individual device, and there were more than a thousand of them in the list. If we'd been attacked by monsters, I wouldn't have been able to get the shield back up. But nothing went wrong. I spent the next hour turning the hulk into dust, and not a single monster stopped by to see how we were doing that whole time. Of course, Grust had the drone up and was patrolling the area with the drone ready to defend me. But he didn't have to.

The last block on the list was an enormous vat that melted away, and the area shook when it did. The gaping hole leading somewhere deep into the ground closed. I felt a sense of relief emanating from every pebble in the area, a strange sensation, indeed. It was like the planet was alive, and I'd helped it patch up a horrible wound. Pulled the splinter out of its finger.

Something glowing brightly attracted my attention. For a long time, I couldn't figure out what it was, though when it dawned on me, I got up and wobbled over to it like I'd been bewitched. It looked like a stone made of concentrated energy. Floating above the ground, it glistened with all the colors of the rainbow, and there was a lightning storm going on inside it. Somewhere off to the side, Grust yelled at me, but I wasn't listening to him. All my attention was fixed on the miniature ball of lightning in front of me. Throwing caution to the wind, I took it, and the world around me stopped. A message exploded in my head.

Earthling!
You hold in your hands something I need.
Give me the noa, or humanity will forever be wiped from the game's memory. I will delete your data as soon as I'm finished with Earth, and none of you will be permitted the eternal life granted by rebirth in a new world.

My thoughts turned over slowly, almost as if I'd been transported to the Arctic and dowsed with liquid nitrogen. *So, this sphere is noa? And whoever's behind all this chaos needs it?* Olson popped into my head, and I remembered how happy he'd been to tell me how much more powerful he would be in his next life. He was going to have slaves, different functionality, and really, when was humankind going to die off already so he could get on with it? A new planet, new functionality, and a new lifeless wilderness. The joy of destruction stretching into eternity. *But at least humanity won't disappear...*

I squeezed my fingers, making the decision on behalf of everyone else still alive. At least, the decision had been made a few days before when all the big cities had been destroyed by nuclear bombs. When it comes to stopping a fearsome enemy, humans will stop at nothing. Even the destruction of their own race. The noa flattened out, trying to resist, but it eventually gave in and exploded in a shower of sparks. A wave of blindingly white light hit me, and the world around me began moving once again.

"...don't touch it!" I heard the end of Grust's yell, but he froze suddenly, staring at the messages in front of him. I didn't need my phone or my helmet to understand what was going on. The notifications showed up in my head all by themselves:

You destroyed an Earth noa concentration plant.

Title: Destroyer changed to Hero.

***

You're the first player in the past 4 seasons to earn the title of Hero.

Level +30 (96).

30 free attribute points received.

***

The hexagon general labeled *Together to the End* personal enemies. From now on, all the monsters in this hexagon will do quadruple damage to you. You will receive four times as many coins for each monster killed.

Level +10 (106).

10 free attribute points received.

You can collect any level four item in the store for free.

***

You're the first player on Earth to reach level 100.

5 free attribute points received.

Attribute parameter limits removed.

***

You stole Earth noa, but then you dispersed it.

The game owner is displeased with you.

Penalty received: Tough response: From now on, you only have access to named and level one items for personal use.

***

You're the first player in the past 10 seasons to receive the tough response penalty.

Store access to named items unlocked.

You can collect any named item in the store for free.

Level +50 (156).

50 free attribute points received.

***

Location 554, hexagon 118, was cleared of monsters and declared a safe zone.

Notification sent to all players.

You're kidding me! I read the whole thing a few times before it hit me that killing monsters was going to be much harder. It took some doing to kill the weakest level three monster with a level one gun, not to mention bastards like Gray and Wax. I couldn't forget about them.

"We got him, Mark!" Grust yelled, for some reason overjoyed as he pulled off his now-useless level four armor. "We hurt that bastard, whoever it is!"

"And took ourselves out of the picture in the process," I muttered, though he was too excited to let me get him down.

"Ah, screw that. Do you understand that the more of those plants we destroy, the better it will be for the planet? Sooner or later, we'll come across someone that will be too much for us. But for now, we cleared a location and hurt that thing! Screw it! You take the picture—this field is yours. If it weren't for you, there's no way we would have survived. So, enjoy your spoils! I'll go check out what those named items are in the meantime."

I held out a hand, and my phone flew over, intact, to meet it. Neither my drone nor the ATV were personal use items, so they were still under my control. But that didn't make things much better. The game owner had pulled our fangs.

On the other hand, I couldn't help feeling better after taking a picture. It was hard to believe that Grust and I pulled something like that off.

You took the first picture of 3566 dead inferior monsters. 14264 coins received.

You took the first picture of 8213 dead superior monsters. 164260 coins received.

You took the first picture of 538 dead champions. 645600 coins received.

You took the first picture of 20 dead players. 800 coins received.

I looked down at my screen and smiled—there were almost nine hundred thousand coins in my account. *Sure, it's going to be harder to kill the monsters, but whoever said we're afraid of a little rough going?*

"You know, Grust, you're right. As long as we're

still breathing, we're going to keep fighting. And who cares if they limited our level? We'll take the bastards out with sticks."

"You think they limited us?" Grust looked over at me with shock in his eyes. "Have you seen the store?"

Chapter 15

I DIDN'T HAVE ANY REASON not to trust Grust, so I closed my eyes, focused on my phone, and pulled up the store. Setting a few filters since most of what was in there was pointless for me, I found myself looking at a very different list. *Yeah...* Grust was right—nothing was ever simple in the game.

I didn't have a weapon, armor, or protection, so I needed to be very careful about everything I was going to do in the game. Protection would have been nice, but then I wouldn't have been able to kill anything. And sitting off in some safe zone would have been pointless. So... The choice was obvious—it had to be a weapon. I couldn't stay swinging my fists, and I skipped right past the sharp stuff with the flowery names. The different bows, crossbows, and slingshots went by, too. Rambo had never been a favorite movie of mine. That left ray weapons, and the selection there was awfully limited: one rifle, one pistol, one automatic. At least, they were what I associated with rifles, pistols, and automatics. In reality... They were something futuristic and impossible.

The pistol was my first and only choice. All I had to do was pull up the description, and a projection of the weapon appeared in my hand to give me a good idea of what it would look like.

It had a powerful, Magnum-like barrel. I'd seen a weapon like it in some action movie or other. Then, there were the cylinders fitted to the barrel that changed the ammunition type—energy, fire, electric, explosive, flammable, and freezing, the one I liked the most. The hilt was a direct extension of my arm that connected to my wrist. Even when I relaxed my grip, it still didn't fall out of my hand. And it fired either when I pressed a button, or when I gave it a mental command. I did have to get my device control higher before I could connect to it directly, however. My current level just wasn't enough. *What else... Ah!* Most importantly, something that made the pistol stand out from the rest of the game's arsenal was the ability to upgrade it. I wasn't exactly sure how that worked, though I knew I could figure it out later. Finally, spinning the projection around and deciding I liked it, I hit the button.

Valkyrie. *Description: Universal automatic pistol linked to Mark Derwin. Initial* Valkyrie *level: 1. Drum with 6 types of ammunition totaling* Valkyrie *level*300 rounds of each. Ignores all armor types through* Valkyrie level. *Blocks regeneration. Blocks 2 random abilities. Cannot be blocked in the game world. Range: 300 meters. Requirements: Pistol shooting (40), agility (30), strength (30), monster knowledge (40), perception (30), resilience (30), device control (30). Cost: 10000000 coins.*

Initial setup complete.

You destroyed a larva-level creature. Valkyrie level increased by 1 (2).

You cleared a location of monsters. Valkyrie level increased by 1 (3).

There was no holster. When I was on the move, Valkyrie just pulled back into my forearm, changing to battle mode in fractions of a second. All I had to do was think, and it began shooting. But there were drawbacks, too. The main one was the cost of a clip for each ammunition type—2,000 coins each. *Unbelievable!* The lower the level, the more upkeep cost. But I wasn't about to skimp, and so I bought a clip of each type. *I'll figure out how much it's going to run me later.* All I had left to do was get myself to the levels I needed to be at to meet Valkyrie's lofty requirements.

Strength +20 (30).

Agility +20 (30).

Stamina +20 (30).

Pistol shooting +29 (40).

Monster knowledge +31 (40).

Perception +21 (30).

Resilience +23 (30).

Device control + 20 (30).

The system apparently tracked the number of free attributes I had, because I had one syringe left after all the changes. I used it to boost my regeneration to level 16. The thing I was most happy about was that I didn't need my main attributes after level 30, as they stopped impacting my skills. I could get the latter as high as I wanted them.

Grust was muttering sweet nothings to the rifle in his hands, and he flatly declined when I asked him what its attributes were. All he would say was that his baby was at level three. He needed a monster settlement to see what it could do, and he needed it right then. I was fine with that, even though I knew the practice run wasn't going to be cheap.

Once we'd taken care of our weapons, we found ourselves at a loss. Both of us had a level four bonus to pick, but that didn't do us any good—we couldn't even grab something and hand it over to Little. The game had everything above level one blocked, leaving us with trash like the pistol for 100 coins or a force field for 20 that we would have been embarrassed to wear. Still, I bought a BRO-I outfit for 300 coins and the helmet for 12,000. I wasn't about to go running around barefoot, and I preferred watching the feed from the drone in my helmet rather than on my phone. One thing I hadn't learned how to do was watch it right in my head. Apparently, that was a separate skill, something like "decoder."

But we ended up finding what I thought was a good option: two modifications. There was protection for the Mark-2, and what I was most thrilled about, an invisibility field for the Mark-1. There wasn't any question about the protection—we spent most of our time driving around in the ATV, so it made sense to keep it safe. But the field for the drone was a whim of mine. I'd had my eye on it the last time, only the price had scared me away. I was tired of everyone being able to catch a glimpse of and take a shot at my Mark-1.

We'd already started planning our next move when our phones got an unexpected notification:

Mission failed: *Help Aspen grow.*

With just one look at each other, we dashed off toward the vehicle and gunned it in the direction of Aspen.

Something had happened to Little and his team.

It took us thirty minutes to get to the resource gather point, and by the time we jumped out of the

ATV, it was all over. Charred body parts and the remains of carts littered the ground around us. I went around to almost all the bodies, jabbing a regeneration syringe into them, but it was too late. They were all dead.

Suddenly, Grust let out a dull whine and fell to his knees. Picking a burnt rifle up off the ground, he started stroking it like some kind of small child. It took me a second to realize why he seemed so taken with someone's gun. Then, chills ran down my body when it hit me that it was the rifle he'd handed Little before we set off to find the other farms. My head throbbed. *Not the kid!* Valdemar and his women didn't bother me—we'd bought them a little more time than they had any right to expect. But Little... *Damn, why does everything have to be so bad?*

I went over to the vehicle on wobbly legs. We kept a few shovels around for just such an occasion, and Little definitely deserved—

A deafening explosion and the subsequent shockwave threw me far off to the side. I rolled down an embankment and splashed into the river at the bottom. My protection had held up, but my head was spinning. A concussion, it felt like. My complete BRO-I kit gave me ten minutes without air, so I stayed underwater to buy myself time to calm down and recover. Catching my breath, I... *What the hell?* The screen caught my attention—red dots were flashing across it. Fifty-two players had appeared in the clearing as if out of nowhere. *How?!* I'd purposely checked, and there hadn't been anyone within two kilometers. *Where did they come from?*

"Grust, it's an ambush! Get out of there!" I yelled into the microphone as I flew the drone in closer to get a better look at what was going on.

Only Grust didn't reply.

In the spot where I'd seen him last, there was an enormous hole, and what really clouded my mind and made me want to scream was that his marker was missing from my map. A couple mental commands, and I was looking at the player ranking for the location. I was there at the top. In second place...was someone else. Grust was nowhere to be found in the top hundred.

He was nowhere to be found anywhere.

There was a long flash, and several bazooka rounds smashed into my Mark-2. The protection held up, though the energy from the explosion knocked it upside down. A rattling machine gun elicited another explosion before I had time to pull it into virtual reality.

Mark-2 destroyed and removed from your equipment list.

With eyes wide in horror, I looked at the burning remains of my ATV, not believing what was going on.

Everything had happened so fast that I hadn't had time to react. The only thing I knew was that the ambush had been set up to catch us by someone who knew what they were doing. Bringing the drone closer to the trees, my eye twitched when I saw who was down there. A motley crew of high-level players. My perception told me what level and race the bastards down there were—not a single human, and not one player below level 50. I opened the ranking once again to find that everyone from second place down was right there in the clearing. A miniature destroyer was in charge, a robot on a flying platform labeled 54X-12. The game owner wasn't just upset about the noa; he was out for vengeance.

"He's still alive!" I heard a lifeless metallic voice call out. "Find him!"

They were obviously talking about me. For a few moments, I wanted to go out in a blaze of glory, taking at least one of the bastards out with me, but common sense told me to get the hell out of there. The latter option held the promise that I could take out the whole gang instead of just one or two of them. And that was what I wanted.

The emotions lost out, and I swam away with the current. With just five minutes of air left, I needed to get as far away as possible. The drone stayed where it was. That let me see the gang roll out some kind of device and start pressing buttons.

"He's gone!"

"The scanner isn't showing anything!"

"No tracks! He was standing here, and then he just disappeared. What the hell, Twelve?"

"Head back to Olson!" the robot barked. "Mark will show up himself. In the meantime, watch for the drone—that will tell us he's nearby. And collect your loot. You earned it!"

I crawled out onto the bank and quietly buried myself in the sand. *Scanner... Olson...* The game had decided to wipe itself clean of my memory, sending its best thugs after me. Little, Grust... My heart was heavier than it had ever been before. We'd just gotten used to working with each other, just put together plans, and there... The thought flashed through my mind that I needed to give them a good burial, and I clutched at it like a drowning man grabbing for a life vest. It was bad, almost bad enough to put a bullet in my own head. But I couldn't. There was no way I could leave Grust and the boy out there to be eaten by the monsters, and I was somehow glad that Squirrel was buried deep underground. The game owner apparently couldn't break their own rules, otherwise she would have been up against a wall somewhere long before.

My shovel was back with the Mark-2, but I figured it had probably survived the blast. The drone told me the bandits were gone. I wasn't about to go running into the middle of the clearing, however. For some reason, my scanner hadn't caught them, and that meant there was probably someone still there. And why had my level four scanner missed the gang? The only answer was that, their concealment was higher than my perception and detection. I needed to fix that. The system started printing attribute syringes en masse, barely keeping up with me.

The game owner had declared war on me. *So be it—we'll play by their rules.*

Detection +24 (30).
Anatomy master +15 (15).
Agility +10 (40).
Concealment +30 (30).
Camouflage +30 (30).
Silence +30 (30).
Scanner +30 (30).
Device repair +6 (15).
Melee weapons +32 (40).
Willpower +33 (40).
Fortress +40 (40).

I added everything I could. If there was so much as a word in an attribute or skill about improving me, my protection, or my stealth, I took it no matter the cost. A full 280 needles turned me into a sieve, and I spent the next three hours unconscious. The update was unlike anything I'd been through before. And coins meant nothing to me—if they killed me, they'd get them, and I couldn't buy anything with them right then. I definitely wasn't going to be saving up for a new vehicle. But there was something else I could do. My necrospear, the one I'd gotten in my one and only dungeon, was still off in my storage. I grabbed the broken part and pulled out my repair kit. It had been enough to kill a champion, turning it into a skeleton, and I very much hoped the wolf had suffered. And that meant it was exactly what I needed. The game's servants dreamed of respawning in the next release? *They're going to pray to their creator that I won't be in that one, too.*

Device repair level insufficient for this part. Required level: 40.

I felt nothing but bitter hopelessness. *Whatever...level 40 it is.* I was tired of stabbing myself, but 50,000 coins, 25 holes, and ten minutes later, I had the piece back in my hand.

Select a form.

My phone showed me a variety of jabbing and cutting items, but I already knew what I wanted. Spears weren't my thing. Something like a machete, that very much was. And I already had the skill for it.

Enter a name.

"Fang," I blurted out, surprised by how long things were taking. There hadn't been anything like that with the plant. And it hadn't asked for a name, either.

Name accepted.
Repair and update successfully completed.
You're the first player on Earth to restore a named item.
Level +5 (161).
5 free attribute points received.

Fang. *Description: A ritual knife belonging to Mark Derwin. Initial Fang level: 1. Ignores all armor types through* Fang *level. Inflicts necrotic damage on opponents, draining stored up energy into them. Cannot be blocked in the game world. Requirements: Melee weapons (40), agility (30), strength (30), monster knowledge (40), anatomy master (40), resilience (30), necrotica (40). Cost: 15000000 coins.*

Fang also picked up two levels, and I opened the store. *Where's my wholesale discount?* Another 25 syringes for anatomy master, 40 for necrotica, 130,000 coins gone, and I was again out of it for three hours.

When I woke up, the first thing I saw was a red

dot where Grust had died. And it wasn't some wandering monster. It was a carefully concealed player the drone couldn't pick up visually even though it knew exactly where he was. The fighter's camouflage was masterful, only he'd forgotten one thing: the damn game limited player attributes to level 15 until they reached level 100. I was the only one in the location to break level 100, and that meant the bastard was in for some unpleasant surprises.

I pulled out Fang, whose blade was enshrouded in a black mist, and buried it in the nearest bush. Each plant now had its own aura, or energy that Fang could suck in for its necrotic energy. A slender ray formed between the blade and the plant. The hair on the back of my neck suddenly stood up, and the plant aged and dried up as if the life had been sucked out of it. All its energy.

But the bush wasn't enough, and I had to destroy a couple trees the same way. Finally, the mist soaked into Fang's blade, which turned virgin clean. My ritual knife was ready for an execution.

The red dot was right where I'd left it—the fighter was patiently awaiting my return to the field. I took a few steps and grinned. It was incredible how silent I was. On the next tree over, I noticed a bird going about its business and paying me no mind. I decided to see how close I could get without scaring it. After a dozen strides and a leap onto the branch, I settled down just a couple centimeters away from the sparrow. It continued grooming itself as if I wasn't even there. In fact, it was only when I touched it gently that the creature hurtled into the air and flew off screeching. *Excellent, my concealment is working.*

It took me ten minutes to walk back to where my partner had been killed, and I finally laid eyes on my opponent. My perception and detection worked far better in person than they had via the drone camera. The guy had settled in among some building stone ready for transport to Aspen. I wasn't sure how it was able to blend in with the rocks so well—apparently, the Alturian race was able to transform their bodies in a way humans couldn't. It had a weapon, too, a level four rifle. I immediately recognized it even hidden under the creature's flat body. Well, no, I didn't recognize it; I sensed it. The closer I got to the spy, the clearer I sensed its weapon and armor. Suddenly, I felt the need to freeze. The Alturian picked its head up slightly and looked in my direction, leaving me with an incredibly strange feeling. We were there looking right at each other, only I was able to concentrate on its smudged body, and it wasn't able to see me. It was looking right through me.

Convinced that it was alone, the fighter blended back in with the stones, though that was its last move. I had no intention of taking it prisoner. Everything I needed to know, I already knew. I was there to kill it and kill it cruelly. Crawling right up to it, I was able to take control of its game items. *That's device control to you, bitch, and you're covered head to toe in devices! Tough luck.*

No longer bothering to hide, I stood up. The Alturian was trapped inside its impenetrable cage the same way Grust had been. If I'd left it like that, sooner or later it would have run out of oxygen, but what did I know about its race? Nothing at all. They could very well go into anabiosis and stay there for years, which was not what I was looking for. *No, let's do this the right way.*

I pulled Fang out and slowly slipped it into the rocks. There was no resistance from the spy's protection.

It was terrifying to watch in person what Fang could do. *I wouldn't want to die like that.* The Alturian suffered for a good ten minutes, finally falling silent when the decay reached its head—the creators had had the horrific idea to make the weapon start with the body. But I didn't feel a drop of sympathy for the creature. It would have killed me without a twinge of conscious, and it knew what it was getting itself into. Digging around in the remains, I found a phone. And it didn't take long to hack into it. I didn't care about the contacts or purchases—all I wanted was information on where the spy had been. The gang presumably had a base somewhere.

And I wasn't wrong. There certainly was a base, and it was off in the next location over. The deceased had been to a particular point too many times for it to be a coincidence, and I noticed something we'd done, too. The Alturian had made a detour before heading over to Aspen. Olson had given them the coordinates where the miners were hard at work, and where else would a spy at that level go? The creature needed to get ready for the attack. And that meant I'd found their base.

The drone set off before I'd even finished giving the order. It took half an hour for it to close the forty kilometers distance, and finally I had a quality image of a fortified military base in front of me. And I'd been wondering where the military was the whole time. I'd assumed some of them had been players, and that meant they should have put up a solid fight. After all, one lonely guard at a checkpoint had been able to wreak havoc. But the answer was right there in front of me: the military was gone. The base had all kinds of armed creatures, and none of them were human.

But there was something else there.

Surrounded by an enormous wall, there was a familiar area cloaked in gray fog—a steam boiler used to concentrate Earth noa. And I counted a solid fifteen hundred armed guards comprised of the different beasts the game was full of. The artifact had its protection.

Book 1: ∩o ∏istakes

There were 23,444 coins left on my victim's phone. It wasn't a bad haul, especially not when I threw in the game items I was going to sell and the 40 coins for the picture of the body. Of everything I got, I couldn't use a single thing. It was all higher than my level one limit, though it was at least expensive. Most important was to find a fence—Olson was probably not going to live to see the other side of our next meeting.

I wasn't able to restore the Mark-2. Twelve had gutted my ATV. Really, it wasn't an ATV anymore, and just hunk of metal. One of many monuments to a civilization whose time had come and gone. There were lots of them out on the roads, and nobody had cleared them away over the previous couple weeks. Lifeless, abandoned cars.

That just left the most unpleasant part. I'd been putting it off as long as possible, but I eventually had to pick up one of the many shovels lying around. There were plenty of holes, too—the people there had been digging up sand when they were attacked. All I needed to do was gather their remains, dump them in one of the holes, and cover them, saying a few words as I did. Of course, there was nothing to say. And no point, as there was nothing I could say that would do them any good. In keeping with the tradition my partner had started, I scratched an inscription into the stone. *Our descendants will know who was buried here.*

But Twelve was wrong if that thing thought I

was going to come barreling after it. Our next meeting was going to be on my terms.

Chapter 16

BLENDING IN WITH THE SHADOWS, I slipped between the apartment buildings, fighting more with myself than the need to be quiet. Wandering around abandoned villages and seeing the empty buildings was one thing; finding myself in a dead city was quite another. The difference was astounding. The apartment buildings, former beehives of activity twenty-four hours a day, pressed down on me with their indifference. The stone didn't care who lived inside it, be they homo sapiens or monsters. It would outlast them all.

Water was pouring out of one of the windows, the last witness to a sudden initiation in the bathtub. The water pressure had stayed steady for the previous two weeks. And it would keep going, I figured, until something broke. A red dot standing for a human flashed on my radar yet again. My mood dropped still further. Over the past hour, I'd seen at least fifty of them. People were hiding in basements, garages, attics. Everyone was doing their best to survive, though they all knew they were doomed unless a miracle happened. And in that moment, a miracle was walking down the street cursing himself with each step. Because if I didn't carry out my plan, there wasn't any sense helping people in that moment.

I didn't end up going to Aspen. Instead, I sent the drone around it a few times to make sure there wasn't anybody left there. Olson had gotten rid of everyone, and Twelve and his gang had taken up residence there, assuming I'd come dashing up to get my revenge for Grust. A few champions were even positioned not far from the safe zone. I was up against some solid firepower. There was no point taking them on with a frontal attack, and so I was off to take care of business before I settled my personal scores.

But my business wasn't easy, either—there were those three larvae to knock out.

The third farm was right in the middle of the big city. After scoping it out, the only thing I could do was curse helplessly, as I counted fifteen hundred tubs. A long line of monsters was collecting the cocoons as they were birthed and carrying them away. Apparently, they were off to feed the general, while the girls were loaded up and sent around again. All three centipedes worked ceaselessly with their feelers, only themselves stopping to eat every once in a while. And the game had moved to a defensive stance. There were more than a hundred and fifty champions, most of which

277

were mages. Dumb animals weren't any use for organized defense.

After crossing another street, I stopped. There were several red targets in the apartment building next to me—a human and a couple inferior monsters. The person was hiding on the eighth floor; the monsters were down on the first. And I was going to keep on walking the way I had every other time, only something about the monsters didn't sit right with me. They were dashing chaotically between the apartments. *What, are they clearing the whole city? Or is that just those two idiots out on their own?*

Whatever the case might have been, I couldn't keep going. The other people I'd passed hadn't been in immediate danger, though the guy in that building had minutes to live. I slipped past a few patrols on watch around the buildings and disappeared like a noiseless shadow into the downstairs door. Shooting was out of the question—that would have attracted attention. *Melee it is.* Valkyrie disappeared, giving way to Fang, as the two shared real estate on my right arm. The downside was that I could only use one at a time. The knife wasn't charged, as I hadn't stopped to fill it up as I ran the forty kilometers between Grust's grave and the third farm.

But that was fine—the monsters were weak enough for me to take them out even like that. I headed up to the fourth floor, where one of the apartments had just been cleared. And when a scowling face flew past a broken-down door looking to head up to the next floor, a bone blade buried itself in it from above. It was only a moment before it was sent off to the afterlife that the creature saw me. I turned toward the second and pulled the dagger out of the dead body, but that was when time stopped. Literally.

The second inferior monster had already leaped out of the door and was frozen in midair. It hadn't noticed me, though it was aware that something had happened to its friend. I froze, too, my hand wrapped around Fang's hilt as I prepared to poke a hole in the second monster. And even the spit flying out of the mouth of my first victim didn't hit the ground. The only thing that didn't freeze was my perception, as I was anything but oblivious to the still space, my own body, and my inability to move. I could also see Fang living its own life. The dagger was pulling its own tricks—a dark mist started to seep out of the wound and enshroud the dead monster. And where the mist hit touched the body, a horrifying transformation began taking place. The body deflated and dried up. When the monster was finally engulfed completely by the dark glow, it twitched and turned into a small chunk of dried flesh. The mist disappeared; the dagger freed itself completely of the wound.

Time once again began ticking.

The second monster was the last thing on my

mind, but my body was already on automatic. The blade buried itself in the creature. That time, nothing slowed down, and it just dropped to the ground, a dried-up corpse. My terrifying necroknife flashed cleaner than ever before. Fang had all the necrotic energy it needed.

I crouched down in surprise to check through the logs. Unfortunately, they didn't tell me much. One inferior level three monster had charged my knife up to 50%, and the second had finished the job. I was all set to find and make a sacrifice. That last word caught my eye, and I dug deeper into the logs. The only other time I'd made a sacrifice, I hadn't paid much attention to the string of messages that had popped up. *What does that even mean?*

A cold sweat broke out on my back when I realized the kind of weapon I was holding. It took some doing not to hurl it as far away as I could, in fact. No, the necroknife didn't just make a sacrifice; it cut off the victim's connection to the restore point. Basically, though this was just my guess, it completely nullified the monster without letting it come back in future releases. Alternatively, it might have wiped their memory clean of their time on Earth, as it must have had some vague consciousness. The game owner would just pull it from its data bank the next time. Suddenly, a nasty smile flitted across my face. *Olson!* The piece of functionality was doing his best to stand out so he would earn a promotion in the next release, making sacrificing him a great option for me. *Yes, I think I'll do exactly that.*

I had to wonder if I could sacrifice larvae, too.

It really is true that humans are too opportunistic. Even rats have nothing on us. Just a moment before, I'd been shaking just from the thought of how the tool in my hands inflicted death in its complete finality, and there I was right then off looking for a superior monster. Before I went to find the larvae, I needed to run some experiments.

The superior beast froze and shrank away in the middle of a wordless howl when I emptied the knife into it. A minute later, all that remained was a skeleton and 40 coins for my wallet. It turned out that I could charge Fang using either inferior or superior monsters so long as I landed a fatal strike. That lesson was learned when I started hunting a patrol. On the other hand, things were trickier with champions. They made for excellent sacrifices, rotting away just like the rest, though they refused to charge Fang no matter how many times I jabbed them. Even dead, it didn't work. Either Fang's level wasn't high enough to charge using champions, or it wasn't able to at all. But it was fine—I took care of the entourages trailing behind two test champions and set off for the city center.

To be honest, when I saw the variety of monsters in the square, I had second thoughts. I knew very well that there was no way I could take them on myself. But I couldn't turn back, either. Pulling out my phone, I decided to take a couple pictures. *That's larvae we're talking about!*

You took the first picture of 165 live champions. 13200 coins received.

You took the first picture of 3 live larvae. 12000 coins received.

You took a picture of a live larva-level monster. 4000 coins received.

Wait, what?

I brought the drone over and scanned the square one more time. Three larvae, a crowd of champions, and a horde of superior monsters. *There's no fourth larva! Where?!* But still, it was there—the game had given me 4,000 coins for it. Remembering that I'd already come up against a description like that, I took a closer look at all the vehicles and was rewarded for my efforts. All fifteen hundred tubs set in what looked like different storage levels were actually inside an enormous mechanical creature. The monster's body took up the whole square, which was why I hadn't noticed it right away. And it had even managed to avoid a level four scanner, which spoke volumes. The first thing it told me was that I needed to get out of there.

I noticed the red dots denoting players immediately, giving me time to hide in the shadow of one of the buildings. A column of armored vehicles modified to meet the needs of the world we were living in appeared on the road. For myself, I called them Hummers, as that was the only kind of military off-road vehicle I knew. The monsters watched them go by lazily, then went back to the apartments they were searching.

"Here!" a metallic voice called, and the column came to a halt. *Twelve!* "From the data we received, the monsters were killed here. Roll out the scanner!"

"Clear!" came the reply, and I breathed a sigh of relief. I'd been worried that my skills wouldn't keep me safe from the device, but they had. A suspicion of mine was confirmed, however—the game told the robot about my kills.

"He must have headed toward the square," Twelve said. *Smart bastard!*

"You don't think he'd go after three larvae, do you?" one of the fighters asked in surprise.

"Four," Twelve said. "The farm is held in a container to make it easier to move if anything comes up. And as far as that Earthling goes, I have no idea. He's hard to read, so let's assume he's crazy enough to risk it. Can you imagine what he'll do when he finds out the humans have almost completely regained control of the north? Stupid planet... I hate it. The sooner we pump all the noa out, the better."

"Yes, that idiot just dispersed it," one of the fighters said with a laugh that engendered a wave of indignation from me. *What, did I do something wrong?*

"We got lucky. If he knew how to use his planet's strength, he would be much more of a challenge. Crindar, stay here with the squad and scan the area once every minute. Don't let Mark by you. And take care of those three low-levels—we need to crush the humans like cockroaches. Move out!"

The Hummers set off, though I could see very well an inconspicuous shadow slip out of one of them and melt into the grass. *Sniper cover.* Crindar was the bait, and the Alturian was the hunter. The problem was that they didn't have any prey to go after, because I wasn't about to turn myself into that. And while the drone lost the spy, I could see it right there. I stuck to the shadows and slowly moved in that direction. The fighter assigned to the scanner stayed in the vehicle, while the other two headed into the houses. It looked like luck had run out for the guy on the eighth floor.

"He was here!" One of the fighters poked their head out of a window on the fourth floor. "Look what he did with these inferiors!"

Two dried-up bodies flopped down onto the ground. Crindar bent over them, touching them with a concerned hand.

"Completely drained," he said in surprise.

"Mummified! How did he do that?"

"No idea." The character on the fourth floor was clearly nervous. "He definitely isn't showing up on the scanner?"

"No. Do your job!" Crindar barked back. "He's somewhere in the center. Twelve will find him."

"What the hell are we doing here?" the insistent fighter asked. "Why did we split off?"

I paused as I looked up at him, and then I was hit by an unpleasant thought. *Really, why did Twelve leave a vehicle here?* Even covered by a sniper, it was an obvious trap. The drone set off after the group that had left, and I had my answer half a kilometer later. There were another two snipers on the top floor of another building. Our position was right in their line of fire, which meant that Twelve had known I wouldn't be able to leave the troops there be. Even the Alturian was a trap. *That sneaky bugger!*

I didn't stop until I'd found all the players. The rest really had headed over to the square, though their attention was clearly trained in my direction. The robot was expecting there to be fireworks, and I wasn't going to let him down.

The drone flew over to the two snipers. They were hairy beasts, one at level 63, and the other at level 67. Making sure that there wasn't anyone else in the building, I gave a terse order. *Fire!*

It's hard to fight back when you're up against a

machine worth more than two million coins. I had no doubt that the players were wearing level two personal protection, and possibly even level three, though the problem with that was the level four automatic pistol my Mark-1 was armed with. It couldn't have cared less about trivialities like that. Sure, the protection held up for a bit, just letting half the energy through, but even ten shots apiece was enough to free up some game resources. Like a true hero, I came at them from the rear. I didn't want Twelve to know how I'd taken out its troops.

The thought flashed through my mind that I really should invest in some kind of grabber, as the phones with the loot I wanted were up there in the building. But I quickly forgot about that when the building the snipers had been in turned into a firestorm. The explosion was so powerful that the shock wave hit us almost at full force, throwing the players in every direction. Even the Alturian was knocked out of its tree and thrown against a wall. Sadly, their protection held up. All of them survived.

As did my drone. It was battered by a good bit of stone and hurled high into the sky, though it was whole and undamaged. Just a little singed. At least, I'd learned that fire wasn't enough to bring down my bird. It was going to take something much more.

But, damn it, that Twelve was a dangerous opponent. It had read me like a child. I hadn't thought to check for a second ambush until the last moment, and a third hadn't even occurred to me. If it hadn't been for the drone, I would have been gone from the land of the living.

"What was that?" A surprised fighter poked its head out a window.

"They got Mark," Crindar replied. "Get down here and help get the vehicle back upright."

"No, they didn't. He's still in the ranking." The Alturian pulled itself off the wall, showing itself in all its glory. My closest association was a jellyfish—formless, colorless, and unpleasant.

"Yeah-h-h..." came the amazed exclamation. "Where did he get that strong?"

"Who cares? Let's move out! There's a general assembly." Crindar roared and heaved the Hummer upright. By himself.

Both fighters followed orders, jumping out of the window down onto the ground. *That guy on the eighth floor really is a lucky duck!* If the game gave rewards for achievements, he was definitely getting something that day. Crindar started the Hummer and waited for the jellyfish to climb aboard, though that was the last thing he did in his game life.

My leap was as imperceptible as it was precise. My knife found a home in the jellyfish, the opponent I figured was the most dangerous. A charge of necrotic energy, and I brought it around to disappear in

Crindar's back. A left hook with my strength was enough to knock out one of the two soldiers. Forming in my hand, Valkyrie turned the head of the fourth member of the team into Swiss cheese with a couple shots. *You really need some level four armor, idiot.* Then, I deactivated Valkyrie and ripped Fang out of Crindar's chest so I could finish him off with a blow to the head. But there was no head inside his helmet—the player's body had already shriveled up. Fang had only charged halfway, so I stabbed the stunned character with it.

And it was only after that that I released control of their BRO-III outfits. Hacking and blocking four outfits at once had turned out to be so difficult that I very nearly panicked. Apparently, five items, my Mark-1 included, was my limit for the device control level I was at.

The controls for the Hummer were old-fashioned pedals and a steering wheel. I threw Crindar's body onto the passenger seat and beat a hasty retreat out of the city. There was no sense going after the larvae—the numbers were too lopsided.

I dumped the car ten kilometers later. Gas vehicles were useless, as was hacking the phones in the Hummer with me. The hairy beasts had been born in Aspen, with the Alturian making the same journey as the other one. There wasn't anything new or interesting there besides 160 coins for the pictures and

23998 coins from their wallets. And there wasn't anything they were wearing that I could take, which told me that I needed to find ten million coins pronto. That's how much named armor cost. It wasn't that I didn't want to take on the larvae without it; I knew I didn't have a shot otherwise. Tossing everything of higher value into my virtual storage, I dropped the rest into my pockets. *Olson won't be able to overcome his functionality, so he'll have to buy everything off me before we start shooting at each other.* And the fact that I was only going to be able to trade it all in for coins once meant that I had to be ready. For example, I needed to drop by the dungeons, one of which was on the way, and check in on a couple caches. It was just a shame that I couldn't sell the Hummer. It wasn't a game item.

Setting a good pace, I ran off. There was an explosion behind me—my grenades had gone off. I wasn't about to leave the enemy with another vehicle if I could help it. The dungeon was just ten kilometers away, located not far from the military base. But that, of course, was where I was going last, and only after I took care of where the jellyfish were spawning in the next location over.

They probably store all their loot there, and I wouldn't mind acquiring it.

It was a great plan, though I almost tripped when the game made its next move:

Monster levels increased by 1 (current level: 4).

Bastards! The promotions were coming less than a week apart, which meant I had to hurry. Another one of them... I knew if I didn't take care of the larvae then, I never would. Scrambling down a steep incline and reaching for another branch, I got to where I was going. The entrance to the cave was shrouded in a glowing film. It was inside the hill. The drone told me there weren't any creatures in the area, though I still wasn't about to jump down and dash over. My perception and detection were eating at me. Something was wrong, though I couldn't figure out what for the life of me. All of a sudden, I had grave misgivings about going through the dungeon. I even wanted to run off in the opposite direction, though I took a deep breath to calm myself. Thankfully, I'd moved silently, and so nobody knew that a player had appeared in the tree I was in. Even the squirrel next to me was too busy going about its business to notice me.

Ten minutes spent watching the entrance to the dungeon yielded zilch. Nothing suspicious happened, although I was all the more convinced that I needed to get out of there. It was a bad feeling. After the squirrel ran off, I dipped a hand into its nest and pulled out a few pinecones. Then, after loading up a branch with them, I sent my improvised grenade hurtling toward the ground in front of the entrance. If anything was waiting, it would be waiting—

Right there!

No sooner had the pinecone touched the ground, than it erupted into an enormous maw. There was a snapping sound, and the creature disappeared back into the ground. Finally, the drone went crazy, and new information poured onto the screen. It turned out that my smart little guy had only scanned the ground, not bothering to look under it. Once I'd corrected that oversight, I was told quite a bit. For example, I was looking at a larva-level monster called a shrew that had crept over from a neighboring location. And how was I so sure of that? Because that was the direction the tunnel the monster had dug led off in. But the most important part was that there was a whole network of tunnels under my feet, and I sent the drone off along one of them only to find that it opened out into the military base a couple minutes later. Skipping right past all the obstacles and guards, it led right into the middle of the gray mist.

I'd cheated death yet again. A plan began to shape in my head, and I couldn't wait to get started. Six plasma grenades lashed together flew in the direction of the dungeon. The monstrous shrew didn't let me down, popping out and chowing down on my little present. There was an explosion, and earth, stone, and flesh flew in every direction. At first, my hair stood on end when I realized the level four shrew was still alive. But my instincts took over, I dashed over to where the beast was writhing around, and Valkyrie had the final say. Ten explosive shots, a couple electric bolts, and one shot of fire were enough. The monster couldn't use its protection with me that close, and the scorched body finally gave up the ghost.

You destroyed a shrew.
Valkyrie and Fang levels increased by 1 (4).
Level +10 (171).
5 free attribute points received.
You can collect any level four item in the store for free.
***
You took the first picture of a dead larva-level creature. 80000 coins received.
***
Congratulations!
You're the first player in your location to discover *Limbo's Cave*.
1 free attribute point available.
Level +1 (172).

Wait a second, Wax was never here? How did he know about the dungeon then? I'd gotten the coordinates from his phone, after all. *Or was the whole thing a trap?*

Chapter 17

You destroyed the third round of monsters.
The dungeon has been updated, monster levels bumped up twice (current level: 7).
30 players entered the dungeon, synchronization complete.

THE CLATTER OF AUTOMATIC WEAPONS broke out somewhere in the distance as the players started cutting through the fourth round of monsters. And it took me just a few seconds to start berating myself in my head—how could I have forgotten that the game would tell Twelve the instant I started killing things? I'd been so focused on beating the dungeon that I'd completely forgotten about my own safety. *Idiot! Moron! Nincompoop!* And they'd caught me at the worst time, too—I was all the way at the far end of the dungeon. To get to the exit, I was going to have to make my way through the entire thing, full as it was of monsters and players alike.

And it had all been going so well...

I hadn't had to pull Valkyrie out once during the first three rounds. Even Fang had only been called into action twice, stuck into large overgrown worms. The rest of the time, I'd just used my fists to overpower their mortal frames. The monsters died like seconds in a cheap blockbuster, quickly, impressively, and without a second thought. I was even starting to think that I just had the single combat in front of me when the dungeon threw me a curveball. Two, in fact. The first was the fourth round; the second was the 30 unexpected players. And Twelve had had exactly 30 fighters left after the skirmish by the third farm. *Did he really send them all in? What about guards at the perimeter?*

Anyway, they'd just barely entered the dungeon, which meant they were a long way from me. The broad, multi-level network of tunnels spread out like an old fungus on a giant plant. There was a main room, too, presumably the scene of the final showdown with the boss. Sticking my head in there would have been suicide—I'd checked every nook and cranny, and there weren't any good hiding spots. And that meant I was going to have to run around the tunnels setting up ambushes.

But reality had unpleasant surprises in store for me the way it always does.

A fourth-round opponent popped out from around the nearest corner. It looked reminiscent of an

Alturian, though there were some pretty significant differences. The similarity was that it was a shapeless amoeba washing around in its movements. And the main difference was that it didn't have a body. It was made up completely of fog, with just a pair of red eyes fixed on me in defiance of my concealment and camouflage. *It can see me!*

Activating Valkyrie took less than a second, and pure energy went flying at the creature. But it cut through the fog like a knife through butter without meeting the least bit of resistance. Only the monster wasn't dying of its wounds—it came at me, a clump of danger. I had no desire whatsoever to let the thing touch me, so I switched ammunition types and fired once again. Energy rounds had worked. Neither did fire, napalm, or explosives, just passing right through the creature's body. Electricity just lit the monster up for a couple instants in a weird kind of beauty. But finally, I got a result from ice: the monster was covered in hoarfrost that slowed its movements drastically. Changing the ammunition type, I tried again, though the frost melted too quickly for anything to do any damage. It came at me once again.

Ice and Valkyrie gave way to Fang, a quick step forward, a lunge, and a sound wave that hit my ears so hard even my helmet couldn't deaden it. I blacked out.

I regained consciousness almost immediately. Holding my hands out to catch myself as I fell, I pushed away from the floor and jumped back to create distance. But there wasn't anything to create distance from. All that was left of the monster was a handful of gray ash. Fang had sucked the creature in completely, although it had managed to do a number on my ears as it died. Somewhere deep in the tunnels, there was a horrified scream that gurgled to a close with an explosion. The dungeon shook, and a chill ran down my body. The damn jellyfish were reaching all the way to me with their dying howls. The drone didn't work in the dungeon, so I was blind, unsure of what was going on. All I could do was keep going in the hopes that I wouldn't come across anyone around the next bend.

Twenty minutes later, I realized that if I wanted to go unnoticed by Twelve's fighters, I was going to have to stop killing the fog monsters. When they died, they let out their howl that was heard throughout the whole dungeon. That attracted friends and made sure everyone knew where I was. Finally, I had to back off, hide in a burrow, and wait for everyone to forget about me. At least, while I was sitting there, I was able to figure out the enemy's strategy. The other players were knocking the fog monsters out with plasma grenades. It hit me that they were spending my money—after all, I was going to strip them of their earnings once I'd killed them. They were going through grenades by the bucketful. And they cost two grand each, the damn cheaters.

A couple times, grenades detonated not far away, and I had to go through the heat wave followed by the death scream of the monster they were sending into the great beyond. Coming to once again, I froze. Players were walking by.

"Clear!" I heard from three separate players, and ten of them stepped into the cave I was hiding in. They were all from Twelve's detachment. Rolling out a device, they scanned the whole area, after which Zharmund, a level 74 player, stated the results.

"Clear where we are. No, he's not here. Yes, we took them all out with grenades the way you told us to. I guess, he's over on your side. Okay, heading out. Over."

Zharmund turned to the rest.

"Move out! The boss found a passage. Mark should be there."

Yep, I know that passage. It was narrow and almost vertical. When I'd found it, I'd thought there would be something interesting or another level up there, but it just turned out to be a dead end.

I could have let them go and made a break for the exit, but Grust's ghost wouldn't have let me sleep at night. Waiting for them to turn away, I leaped out and began gunning them down with deadly accuracy. I didn't even have to take my finger off the trigger button, just turning Valkyrie from target to target. And it didn't bother me in the least that I was shooting in the back. Those bastards didn't deserve a fair fight.

A few moments later, it was all over. The bodies had dropped to the ground. To make sure they were dead, I pulled out my phone, as that many kills should have given me 400 coins. And that's exactly what I got. Zharmund and his troop had been wiped out completely.

Their phones all went into my pockets. I would have time to deal with them later. Taking a quick look at the bodies, I sighed—leaving BRO-III costumes there to rot went against everything I stood for as a person. The same went for their weapons, as the whole squad was armed to the teeth. I ended up staying there at the risk of ending up trapped. Gathering everything into a pile, I was looking for somewhere to stick it all when I heard another far-off explosion and got a notification:

You destroyed the fourth round of monsters.
The dungeon has been updated, monster levels bumped up twice (current level: 9).
Final round. Single combat.

That was bad. *If Twelve kills the boss, it'll collect all the loot.* That would have meant I'd wasted the previous three hours. The thought was so unpleasant that I even let out a growl. I wanted to fall on my hands and knees, whine and jump around like a little puppy until someone carried me over to my mother and laid me on her neck.

And I did just about that. Falling onto my knees, I scowled, and just as I was about to let out a whine, I heard someone else howling in the distance. I shivered; my stomach emptied its contents right into my helmet. That cleared my head of the delusion. Yanking my helmet off, I crashed to the ground. It felt like the strength had been drained right out of me, and it was only when I heard a heart-rending cry off in the distance that I pulled myself to my knees and crawled forward. I rocked back and forth, banging my head against the wall of the cave.

"No-o-o! Ah-h-h! Please, no!"

The screams sounded one after another as if carried forward on a conveyer belt. I crawled the final meters to the big cave on my stomach, barely hanging on to my sanity. It was obvious what was going on— the boss commanded a powerful brand of hypnosis. A level nine dungeon, level four monsters in the outside world, and that meant the strength of the call was about 36. It was no surprise that I was having such a hard time, just my level 40 willpower keeping me going. Finally, I peered into the cave and saw my opponents. All of them, in fact.

There was a ball of fog with lightning running across it in the middle of the enormous space. Players stood motionless around it, all staring stupidly at a single point. The sphere pulsed, the lightning intensified, and a naked skeleton dressed in a BRO outfit came flying out. That was all that was left of the player. A fat feeler reached out of the sphere to grab a new victim, and an already familiar scream resounded in the cave.

"No-o-o! Ah-h-h! Please, no!"

The scream gurgled away, and the body was swallowed up by the boss. The lightning slowed—it was as though all its energy was going toward digesting the suddenly appearing piece of meat.

I counted ten players and the remains of six more. Adding the one in the boss gave me seventeen. Twelve wasn't there, and that made me nervous. It was presumably somewhere in the dungeon, possibly right by one of the cave entrances watching the odd sphere swallow up its troops. They definitely weren't its friends.

The fact that not all the players had made it to the boss gave me control over my body once again. I was even able to stand up, though I was certainly unsteady. Thought fragments about running over to my mother and giving myself to her popped into my head. I found a way to resist, however, and I pulled up my map before setting off slowly along the edge of the main cave. I needed to check the approaches.

I found Twelve by the fifth entrance. The robot was standing on its platform, arms crossed as it watched the sphere finish digesting its fighters. The boss' mental pressure was growing with each passing minute, and I thought seriously about stabbing myself with a few syringes to boost my will. The only problem with that was that I would've been killed three times over in the three hours that would have taken.

For a couple seconds, my head was the battleground between caution and the urge to rip the robot apart with my bare hands. I didn't know what it was capable of, and so I ended up deciding to keep my distance despite the difference in levels between us.

"You've caused me quite a few problems, human." Twelve suddenly turned toward me, which served as my signal to end the whole farce. Valkyrie popped into my hand. I smashed through the robot's shell, at least, I thought I did. The bullets flew right through as if it were a ghost.

"I've had to do a lot of running around after you." The robot continued talking, ignoring my gunfire. I'd been through that before, so I just switched to electric bullets. *Shut your trap, you piece of metal!*

"Only the knowledge that the general will reward me for my efforts has made the temporary inconvenience worthwhile." Electricity was useless. I switched to ice.

"Time to go!" The last thing I was expecting was that the space around me would solidify into a mechanical arm belonging to Twelve. I didn't even have time to jerk away. With one practiced motion, the robot gave me a shot right between my helmet and armor, after which the world swirled around me, and I fell heavily to the ground.

"It irks me to say that you managed to screw with me even here." The rest of Twelve materialized on the other side of the mechanical arm. "I can't kill you in a dungeon, otherwise your data will be saved, and you'll respawn in the next release. I'm going to have to do something I hate more than anything: touch an organic life form. I hate your soft bodies."

With a sweep of its leg, the robot threw my body onto something resembling a tarp, after which it scrambled back onto the platform and dragged me off. My brain churned slowly, as if frozen. I couldn't move my arms or legs. Even my eyes remained fixed in one direction. My body was no longer under my control. *How? That was just one needle!* I had level 16 regeneration, and I had no idea why I couldn't feel anything.

At the same time, Twelve continued like some kind of movie villain.

"You've really made strides since the beginning of the game. Not like me back in the day, but still solid. Although, what cracks me up is that you think I need a scanner to find you. How is it possible to be that naïve? Sure, your concealment and camouflage are excellent—you broke level 100 just in time. But everything else... It couldn't be simpler. You humans only know how to shoot and die. You need to do more than just take care of yourself, though. There's covering your tracks, masking your scent, completely clearing your consciousness, and that didn't even occur to you. But what does that matter? The important thing is that you know how to die like the rest of organic matter. The sooner this damn planet is sucked dry, the better."

The tip of my finger twitched, telling me that the poison was wearing off.

"But the funniest thing is that you trapped yourself." The robot was dragging me up the last tunnel. The exit was fifty meters away. "Dungeons make everyone equal—you could have done some damage out there, but you're the same as everyone else in here. Level fifteen. You have an interesting knife, though. I'll look forward to getting my hands on it once you're dead."

As we continued uphill, my hand bounced off my chest and landed on the ground. My fingers felt a crevice, and I tensed my muscles to pull myself off the tarp. Twelve kept on going; I slipped off and rolled back where we'd just come from. The robot reacted instantaneously. No sooner had I gotten to the bottom, than a shadow flashed by to stop my flight with a steel leg. I heard an unpleasant snap and was happy I couldn't feel anything. My body had been bent entirely backward. Carried over by the momentum, my arms wrapped themselves around Twelve's legs. A message popped up in my head:

Devices available for connection.
Would you like to take control?

What?! Yes, of course!

Hijacking control block... Successful.
Hijacking protection block... Successful.
Hijacking attack block... Successful.
Hijacking platform... Successful.
You connected to the 54X-12 life support systems.

Block!

That was the last thing I did before whatever had been in the shot wore off to the point that the pain from my broken back bereft me of consciousness.

A lovely metal statue greeted me eight hours later. Twelve was frozen inside its body, unable to do anything. I spent a good while looking it up and down before I found the strength to pull myself up. Everything I'd done to try and penetrate its defenses had come up empty. As it turned out, all I had to do was touch it for my skill to win the day.

I stood up, my wound gone without a trace, though I was still a bit shaky. And while what served as the robot's eyes weren't moving, I could tell that they worked. It was a serious opponent. So serious, in fact, that I got butterflies just looking at it. Smart, powerful, strong. The adjectives came one after another. If the game owner hadn't been looking to wipe my data, my little adventure would have been over. I'd gotten lucky.

"It's over!" I activated Fang and buried it in the robot's head. The body twitched and convulsed, the eyes went dead. Robots apparently didn't shrivel up the way organic material did, and that was definitely a point in their favor.

You destroyed 54X-12, the twelfth spawn of your hexagon's general.

Level +5 (177).

5 free attribute points received.

***

The general in your hexagon recognized you as a threat. From now on, all the monsters in this hexagon will do quintuple damage to you. You will receive five times as many coins for each monster killed.

Level +10 (187).

10 free attribute points received.

You can collect any level four item in the store for free.

Oh, so that was the twelfth spawn? That explained a lot. The experience, the skills, the equipment, all of it. I wouldn't have minded a sugar daddy like that, either. Making a mental note that there were another eleven "kids" like that who were players, as well, I resolved to regularly check the location ranking.

I placed my hands on the robot's empty body and found ten items I could extract. In with the armor, weaponry, and protection I couldn't use because of my limitation was a phone. I paused, turning it around in my hands. *No, I need another attribute before I open it.*

Hacking +40 (40).

I was down to just two syringes, but that was fine. Sitting down on the platform, I let the game start the update while I dug into the list of level four items. I had something flying and mobile again, so I knew I had to be smart about what I spent my two bonuses getting.

Hacking personal data... Successful!
Hacking contact list... Successful!
Hacking store... Successful! Access to level five items unlocked.
Hacking map... Successful! Would you like to download the map?

If Twelve had come back to life, I would have hugged it right then and there. Not only was it advanced, it also had incredible equipment. There were some bonuses I got to download to my phone besides the 1.5 million coins.

Virtual storage-V. *Description: Phone expansion. Lets you store up to 40 game items in virtual space. Item materialization takes 30 seconds. Cost: none, is a title reward.*

Virtual exchange-V. *Description: Phone expansion. Lets you exchange game items for coins at 50% of their value. Cost: None, is a title reward.*

I actually jumped for joy when I was able to hack into the phone and download the updates to my own. That went a long way toward resolving my problems, as I didn't need to come to terms with Olson anymore. And most importantly, I knew where to find the general. Twelve's main deployment position was in the second-largest city in the hexagon, one with a population of just under a million. That looked to be where the general was, too. And that was great news—I was going to give that area a wide birth. Locking horns with the general after what its most junior spawn had nearly done to me was not in the cards. *The troops who recaptured almost all of the north can deal with that character.*

Would you like to sell 32 items for 2557000 coins?

I smiled as I rubbed my hands together. *You bet I would!* Things were making progress, and that named armor was starting to look like it was in reach. The levitating platform stayed with me. I'd already selected expansions for it, though I wasn't looking to buy them just yet. Finishing the dungeon was first.

That people-eating sphere had waited long enough for me. It was time to pay it a visit.

Setting Valkyrie to ice, I made my way to the main cave. The other players were long gone, a fact attested to by the pile of armor and bones. Raging lightning played across the surface of the boss with such intensity that it looked halfway to hysterics. And that made sense—there was yet another piece of meat in the dungeon, and it wasn't walking toward the sphere with a happy grin on its face. Having made sure the boss couldn't go anywhere, I opened fire. The ice was perfect. After just twenty hits, the boss' body was frozen solid, making the fog solid enough for me to attack. I buried a couple explosive rounds in it that performed admirably. And even though the game gave me just 10% damage for each shot, the third one finished the deal. The sphere shattered. Something told me it was safe to walk up to the creature with Fang in my hand, and I'd learned to trust my gut over the previous few weeks.

Congratulations!
You won the single combat.
Limbo's Cave cleared.
Level +3 (190).

***

You beat a dungeon in a group of less than 4 people. Reward level increased by 1.

You beat a dungeon alone. Reward level increased by 1.

You beat a dungeon while being impeded by another group of 30 players. Reward level increased by 1.

***

Would you like to collect your reward?

A bitter smile spread across my face when I read the words mocking me. Five level four items was a prize I would have given anything for a week before, though they were nothing but expensive toys for me then.

But, as always, the game had a different idea.

Modifier for LP-12. Propulsion system-IV.
Modifier for LP-12. Reinforced chasse-IV.

Modifier for LP-12. Universal force field P-IV.
Modifier for LP-12. Security system-IV.
Modifier for LP-12. Magnetic cushions-IV.

As I looked at my reward, my jaw dropped wider and wider, unable to cope with the shock. Adding a camouflage system and invisibility like my drone had was going to make the LP-12, Twelve's levitating platform, something I could really use. Experience had shown that running around on my own two feet just wasn't a good idea. The LP-12 worked beautifully inside the dungeon, so I brought it over to the main cave and got to work. The most important thing was to change the name.

Mark-2. *Description: Modified flying transport built for Mark Derwin. Maximum altitude: 10 meters. Maximum flight speed: 180 km/h. Number of seats: 1. Maximum load: 1000 kilograms. Protection: universal force field (P-IV), camouflage field (MP-IV), invisibility field (PN-IV). Cost: 25000000 coins.*

The first thing my new ride reminded me of was a flying Formula One car. The driver didn't sit; they laid down, hidden completely in the vehicle's body. At least, completely with the exception of their head, of which just the eyes peeked out. It was controlled mentally through my device control interface. The only problem was that there wasn't any storage or weaponry—I'd run out of integration slots. If I wanted something better, I was going to have to buy a level five base.

Then, I got to work looting, a process that netted me 2.3 million coins for the items I sold and 800,000 from the phones of the dead players. I made sure I hacked into every phone I could find, though there was nothing interesting in there. Almost all the animals had come with Twelve.

I was 2.5 million short of the armor, though I didn't have anything else to sell. There was no way I was going to sacrifice Mark-1 or Mark-2 even for my bodily safety. Making sure that the dungeon was completely clear, I took a deep breath and ran through the glowing film, a plasma grenade at the ready. There was no doubt someone was waiting for me outside.

The only question was who.

Chapter 18

IT'S SO NICE TO BE WRONG sometimes. I was standing right outside the dungeon, the drone was hovering above me, and my soul was happy. There was no need to fight for my life, run from other players, or even fight off monsters. Of course, that was all in the cards. But not in that moment. There was nobody in the vicinity, almost as if they'd all forgotten about me. The general had yet to assign a new group of players.

Taking in another lungful of cool forest air, I activated my Mark-2. There was too much to do for me to take a break. The good news was that climbing into and out of the vehicle was a piece of cake—I'd been worried there would be some kind of hatch I'd have to wiggle my way into. But Mark-2 just threw back the body and offered convenient handles. Once again making sure that everything was good and I wasn't being followed, I made a beeline for the base. Just not the military base packed with players and monsters. No, I was off to see the spot the Alturians frequented. One time was a coincidence; twice was a pattern. It was time to see what was going on.

Flying along in invisible mode was a blast. I hurtled through villages, small towns, and whole groups of monsters, none of whom paid me the least bit of attention. Of course, a few champions perked up oddly and sniffed the air threateningly, though they were just mindless animals. And there were fewer of them with each passing day. For the rest, I didn't exist. On occasion, I thought about stopping to hunt, but I thought better of it. They would all come running the moment I went to work on the Earth noa concentrator. And there would be time enough to deal with them then.

Stopping a few kilometers away from my destination, I sent the drone in to scout it out. My smile grew wider in anticipation of an easy victory until it was suddenly replaced with a stony mask that betrayed a lack of faith in myself. The Alturians really had set up a small base. But the reason it was there was to protect a small monster city centered around a larva farm with 300 tubs. The larva itself was nowhere to be seen, presumably because it was back in my location.

The Alturian base was located in a shopping mall. I flew a loop around it, checking carefully to see who was alive. There were ten jellyfish inside, three on the roofs of neighboring buildings, and two positioned in trees. From what I'd been able to glean about the odd race, they were capable of standing guard twenty-four hours a day, not needing sleep, rest, or trips to the bathroom. That made them the ideal scouts and spies that they were. Really, the best idea would have been to beat a hasty retreat, only the player ranking in the location told me that nobody there was above level 30. And that was too tempting to pass up. Plus, there was the damn farm... I was no superhero—I knew very well what I was and wasn't capable of. Winning the war wasn't something I could do by myself, and I was perfectly happy to let the troops in the north take care of that, though big wins are always made up of smaller ones. And I could deliver small wins. To do so, I needed to clear as many locations as I could of the alien scum.

I made my final decision on the way to the shopping center. For some reason, I was convinced that I wouldn't make it inside undetected even with my skills, which made taking out the guards a priority. There was no sense just opening fire on them. Any direct hit they managed to land would have been fatal, after all. No, I had to play the role I hated most: the ninja.

Taking inventory, I counted five fighters about thirty meters from each other. That wasn't so terribly far, though it definitely wasn't as close as I would have liked. After making a mental note of their location, I deactivated my Mark-1. It would have just gotten in the way. I'd never had to control the armor of players that far away from each other, and so I was feeling nervous. It was going to be risky.

I decided to clamber up the outer wall on my way to the roof. There were definitely going to be traps waiting inside for unexpected guests, at least, unless I was overestimating the jellyfish. Once I made it to the top I glanced over at the roof. The Alturian had taken up a strong position spread along a ledge. That gave it a great view of the whole space, and it would have been practically impossible to see it if it weren't for my perception.

Reaching toward its outfit, I hijacked control and blocked the alien inside. It was a simple BRO-II, nothing too complicated there. I very much hoped that their race didn't have anything like telepathic communication—that would have put paid to my entire plan. But it looked like everything was fine. Nobody came after me. The other four were right there in front of me, and I reached toward the one who was farthest. That just elicited a curse. *Too far!* I tried with the ones in the trees, but that didn't work, either. Next was the closest, the one in the next building over. Nothing. *Damn it...* I was as good at planning as Twelve was at people-pleasing. Realizing that I needed to take care of the situation quickly, I sent the drone flying into the air. *Let's try this the old-fashioned way.* My simple U-I rifle scoped in on one of the players, and I grunted. Even a shot to the head was pointless. I'd only ever seen numbers like 0% once, back when I was hunting the destroyer, and even then, I'd at least gotten a small percentage. Here, it was zero. That meant my rifle simply wasn't capable of penetrating the player's protection. *I'd better sell this thing before someone sees me with it and starts laughing at me.*

The only option remaining was to risk it. Sticking Fang into the body of the frozen player, I tossed everything I could pull off it into my storage and crawled back to where I could climb down the building. And it was a good thing I hadn't stayed there. The spot where I'd been lying erupted in a hail of bullets, one even catching my leg. The Alturians were incredibly fast. The one on the nearby roof was the most immediate threat, so I sent the drone over immediately. His camouflage gone, the deadly fighter was right there in the camera. Mark-1 got right up behind what was presumably its back before opening fire. But with that, one of the Alturians turned its attention on the drone, and it lit up. Its protection held, though the level dropped unnervingly. When I saw that, I sent it hurtling over to the next target, a move that forced both of the two in the trees to switch over to it. They forgot me and started shooting at a more visible target.

That was their undoing. The drone was protected against up to 300 hits from weapons through level four. That was a solid number, though it took more than 200 hits as it flew between the buildings.

But the jellyfish were distracted. That let me switch over to and show the world why Valkyrie cost so much. Just ten shots later, and the Alturians in the trees dropped out of the branches. The drone gunned down the one on the roof from point blank range. Immediately turning my Mark-1 invisible, I focused my attention on the shopping center. There were another ten creatures in there, but everything was quiet. Either they were getting a surprise ready for me, or they were ignoring my attack.

I decided not to touch the two Alturians who'd been on the roofs, leaving them as a message to their kind. But I collected everything from the ones I'd knocked out of the trees. Selling their equipment netted me 58,000 coins, with another 12,000 coming from their phones. At my rate of expenditures, that was nothing, of course. The scanner told me the creatures in the shopping center were all on the first underground level, so I carefully opened the door and stepped inside.

It had been so long since I'd last been in a store that I felt a rush of nostalgia. Clothes, different goods, jewelry—all of it was lying there untouched. The alien players couldn't have cared less, and the only ones of ours who'd gotten there had been in the bellies of the monsters. I glanced over at a jewelry shop window. A couple months before, Squirrel would have sold her soul to have a free go at the contents. I felt the sudden urge to give her a call, though I suppressed it. There was no reason to work her up into a panic again. *Let her sleep.* It was also better not to remind the game that I had a weakness.

Being as careful as I could, I made my way down to the parking garage. That's where the creatures were. The scanner told me they were all sitting right in their spots, almost as if they didn't care what was going on above them. Stepping past yet another car, I finally saw them. What had once been a tire shop had been looted and outfitted as a storehouse for game items. There was no point hiding anymore, so I stepped forward openly—none of the ten creatures in the storehouse were a threat to me. They were all caged.

Three hairy Shurvans, three dark, long-eared thugs, three small green bastards, and one Alturian. The jellyfish was being held in a cage made out of a force field. When I showed up, they all went into a frenzy, doing their best to attract attention, only without making a sound. Either the cages were soundproof, or the creatures weren't able to talk. Only the jellyfish remained spread across the floor of its cage.

Waving hello to everyone, I rushed into the warehouse. I wasn't sure how long it would take for the Alturians to find out about the intrusion, so I needed to make the time count.

There were quite a few items, though, to my

great disappointment, most of them were level one. Cheap, useless goods they'd gotten from players who had just barely been getting started, presumably. A mountain of pistols, BRO-I suits, and force fields—the Alturians had pulled all the tires out of the shop and packed it with game devices. *I never would've thought they'd be hoarders. Although... What did I really know about them?* When I found some level two items, I smiled. Level three items earned themselves a happy shout. But it was only five times that I saw a level four item and jumped for joy. Two hours spent going through it all left me a happy camper—I was 3.6 million coins richer. All of a sudden, the Alturians were my favorite players. *I think I'll even start killing them quickly to make sure they don't suffer.*

The store section I was looking for popped up, and I spent 10 million coins without a second thought. Finally, I had what I needed to survive a few hits.

Ulbaron. *Description: Universal adaptive tactical outfit for Mark Derwin. Initial Ulbaron level: 1. Built-in universal protection capable of withstanding Ulbaron level*50 hits from any weapon through Ulbaron level. Regenerates when up to 50% of the surface area is damaged. When activated, is airtight for Ulbaron level*10 minutes. Heat resistant, cold resistant, built-in cleaning system. Integrates with microphone. Cannot be blocked in the game world. Requirements: Strength (40),* *agility (40), stamina (40), fortress (30), resilience (30). Cost: 10000000 coins.*

Initial setup complete.
You destroyed 2 larva-level creatures.
Ulbaron level increased by 2 (3).
You cleared a location of monsters. Ulbaron level increased by 1 (4).

The only requirements I didn't meet were for strength and stamina. Five attribute syringes were already in my pockets, which left 15 more to buy. That knocked me out of the game for three hours. It was a risk, of course, but it was my only option.

Once I'd stuck myself, I made sure I stayed awake, heading over to the prisoners. I needed to do something with them—there had to be a reason they'd been locked up. The cages were held shut with electronic locks I was easily able to hijack. I decided to start with the Shurvan. Stepping away, I pulled out my pistol, letting the creature know I was willing to use it the moment anything went wrong.

The hairy player took a few tentative steps out of the cage as if not believing what was going on, its eyes fixed on me. Finally, my perception kicked in, and I was able to read its status.

Crawlson, level 12 player. Status: Active.

"Who are you, and why were you locked up?" I asked Crawlson, though it responded in a way we hadn't agreed on at all. With a bestial roar, it leaped at me. A smoking hole appeared right in the middle of its forehead, the shot sending it rolling backward a few meters. *Okay, no luck with the first. Let's see what the rest have to say.*

Not counting the angry growling, the rest also kept their mouths shut. The hairy ones, the dark orcs, even the goblins. None of them ran away, none of them tried to talk. No sooner were they out of their cages, than they all rushed me with arms thrown wide. I had to doubt they were looking for a hug.

That left the Alturian, who hadn't yet taken part in any of the excitement. Knowing all too well what to expect, I still deactivated its cage. I was going to have to be careful—the jellyfish had good protection. It rolled out onto the floor as soon as the force field disappeared. But then, it surprised me by speaking up instead of charging.

"You don't need to shoot, human. I can control the possession, at least for now."

"You're possessed?" I asked in surprised. "With what? Tell me, Nriman, level two, who are you, and what were you doing in a cage?"

The jellyfish wanted to launch itself at me, but it held itself where it was.

"Possession. An obsessive urge to kill all things

living, a side effect of the release. It happens. They have us here to study—Alturians like learning new things."

The creature had my attention. *Did I finally find someone who can explain what's going on around here?*

"The whole game is one big new thing for me. Why did you attack Earth?"

"For the noa," came the straightforward reply.

"I got that far. But what's noa? And what does the game owner need it for?"

"Noa...is noa... There isn't a better synonym—your language doesn't have a word for it. Noa is what gives life. It's what makes your planet unique."

"The soul of the world?"

"Planets don't have souls. They're lifeless. It's just noa."

"So, the point of the game is to collect noa?"

"The game is there to offer cover while they collect noa," the jellyfish replied. "While humans are busy trying to survive, they don't have time to care about what's being pumped out of Earth's core. If we'd just come for the noa without the game, you all wouldn't have been so happy to see us."

"What do you need noa for?"

"You're asking the wrong creature, Earthling. All I can tell you is what will happen to your planet once the noa is gone. And I can tell you how items are made. How the game started. Our scientists found all that out before our world disappeared, though we couldn't figure out why the game owner needs noa."

Nriman was in his eighth release. Every other time, he'd ended up a regular technician repairing and supporting game machinery, though he'd gotten unlucky that time—he'd been overcome with a crazy urge to kill. The curious Alturians had grabbed all the possessed creatures they could find and locked them up there in the storehouse so they could study them later. For his part, Nriman sat there so he could get a fresh start in the next release, maybe even a better role. Ultimately, from what he said, both your coins and the game items you picked up counted for you. The better your final score, the better your position in the next release would be. And that was all interesting enough, but I brought the conversation back around to the game itself.

Noa gave life. It was a vague way of putting it, but that was all Nriman had. Without noa, the planet would die. The jellyfish wasn't sure how it appeared, though it was a fact that everything would die off when it ran out. It told me about how the game started, too. The owner showed up on the planet in its ship, using the most widespread tool available for communication. In our case, that was our cell phones and towers. The owner's servants spent a little while modifying our equipment, after which the planet was sprayed with nanoparticles. They were what was responsible for all the mutations and modifications. They printed out all the different game items, and they were what the items dissolved back into when they were deactivated. But for the nanoparticles to work correctly, they needed something controlling them—in our case, cell towers. And the reason humans had been successful in the north was because there weren't as many cell towers up there. Just like in Africa, South America, and other developing countries, we didn't have them everywhere. Which was a shame, really. The more advanced you were technologically, the worse your chances of surviving the release were.

"So, there are noa extractors in all the different locations?" I asked in horror. "How long does it take to pump it all out?"

"No, not in all of them. To get noa, you need a fault line, so they stick noa concentration plants next to each other. There are usually two or three together. But there aren't that many fault lines. From what I heard, there are only three in our hexagon. One here, two in the south. And as far as time goes... Nobody knows. That depends on the fault line. Every planet has one million units of noa, and as soon as the game owner gets the last one, the game wraps up. We all die, and the world is left to itself."

"A million?" I asked, this time thoughtfully. "But what if the owner doesn't get one or more units?"

"I'm not sure. You're asking the wrong creature,

Earthling—I'm just a mechanic."

That was why Twelve and his people had laughed when I'd dispersed the noa. It was just extracted by other stations. *What if I hadn't dispersed it? Would the owner go hunting one unit out of a million? Does it need all of it?* I made a mental note to give that a try.

"That's all I can tell you, Earthling. Don't kill me."

"I'm not going to," I replied to my own surprise. "You're possessed. You want to kill all things living, I don't have time to clear the city, and you need to do some leveling-up. There are enough monsters here to last you a while. I already killed all your kind, so nobody will be coming for you, and you can find their bodies and equipment on the roofs of the neighboring buildings. That will help you survive."

The jellyfish vibrated happily in anticipation.

"That's a smart move, Earthling, so let me give you a piece of advice. If you're prepared to risk your immortality and want to save your planet, get your hands on some noa. Don't let the owner have it. They'll hunt you, but you're strong. You'll be fine. The game resources are limited—there are only half a million of us, and the owner can't break the rules of the game. It's just another user like all the rest of us. Survive, and your planet can revive. Okay, goodbye."

Wiggling away sideways to maintain distance

between us, the jellyfish headed toward the exit. I just kept an eye on it as it went. Finally, it disappeared, and I waited and watched as it left the shopping center and headed up to the roof for some armor. And while I was worried it would stay up there and start hunting me, it didn't even touch the rifle. Coming back down, it slipped off toward the city center. That was where the farm was.

The five possessed players gave me 250 coins, though I was much happier about the ten cages. They were game items worth 50,000 coins each. *As much as my sister's cage!* I couldn't wait to get her out and send her north.

Once I was sure there wasn't anyone left alive to threaten me in the area, I headed toward the stores. I stank so badly that it was even bothering me. There was no bathroom with a shower in the shopping center, though I found a mountain of wet wipes and bottled water. The next hour was spent getting myself freshened up. I even found an electric razor I used to shave everything I could. The dirty clumps on my head refused to wash out, so I got rid of them. After pausing a second to think, I tossed the razor in a backpack I found in the next store over. *I'll be needing that later.* And I didn't want to put Ulbaron on my naked body, so I found a high-end store with quality underwear and T-shirts. A couple spare sets went into my reserve. I'd never been able to spend that kind of money in my previous life, so I made up for it then. *If some animal eats me, I'll at least be clean and good tasting.*

Finally, my body was done modifying, and I was thrilled to slip on Ulbaron. As soon as the helmet snapped into place, I was hit by the kind of cool air I'd forgotten about. There was an air conditioning system inside the armor that kept the temperature perfect. It integrated with my phone automatically, also offering a special protected pocket for it. I was ready to find some other players.

Let's get us some noa.

Chapter 19

You destroyed 1 of the larva's 3 farms in this location.

I WATCHED WITH A GRIN as the monsters dashed to and fro, trying to figure out where the attack was coming from. Five plasma grenades had turned the tubs into a scorched soup. If I could have, I would have stayed to bury the dead women, but there was an enormous crowd of monsters I would have had to take out before I could do that. And I had neither the time nor the possibility right then. But the tubs couldn't be left there, so the risk had to be taken. You can't just feed on people to level-up like that.

An hour later, the monsters calmed down. Most of them even dashed out of the city. *Probably to go take up guard over the next farm.* Making a mental note of the direction they ran off in, I headed out slowly. The Alturian kept popping up on my radar, and I watched it engulf its victims, pouring into every crevice it could find. It was a good thing I'd avoided touching the creatures. From what I could tell, Nriman had already taken out a few dozen monsters, so I needed to make sure I stayed away from him. *Wouldn't it be ironic if I died at the hands of my blood-crazed little helper?*

There was a surprise on the way back: a larva came rushing toward me with its extensive entourage. I even had to duck off the road to make sure none of the many monsters accidentally bumped into me. *Perfect!* Before I had it out with the third farm, I needed to head over to the neighboring location and kick up a fuss there. The powerful beast would go dashing off to the aid of its "children," leaving me with just the other larva to deal with. *Well, two, if you count the transporter.*

But that was the end of the good news. The number of creatures around the concentrator hadn't just grown; it looked like all the monsters from the surrounding region had been called in as reinforcements. The champions didn't let the lower idiots attack players, and the latter were doing their best to stay out of sight. And they had a wide range of weaponry at their disposal: from energy rifles to regular automatics. The latter were aimed in the direction of the dome. Not only that, but there was a separate group armed to the teeth with nothing but earthling weaponry. From what I could tell, that was the fast response group assigned the task of taking out anyone who appeared inside the dome. The game owner had taken defense seriously.

So, what was I supposed to do? Give up, toss in the towel, tell everyone to go screw themselves? No, the station had to be destroyed. And that left just one option. I'd had it in mind for a while—get under the dome via a tunnel. They were there, so I might as well use them.

The only entrance I knew of was by the dungeon, over where I'd killed the shrew. The creature's body had already dissolved into nanoparticles. That left nothing but a deep well in its place, and I was forced to spend time flying over to the nearest village in search of a rope and a flashlight. I made sure my expedition went unnoticed—there was no sense spooking the monsters and having them report back on my location.

Ultimately, the day was drawing to a close by the time I started down the tunnel. Doubled over, I crawled along the passageway, my outfit catching on jutting roots. The shrew had done an awfully poor job. The tunnel was narrow, uncomfortable, and constantly ducking left and right, up and down. Without much air to speak of, I soon found myself covered in sweat despite my stamina. *Going to have to get cleaned up again.* The five kilometers between me and the military base made for tough sledding.

But my weariness vanished the second I made it to an enormous vertical shaft. The drone couldn't see me—I was under the dome. And the size of the shaft was staggering, the opposite side five meters away. Well, approximately. The massive pipe made it difficult to accurately gauge distances. Up at the top, there was a solid steel ceiling, while down below... I shone my flashlight in that direction, but the beam wasn't strong enough to reach the bottom. Poking my head out, I touched the pipe. It was cold, lightly shuddering.

Earth noa concentration plant. Status: Active.

A list of available hardware popped up in front of me, though nearly all of it was inaccessible for me. There was just one that wasn't: *noa supply hose*. Pulling up the settings, I sighed. I wasn't going to be able to do anything from where I was, as the only option available from my location was to activate the handrails. When I did that, brackets popped out along the length of the pipe. That gave me a way to climb up, which is exactly what I did. But the problem there was that the iron cover was one solid piece completely free of cracks. It didn't react to anything. I tried device control, not to mention giving it a shove upward and to the side, though nothing worked.

Pulling out Fang, I decided to see how tough the pipe was. *No good.* The knife didn't even leave a mark, not to mention actually penetrating the thing. Shining my flashlight downward and eyeing the pipe the monsters were sucking noa out with, I decided to head into the depths. *It has to end somewhere. Could I get inside the thing?* It was definitely wide enough. Not putting it off any further, I started letting myself down using just my arms. It was faster that way.

It was an odd trip down. I kept going and going, the flashlight I'd strapped to my shoulder the only beam of hope shoving back the pitch darkness. Twenty minutes later, I had to get my legs involved. My arms were so tired they were starting to shake. After yet another twenty minutes, I had to start taking breaks every sixty seconds. My entire body was quivering, and it was cold and uncomfortable. Finally, it started getting lighter down below, and I hurried up, throwing caution to the winds.

From what I could remember, magma gave off a red glow and all kinds of heat. But it was blue, light blue, where I was, and deathly cold. I even had to close my helmet and appreciate Ulbaron's advanced thermoregulation. The lower I got, the lighter it was, to the point that I ended up just turning off the flashlight. I sighed a couple hundred steps later as I leaned against the pipe. *I did it!* I'd made it to the end of the damn pipe.

I found myself in an enormous cave. Or rather, it was more like a separate layer of Earth's core filled with a blue fog. The light was coming from the strange substance. The pipe I'd climbed down ended a bit lower, where it was vacuuming up the fog and pulling it through a system of filters. I checked out my surroundings. I couldn't see the bottom, what with how thick the fog was down there, though it was practically nonexistent where I was. *Already sucked it out, I guess.* Pulling out my rifle and happily noting that game items worked down in the depths of the earth, I looked around through the scope. There was another pipe off in the distance. The Alturian had been telling the truth—there were three noa concentration plants in our area, and I'd already found two of them. I made a mental note to remember the direction of the third. *That will come in handy.*

Suddenly, the pipe jerked, and I almost fell off. I grasped the handles tighter and looked down. The pipe was extending right in front of me, growing new sections and burrowing deeper into the blue fog. *Time to hurry!*

I slung my rifle over my back and clambered all the way down, hoping that Ulbaron would keep me safe from the fog. There was no problem with the noa, though the same couldn't be said for the pipe—it was covered by a variety of filters. Attaching myself to the bottom rung, I swung around the edge and found myself plastered against the bottom of the tube. The vacuum was so strong it held even my hefty body right in place. Fang appeared in my hand, and I fought the stream of air as I slashed through one of the filters. *Got it!* The knife penetrated the metal like warm butter, making a deep incision. Immediately, I flipped the blade around and started cutting away from the other side to make a hole big enough for me to crawl into.

That just about killed me. Quickly realizing that the vacuum was strong enough to hold me in place, I'd let go of the bracket and was using both hands to try and rip my way inside. When the hole was wide enough to fit me, I untied the rope, reached for the new opening, and...

And dropped like a rock toward the noa fog. Because the vacuum effect had disappeared.

My hands slipped, the rope was untied, and with a final, incredible motion, I was barely able to hook the toe of my boot to the bracket. Afraid to move, I hung there head down and noticed the fog beginning to recede. The pipe was being pulled into itself like a telescoping antenna. It picked up speed with each passing second, and I realized I wasn't going to be able to hold on much longer. Without making any sudden moves, and fighting the 2G and even 3G force, I bent my body in two and managed on the second try to grasp the edge of the hole I'd cut. Stretching upward, I crawled inside and was immediately plastered against the bottom. The pipe was going faster and faster.

It stopped so suddenly that the momentum very nearly pulled me off the edge. My rifle saved me—as soon as we got inside the dome, it turned into what felt like a bar of solid concrete. Making sure everything had quieted down, I freed myself of the weapon and froze when I heard voices.

"Damn, look at that hole! Think it hit a rock?"

"No, look how even the edges are. A chunk of diamond, I think. Remember how that happened before?"

"Yeah, but that time the hole was the size of my fist! And here I could just crawl right in. Can you imagine how big the diamond must have been? Have you ever seen one like that?"

"You never know with this planet. I wouldn't be surprised if it really was a diamond. Anyway, whatever, bring the repair kit over—they're going to have questions for us about the delay."

"That's for sure..."

I peered out of the hole to see that the shaft was closed. Not far away stood a pair of technicians, two hairy Shurvans in white jackets. They were busy, completely unprepared for me to pop out, and so all they could do was open their mouths in surprise when I dropped to the ground. A couple hits to the head, and they both collapsed unconscious. But their chests still rose and fell—they were alive. *Excellent. The game doesn't know I'm here, yet.*

It was time for me to look around, and I grinned maliciously—I was surrounded by control panels and remotes. *Am I really in the control block?* Placing my hands on one of the control panels, my grin widened. Suddenly, I had control of the entire plant. And with the exception of the noa feed hose, it was working perfectly.

I started flipping through the monitors. The plant was automated, the two technicians locked in the control room servicing the whole thing. There were ten guards around the perimeter. Another few dozen were by the dome, and everyone else was on the other side of it. Unfortunately, the plant didn't have its own weaponry, otherwise I would have been able to just blow it up.

Going back to the list of unfamiliar names, I went back and forth from block to block, unsure of what to do, until I found something called the *storehouse*. The screen pulled up an image of a small room with two glowing rocks protected by several force fields. *Concentrated Earth noa! Two units!* A few taps on the keyboard, and both were delivered to the control block. One of the walls opened to show off a small niche with my prizes.

I grabbed them and dropped them into a pocket, and the dome immediately disappeared. The entire army outside went on full alert. Players and monsters alike dashed toward the machine, glancing around to find the spy that had gotten past them. The game owner knew the noa was gone, though there was no way of telling where or how. There was more panic than intelligence in the scatterbrained way everyone was running around. And regardless, nobody headed toward the control room to look for me, which was perfectly fine by me. It really was a good thing I didn't kill the guards. Climbing back into the pipe, I retrieved my rifle, an easy enough assignment with the dome gone. There was no shooting by the big contraption, so I nearly dropped the gun when I accidentally pressed the trigger button. A blue glare shot out of the barrel to leave a dark splotch on the wall. Trying it again, I found that it really was working. *But why?* Grust and I had very nearly met our end because we hadn't been able to shoot.

The answer only came to me a couple minutes later. *What if it's the valve covering the shaft?* I found the control, pulled it open, and grunted—I couldn't shoot. Closing it again, I found that the rifle was working fine. And that made sense, as we hadn't pulled the pipe up at the first plant. That was why none of our game items had worked until I'd dissolved it. Although, the rifle itself had worked fine down by the noa fog. The only conclusion I could draw was the game items went crazy when they were by a plant that had noa, as that was all that explained the facts.

And seeing as how that was the case, I had a plan.

Closing the valve, I pulled up the store. Plasma

grenades weren't the only way to kill at scale. In addition to them, the virtual shelves held a number of interesting options including V-III explosives. I didn't have the attributes for level four, and there wasn't time to bump mine up, so I went with level three. One unit cost a hundred grand, but I was in no position to complain. Judging by the description, it was powerful enough to take out the whole plant, so I bought three. Just in case.

Hanging the charges on the walls, I set the timers for ten minutes, opened the valve, and... The timers stopped. When I closed the valve, the explosives were activated, only without the timers. *That's no good...*

The game was the one that handed me the solution. Paging through the store looking for anything that would help, I finally found a device called a *remote control* in the *recommended* section. Built for the player's device control, it let you control different pieces of hardware remotely. There was no need for timers. Each cost ten thousand coins, so I bought them and stuck them on the explosives. Of course, they didn't work with the valve open, but I had to believe they'd kick in once it closed. The rest was simple. I stuck a hook in the wall of the shaft, tied the rope to it, hit the button to close the valve, and dove into the hole. The cover slammed shut above my head as I flew downward into the shaft the shrew had dug.

It was anything but simple. My heart was pounding so hard, I thought it was going to jump out of my chest. And if anyone else had recommended I give that maneuver a try, I would have called them crazy and told them to screw themselves. But it worked. I checked my settings—the remote control and explosives were working flawlessly. Setting twenty minutes before the explosion, I crawled off on all fours.

Setting the timer was a good idea, too. As soon as I made my way outside the dome, the devices disappeared. I decided against going back to check and see if they were still working—I was going to find out soon enough.

Crawling and crawling, I was so focused on getting as far away as I could that I missed the explosion. At least, I wasn't expecting it. The explosion itself would have been hard to miss—the earth shook so violently that the tunnel caved in. I tensed up, bracing the roof with my back. And it worked without too much difficulty, my shaking arms notwithstanding. The problem was that I was blocked in from behind and the front with collapsed earth. The little Armageddon I'd created was awesome, the image from the drone showing me an enormous crater where the plant had been. The trees had been flattened by the shock wave for a good few hundred meters in every direction. And while there were survivors, both monsters and champions, the number of players had dropped precipitously. Everyone responsible for the defense of the dome had been sent off to their rest, the ones in game clothes turned into pancakes.

You destroyed an Earth noa concentration plant.

The hexagon general declared you public enemy number one. From now on, all the monsters in the hexagon will do sextuple damage to you. You will receive six times as many coins for each monster killed.

Level +10 (200).

10 free attribute coins received.

You can collect any level five item in the store for free.

***

You're the first player on Earth to reach level 200.

10 free attribute points received.

***

You stole Earth noa.

The game owner is unhappy with you.

Penalty received: Sanctions: From now on, you only have access to named items.

***

You're the first player in the last 10 seasons to receive the sanctions penalty.

You can collect any named item in the store

for free.

Level +50 (250).

50 free attribute points received.

***

You were compensated because you cannot receive your level five bonus. 1200000 coins received.

The drone feed disappeared, as did the drone itself. No longer available for me to use, it had disappeared from my consciousness. *You're kidding me! Is the owner off their rocker? How am I supposed to play with all these penalties?* The bastard just wiped out anyone who tried to stand up for themselves.

As anger washed over me, I worked my arms and legs, pulling myself upward. A couple minutes later, a hand broke the surface and was immediately bitten with such force that I was yanked out of the ground. My hand was squeezed hard, but Ulbaron held up. One of the monsters had noticed the ground moving and ran over to see what was going on. Fang flashed, turning the creature into a dried-out mummy, but then the area erupted in joyous howls. I'd been seen. Without the drone, it felt like I was fighting with my hands tied behind my back. I activated Valkyrie and started slowly backing away, gunning down the monsters with deadly accuracy as they rushed me. Finally, the flow started to weaken, and I decided to go on the offensive. A few times, I had to duck to the side and take out a player lying on the ground—my perception kept kicking in. And I could see my drone, too. Stripped of its invisibility, it was sitting off alone in the wreckage of the building. Finally, I took out one last target and swept from side to side, only to find that there was nobody left to shoot. The explosion had made the job much easier for me. I only wished that my named items had leveled-up. *Damn it—I'm not going to be able to use my Mark-2, either!* It was back to my own two feet. *I've had it about up to here with the game owner...*

You took the first picture of 1200 dead superior monsters. 36000 coins received.
You took the first picture of 250 dead champions. 450000 coins received.
You took the first picture of 400 dead players. 24000 coins received.

They certainly hadn't skimped out on the plant's defenses. I wouldn't have been able to break in no matter how much I wanted to. And in that moment, I knew I had to beat a hasty retreat before all the monsters in the location showed up. I tossed Mark-1 into my virtual storage and sprinted off. There was no time to collect the loot from the players—I needed to lie low until the wave of monsters washed past. And they were definitely coming. I could already hear the snapping of trees breaking, and no sooner had I ducked into the forest, than two larvae and their entourages appeared on the opposite side of the clearing I'd created. There were all kinds of monsters over there, too. And so, without waiting for them to notice me, I moved away slow enough that my camouflage and concealment could show themselves off. Players were over there with the monsters, too. I pulled up the location ranking to discover that I'd dropped down to fourth place. The top slot was occupied by Ardan-9 at level 283, next was GR7-10 at level 276, and third was N34-11 at level 257. All three of them were over looking for me with the monsters. And they were all robots just like Twelve.

Once I'd gotten far enough away, I turned and ran without bothering to hide. I needed to create enough space to make my next moves. Two hours later, I decided that was enough. If anyone had been following me, they would have caught me by then, so I sat down under a tree and checked into what was going on with my Mark-2. Yep—there was no more controlling it for me. My device control was still there, only my race car had turned into a simple transport incapable of going invisible. The drone flew around beautifully without sending me a single image. *No scanner, no invisibility.* It was just a flying gun.

I pulled out the two glowing rocks. There was no

way I was going to repeat the mistake I'd made the first time—they weren't going to be destroyed. But I needed somewhere to put them. They wouldn't go into the virtual storage, which meant I had to find a box so I didn't accidentally squeeze and disperse them. Everything I knew about noa popped into my head. It gave life, though it wasn't the soul of the planet. *How does it give life? What does that mean? Who does it give it to, and how? For example, can it give life to someone who already died?* There was Grust, for example. *Heh...* That would have been great. *Grust, I want you to be reborn. Come back, warrior—there's no saving the world without you, yadda, yadda, yadda...*

I sighed sadly. Obviously, nothing had happened. Tossing the stones into my chest pocket, I stood up, joints popping. Before I picked out my third named item, I needed to check in on that third noa concentration plant.

"The hell is going on?!" I jumped when I heard the voice behind me. Valkyrie sprang to life in my hand, and I came oh, so close to pressing the trigger button. A ghost was standing next to the tree I'd been sitting under. With each passing second, it gained density until it finally lost its transparency completely. But that wasn't the only change. The body was bathed in whiteness, almost as if it was being cut out of an elephant's bone.

"Mark, did you pull this off? What did you do?"

The ghost finally saw me and jumped immediately into its tirade. I stood there, unable to say a word, just reaching into my pocket to feel around for the noa stones. But there was only one there. I was positive I'd stuck the other in my pocket, as well, but it was gone.

"Did you forget how to talk? I asked you what happened to me and why I'm back at level one."

"Hi, Grust," I said when I got over my shock. "What's the last thing you remember?"

And that's when system messages started raining down on me.

Chapter 20

"SO, I REALLY DID DIE. And even though I'm alive now, it's just temporary," Grust said morosely, clutching his phone. All he'd done was hold out his hand, and the device had flown over as if it had been waiting under the next tree over. Technically, regardless of his vampiric demeanor, he was alive. As alive as a phantom could be.

"Yep. And you'll stay alive until you're killed or the game is over," I replied. "And it doesn't matter if we win or lose. Once the game wraps up, that'll be it for you."

The main thing I gleaned from the mass of messages raining down on me was that you could use noa to resurrect players, transforming them into receptacles. In other words, that wasn't Grust in front of me. It was a receptacle for noa that had been given dead Grust's memories. He had all his achievements, awards, and bonuses, just not the level he'd gotten to before he was killed. There he was, a complete beginner just entering the game. His attributes were all at level one. But that problem, at least, was solvable—I had money for syringes. The only question was whether they would work on receptacles.

"Okay, I'll be smarter next time." Grust even found the energy to grin. "Who knows when the game will end, right? And we'll keep fighting as long as we're alive. What's the plan?"

I didn't tell him that we couldn't lose the game as long as he was alive. The guy was one of a million units of noa the game owner needed, and so they would have to kill my partner before they could win. Pulling out an attribute syringe, I turned to him.

"You need to get stronger. Try this."

Without asking questions, Grust stuck himself and pressed down on the plunger. His eyes widened in pain, he collapsed to the ground, and convulsions began wreaking havoc with him. All I could do was watch him suffer. Everyone getting started had to go through that—it was part of the damn game. He was going to need eight hours for the first attribute, three for all the rest. And in the meantime, he didn't ask where his rifle was, though I did see him glancing at Valkyrie. It was on his mind. *Incidentally, where is it?* Twelve hadn't had it. The other players hadn't, either— I'd checked all of them. After killing Grust, they'd headed toward Aspen. *Could they have given it to Olson? That's the only option...*

Grust finally relaxed as the nanoparticles went

to work on his body. That meant it was my turn. Twelve had told me quite a bit about how I wasn't hidden enough for experienced players, that it was easy to find me using my scent, my scattered aura, my thoughts, the tracks I left behind... There was a lot a good tracker could determine about their victim if they really wanted to. And I could only assume that the digital trio sent to hunt me had those kinds of skills. I needed to hide myself.

Introversion +30 (30).
Consciousness block +30 (30).
Trackless +30 (30).

One attribute and two skills got me where I needed to go, though I did make an awfully unpleasant discovery. My trip up and down the tube as well as crawling around underground had shown me that I had a problem with stamina. I decided to bump it up ten levels, but that's when I was stymied. After level 40, each additional level took three points rather than the usual one. I checked my strength, agility, willpower, and even melee weapons. But the game couldn't have cared less whether it was a main attribute, a supporting attribute, or a skill—all of them took three points to level-up after level 40. And I could sense that there would be more surprises later. They'd been hidden practically around every corner.

After thinking for a while about what to do next, I figured out what to spend my bonus on. The fourth named item I picked up was an accessory.

Raptor. *Description: An adaptive device for Mark Derwin. Initial Raptor level: 1. Scans the surrounding area with a radius of* Raptor level*10 *meters, revealing all players and monsters, including those with concealment attributes less than* Raptor level*5. *Builds a local map with a radius of* Raptor level*200 *meters. Hacks other players' phones no more than* Raptor level *meters away. Replaces phone functionality. Cannot by blocked in the game world. Requirements: Monster knowledge (40), anatomy master (40), perception (40), detection (40), scanner (40), device control (40), cartographer (40), hacking (40). Cost: 20000000 coins.*

Raptor reached the same level four the rest of my named items had, though none of the others had had the same hefty requirements. I had to jump back into the store and do some injecting. The good thing was that I didn't have to pick up any new attributes or skills.

When Grust came to, I was playing with my new toy. It felt fantastic to have the red dots back where they were supposed to be on the screen. There was only one—my partner—but I could see exactly who he was and what level he was at. Even my Mark-1 hadn't given me that kind of information. Raptor was strapped onto my left wrist, and my phone had disappeared the moment I matched up to the requirements and fastened the device to my arm. All of my phone's functionality had been taken over by Raptor. And the description hadn't done it justice—even though there was quite a lot I still had to dig through, I could tell it was a big pickup. After staring at me for a while, my partner burst out with a question.

"Who has my Swallow? I can sense it, though I can't link to it. It's like someone has their hands on it, someone in that direction."

He pointed toward Aspen.

"There's a lot I need to tell you. Decide how you want to spend your points, and I'll tell you a bedtime story while the game modifies you. I remember how much you enjoy them. Oh, and grab device control—you're in charge of the drone from now on."

"What about you?" Grust asked in surprise.

"I can't anymore. Do you have sanctions as one of your penalties?"

"I don't even have tough response." It was my turn to be surprised. "No penalties at all, and just the regular one-coin coefficient for monster kills. Completely reset."

Three hours later, a video feed appeared on my screen. Grust sent Mark-1 soaring into the sky and flew it around for a while like a kid with a new toy. The drone scanner also connected to Ulbaron without overriding the data I was getting from Raptor. Everything within 40 meters was shown by my device; the Mark-1 took care of the rest. It was a great little system.

I ended up spending two and a half million coins on Grust, though it was a good investment. I was picking up powerful fire support. At my recommendation, he bumped up all the different branches of concealment and protection. We had to be ready for anything.

"Just for one person?" he asked, squinting at my Mark-2. "Nothing you can do about that?"

"There is, I just don't have the coins," I replied with a sigh. "We're going to be hoofing it for now."

We were headed for Aspen—Grust needed his rifle back. But as soon as the drone entered the safe zone, we realized that it wasn't going to be easy. The village had grown to resemble a fortified castle. There were tall stone walls, guard towers, innumerable guards, and even a moat. And an army of monsters had set up camp outside the walls. What bothered me most were the automatic turrets the guard towers were bristling with, and we could only see from a distance how the hotel had transformed into a kind of palace. Olson was really putting in the work to make sure there was a better role assigned in the next release.

"I'm going in alone," I said immediately. "But I

have an assignment for you. Find a village, preferably a ways away, and clear it. I need you to lure the high-level players out of their lair. Sound good?"

"I'd say you can only die once, but who even knows anymore? Sure, that's a smart idea. But will you be okay by yourself?"

"Like I have a choice," I replied with a mirthless smile. "It's time to be done with Aspen—Little died because of Olson."

Grust's face fell. I understood how much he wanted to help, but he couldn't. We'd already discussed that—until we had another unit of noa in reserve, we weren't going to resurrect anyone else. And I wasn't going to hide the stone I had, either. I didn't know what kind of attributes it had, so I couldn't risk it. The thing was fine where it was in my pocket.

"Don't you dare die!" Grust said. "If you do, I'll resurrect you just so I can wring your neck, got it?"

"You be careful, too." I shook my partner's hand. It was tough parting ways so soon, though we didn't have any other options. I needed to pull a couple of the general's spawn away from Aspen.

When we came across a stream, I finally took the time to wash the dirt off me. A change of clothes had me feeling like a new man. There was something wrong with my head, but I really did feel completely different. No longer a modified copy of Schwarzenegger with the agility of Jackie Chan, I was just your regular

Joe.

Getting into Aspen wasn't nearly as simple as I'd been expecting. The monsters weren't just hanging out around the fortress; they were patrolling the area. Champions—mages, in fact—headed up each squad. And with enviable regularity, they sent lightning, frost, or fire sweeping through the area around them, presumably to make sure no spies could sneak up. Half an hour spent observing the whole picture didn't reveal a single weakness in the defenses. The monsters didn't need food or sleep, and they patrolled relentlessly, periodically shaking the ground with their magic.

The only spot that wasn't patrolled was the road to the main gate. Of course, there were plenty of eyes watching it as it was. The towers that had popped up everywhere were one line of defense, and there were lines of champions checking everyone looking to come in. None of it looked good. And I didn't see a way to get in without serious injury.

But suddenly, the gate opened, and something popped out. That something was GR7-10, at level 276, a hodgepodge of different mechanisms: sharp knives made room for a dozen ray guns pointing in different directions, the body was covered in rivets and other reinforcements, and the central processor that served as the thing's heart was hidden deep under layers of armor capable of withstanding ten direct hits from a ray cannon. My perception, scanner, and device control really were fantastic when it came to robots. Just like Twelve, Ten moved around on a levitating platform, and it was heading directly toward me. Grust had already called to tell me he had gotten to work. The game had immediately made its counter, sending an executioner out after him. And that was it, actually—I didn't see a support group coming with the robot. Ten was either that strong or that confident. Either way, no sooner had it gotten within range of Valkyrie, than I realized why it could be so confident. The bastard had level five armor. All I got with my pistol shooting was 0% damage, so I headed to the store. Universal level five armor stood up to 500 hits and could restore five protection units a minute. I had nothing but a fool's hope of standing up to the monster alone.

Or if not a fool's hope, then the hope of someone with nothing to lose and a toy worth twenty million coins.

I'd been most worried about all the players heading after Grust. If they had, I wouldn't have risked it, telling him to get out as fast as he could. But I didn't mind risking an attack on just one, even if it was that advanced. And my position was well chosen—trees kept me hidden from the castle. Ten was going to have to fly by and find itself also hidden. It was presumably scanning the area, but I had to trust my attributes. *If they let me down, it's over.*

It didn't seem like they did. The levitating platform quickly covered the open space and entered the forest, at which point it was within range of Raptor. I found out almost everything—the robot's strong and weak points, where the nodes that doubled as energy support were. Raptor even told me it had almost a million and a half coins in its wallet. *Not bad living as the general's spawn.*

As soon as the platform came even with me, I leaped forward. It was entirely possible that Ten didn't even know it had weaknesses, so it was too late by the time it noticed me. Place a hand on the platform, hack the defenses, hijack control. I also lifted the far end of the platform to send the robot into a bit of a wobble. Once my second hand, which had Raptor strapped to it, hit the player's body...

The battle of skills had begun.

You're trying to hack the defenses of player GR7-10.

Sum total of your skill levels: 160 (device control: 40, hacking: 40, perception: 40, anatomy master: 40).

Sum total of GR7-10's skill levels: 110 (hacking protection: 30, resistance: 20, resilience: 30, willpower: 30).

Probability of successful hack: 31.25 % (1 —

110/160).

>**Attempt 1... Unsuccessful.**
>**Attempt 2... Unsuccessful.**
>**Attempt 3... Unsuccessful.**
>**Attempt 4... Successful.**

Block!

Those four second were the longest I'd experienced since I'd started playing the game. While the first messages popped up immediately, each subsequent attempt took a full second. And that would have been fine if Ten hadn't been putting up a fight in the meantime. In just that little time, Ulbaron's defenses were nearly annihilated. A few hits actually got through, and only my resilience saved me from the waves of electricity sweeping unpleasantly down my body. I'd really gotten lucky with Twelve—the monster hadn't had any of that. *Or maybe it did?* I was getting my intel from Raptor, with none of it available back in the dungeon. I must have just gotten lucky. But in that moment... It was a risk. A big risk, and the only reason I took it without getting my skills up to a hundred was because I had experience hacking robots.

But none of that was important right then. Without taking my hands off the body, I jumped onto the platform and sent it hurtling away from Aspen. There was a plan in my head for how to get into the village, but it took some preparation.

Hacking Ten's phone didn't tell me anything interesting. The million and a half coins found their way to my account, though I couldn't pull the virtual storage or exchange to give to Grust. He had to be there personally for that. *Next time.* What did impress me was the map, as it had the location of noa concentration plants in addition to dungeons and caches. The two I'd taken out already had red crosses, the icon in the next location practically begging me to come after it. Two more fault lines with three plants each were far to the south. Also, my suspicions about the general were confirmed—it was in the second-largest city, almost in the middle of the hexagon.

Disemboweling Ten, I found myself with three level five items and five level four items. *Love it!* Grust was going to be a happy camper—there would be plenty of money to buy him more attributes. But that was later. Right then, I had some upgrades to take care of.

It wasn't hard to create a little alcove in the platform big enough to fit a player. I had device repair, after all. Hiding myself inside the body, I sent the platform and frozen Ten back toward Aspen. That was the weak link in my plan, and I was just hoping they didn't search the general's spawn. Happily, my hopes were realized. The mage champions lining the entrance didn't bat an eye. The scanners couldn't see me, either, and a few long moments later, the gate opened to let me through. I quickly headed in and took my bearings. Yes, Aspen really had changed. The buildings were all made of stone, with multiple floors for each. The streets were smooth and wide as if poured from concrete. Everything was clean, colorful, and idyllic.

Once I got to the hotel, I checked my scanner, grinned unpleasantly, and pulled out Fang. It was time for action.

You destroyed GP7-10, the tenth spawn of your hexagon's general.

Level +5 (255).

5 free attribute points received.

Dumping the useless piece of metal off the platform, I sent the flying machine to my virtual storage. *I'll sell it later.* The hotel door flew open, and N34-11, or Eleven, popped out. But it made a silly mistake for a player of its caliber: when it saw the remains of Ten, Eleven froze, giving me invaluable time. I was standing in the shadow of the door. One step forward, and I got to work. I'd told myself I wasn't going to do that anymore, but there I was... A hand on the platform, hijack control, knock the robot off balance, and grab the body. Mark Derwin's 160 attribute levels against N34-11's 100. My probability was 37.5%, though it just took one attempt to turn Eleven into a statue. It was outfitted worse than its compatriot—just one level five item and seven level four items, not to mention the platform. The good news was that it boasted 2.3 million coins. My knife found a new home in the newly vulnerable body; necrotic energy filled the robot. *There we go.*

You destroyed P34-11, the eleventh spawn of your hexagon's general.
Level +5 (260).
5 free attribute points received.

And I didn't feel bad about it in the least. Those hunks of iron were only in Aspen to hunt me, so they must have known that the tables might end up turning. From what I could tell, Nine wasn't in the village. Nobody else came running to check into the untimely demise of the two high-ranking players, and my scanner told me there was only one other creature within a radius of 40 meters. I stepped into the hotel and saw it immediately. Olson was sitting on the first floor, and it was alone. Gesturing me over, the creature invited me to sit down next to it.

"I've been expecting you, Mark Derwin." The game representative didn't look nervous at all that I was there. "You've really leveled-up since the last time we saw each other, and you've accomplished quite a bit, too. Everybody knows who you are. And I have a mission for you, only we need to take care of a problem first. I think this belongs to your newly resurrected friend. Could you give it to him?"

Swallow, Grust's rifle, was lying on the table. I had no doubt that it was the real thing—Raptor gave me all its attributes right away. At the same time, it told me nothing about Olson, nothing except the fact that the character was a function serving as the head of the safe zone. *So, Olson isn't even a player? Or is it an oddly configured player?* The scanner didn't alert me to any danger, and it was as if the hotel was deserted. When I picked Swallow up, I noticed that I couldn't drop it into my virtual storage since it belonged to Grust. Still, it fit snugly on my back.

"Now that we've taken care of the reason you had for visiting me, I'd like to offer you a job. I need you to completely clear this location of monsters, the same thing you did for the next location over. Can you do that?"

Olson's offer was so unexpected that I couldn't find my tongue. I was there to kill him, but suddenly we were sitting and chatting. Just in case, I looked around to see if the scanner was missing anything. But no, it was quiet.

"Don't worry, Nine isn't in Olson. It headed after Grust."

"What?!" I exclaimed as I leaped to my feet.

"That surprises you? Noa incarnate glows in the ether like a lighthouse, so it's hard not to notice it.

Nine wants to finish its service—killing the incarnation will earn it a promotion into the top eight, at which point it won't have to run around like a kid anymore. But don't worry about Grust. His speed is about the same as Nine's, so if he's smart, he won't let the robot get close."

By the time it finished speaking, Olson was on its own. I was too busy calling my partner.

"What do you need?" Grust yelled angrily. I heard a shot in the background. "I'm busy killing monsters here!"

"Get out of there!" I shouted back. "There's a strong player coming after you, so jump into the vehicle and fly around in a circle. Keep an eye on the scanner—don't let anything get close!"

"Mark, why don't I watch my own—"

The call dropped.

"Hm... Nine is much faster than I expected. Well, that changes everything. Mark, you have half an hour before it gets here," Olson said as if nothing had happened. It wasn't the one who'd just lost a partner, after all. "But I think we'll be able to take care of everything. Do you agree to accept my mission? Your knife won't help you—there's no killing me since I'm not a player. I'm a function."

Fang was already in Olson's chest. I cut loose all the necrotic energy I could, but nothing happened. And when I pulled the knife back out, there was no wound to be seen.

"What the hell?" I glanced at my scanner. Servants should definitely have been running over.

"There aren't any players besides you in my fortress. Sure, there are monsters guarding the perimeter, but they arrived with the general's spawn. We're losing time, Mark Derwin. As it is, you can't take Nine on—you need to get out and level-up. The best way to do that is to clear a location and destroy a larva, at which point your weapon will be better, and you'll be able to penetrate your opponent's armor. You don't think you can just go around hacking them all the time, do you?"

"What do you care?" I growled.

"I'm part of the game. With every new release, I'll be there, and I want my next incarnation to have more opportunities. When you were weak and useless, I worked with the owner's players. But you're the highest-ranking natural player in the hexagon now. I could use you, especially since there's nothing else I can do right now with things the way they are—Aspen is as big as it can get. The next step is a whole safe location. And of everyone I know, you're the only one who can pull that off, which is why I'm giving you the mission. We could really help each other out, both now and later."

"How can you help me? You want to sell me off like you sold those miners? The way you sold Little?

The way you sold me the first time by giving out the mission to kill me?"

"Again, my function is to work with whoever is strongest. You were weak, and I didn't need to work with you. And when I assigned the mission to kill you, I was looking to see who was strongest, who I should work with. But if you want to talk about who I've sold, why don't we think back to your sister? As far as I know, she's still alive. Neither the general nor the game owner know anything about her. I'm not a player, Mark; I'm part of the game. And as far as what I can do for you, how does information sound? Information about the game, about your opponents, about their strengths and weaknesses. You don't have much time to make a decision—Nine is getting closer. Mark Derwin, do you accept my mission?"

"Yes, damn you!" I muttered angrily. Olson had made a point of mentioning my sister—the bastard knew which buttons to press. Although, I had already been planning on clearing the location, so there was no point turning down something I couldn't turn down anyway.

New mission: *Clear the location.*
Description: Destroy all the monsters in location 552, hexagon 118. Monsters remaining: 554 inferior, 4332 superior, 898 champions, 2 larvae, 1 transporter.

"I'd recommend not incarnating your partner until you defeat Nine. Of all the players in the hexagon, Nine is the only one who can see where he is. As far as the first eight go, the general never lets them go anywhere. They're the personal guard. If you take out Nine, you'll be doing the whole hexagon a favor. And if you don't... Well, I'll have to go looking for a different strong player."

"Are there any humans left alive in this location?"

"Not in ours, no, though there are in the safe zone you created. Two women and one man, all of which you know: Valdemar, Laura, and Ella. It's amazing they've been able to survive given their levels. Also, you should know that they were the ones who left the miners vulnerable. Little stayed, but he couldn't do anything on his own against Twelve and its fighters. Time for you to go, Mark. Nine is going to be getting to Aspen very soon."

Chapter 21

Warning!
You need 5 free attribute points to boost skills after level 50.

ARE YOU SERIOUS? How hard are you going to squeeze the players? You want all the Earthlings dead? I decided to screw it and go with what I had.

Device control +10 (50).
Anatomy master +10 (50).
Consciousness block +10 (40).
Trackless +10 (40).

I didn't have time to boost my perception or my hacking—they would have taken three hours. And that just left me with my skills. My leg was aching from all the needles I was stabbing it with, but there was no other way. The one problem was that if I survived the battle, Grust wasn't going to be able to do much leveling up since I would have to get all my attributes to 50. *Maybe even 60.* That was going to cost a fortune, more than a couple named items would have cost. But that was the only way to overcome my weakness in the face of the machines being thrown at me.

Although... How weak was I really? Nine was at level 283, just 23 above me. That was 283 reinforcements with an equal number given as bonuses. The main question I had was whether the owner's players could use the syringes. My encounters with Ten and Eleven had shown me that they didn't have anything out of the ordinary in their attributes. Theoretically, Nine wasn't some kind of demigod, either, in that case, and I could take him on right then. The important thing was to avoid getting caught in its sights—Ulbaron wouldn't stand up to a direct headshot from a level five gun.

Suddenly, Olson's voice boomed from every building in Aspen. It couldn't see me, though it knew I was somewhere in its fortress.

"Mark, that's a terrible idea. Nine is significantly more advanced than you are, and it knows you're here. It's going to start destroying buildings one after another. And I can't let that happen."

"If you sit this one out, I'll clear an extra location for you," I called back, figuring that Olson would be able to hear me. The function fell silent as it processed what I'd said. Finally, I had my answer.

"Aspen will be okay if it doesn't lose any more

than half its buildings. Nine is restricted by the rules, so it will take some time to destroy them. If you aren't able to defeat it by then, I'll be forced to go over to its side."

Clear the location updated...

Getting rid of the useless message, I pulled up the store. There was no time to lose. Olson didn't actually seem like such a bad guy, and I started to think we might be friends if it could buy me three hours.

Hacking +20 (60).
Perception +20 (60).

Those forty extra attribute levels came out to a hundred and sixty syringes. I plunged them into myself one after the other, ignoring the pain and hazy vision. There wasn't time to upgrade my skills. But that was okay, as I had bigger problems—no sooner had the last syringe disappeared, than the monsters guarding the perimeter began howling for joy. Nine appeared out of the forest.

It was an exact copy of the destroyer, if smaller. Though, not much smaller. With a wave of an arm, Nine sent drones flying in the direction of Aspen. I counted three of them. *But how many are invisible?* I had my answer a few seconds later—another three. Six drones. Adding in the platform, and... *Damn it!* Either the robots had the unique ability to operate a larger number of devices, or I was up against a player with its device control at level 60. *I'm not ready for this...*

I was in a good spot on the roof of one of the buildings, so the invisible drones flew into raptor's range one by one. It both pinpointed their location and highlighted them, reacting to barely visible vibrations in the air. I froze. It was a serious opponent out there.

The drones hovered over one of the buildings, and what happened next was unexpected, to say the least. Nine launched some rockets. Three fast bolts of lightning hurtled over, and the big two-story building was reduced to rubble. A column of fire shot into the sky, though it was quickly put out. Olson and his helpers were already hard at work.

The robot's flying eyes headed over to the other side of the fortress and paused one more time. Three rockets, and another building was knocked out. I broke out in a sweat regardless of the air conditioning my suit provided. To be honest, I'd been expecting the robot to fly into Aspen and start pulling it apart building by building, not the way it was doing it— skillfully and from afar. My arms drooped, unsure of what to do. Nine stayed frozen at the edge of the forest. Not only that, but it was protected by an entire phalanx of champions apparently there to make sure nothing got in the way of the destruction of Aspen. Another building caught the robot's eye. Three more streaks demolished it.

One of the drones eased its way over to the next building over, and that was my chance. It was time to do something. The device's protection wasn't a problem for Raptor, and I had control a couple moments later. Well, I had a sort of control... All I could do was fly it back and forth, relying on visual contact. The weapons, camera, and scanners were all inaccessible. But even that was enough to send the thing into a steep dive. It clearly hadn't been designed as a battering ram, and so it blinked piteously and disappeared when it hit the pavement. There was actually an advantage to how everything in the game turned off when I gained control. The drone presumably had solid protection that did nothing for it in my hands.

The response from the robot was instant—six rockets slammed into the roof the drone had been over. It was clearly an attempt to finish me off in one fell swoop. Three of the drones hovered over the wreckage to scan for survivors, and that gave me the chance to send them down into the burning rubble. The other two invisible drones were hovering not far away, but still out of Raptor's reach. It was time to take a risk. As soon as Valkyrie appeared in my hand, I leaped to my feet and threw myself off the roof, sending rounds at the flying devices as I went. I saw some flashes out of the corner of my eye—Nine was reacting to my appearance. But that didn't bother me, as the rockets were going to take an eternity to get to where I was. Three seconds. I could have gotten out of Aspen in that time, not to mention getting off the roof.

Two smoking pieces of metal plummeted to the ground, all that was left of the drones. Valkyrie had no problem with their level four defenses. Just as I'd thought, the invisible ones hadn't been well protected. There was an explosion behind me, but that just gave me a little extra shove. My leap took me easily to the next roof, and the next one after that. One more, and I froze in the shadow of a chimney.

Your move, Nine!

It didn't keep me waiting. I'm not sure what the player used, but an entire of barrage of rockets came flying toward Aspen. Buildings began dropping left and right, there were explosions between houses, and the beautiful façades and roads began taking a beating. A few rockets even detonated in the ruins that had already been created. But what I liked least of all was that one of the shells slammed into the roof I was on. The shock wave sent me flying to the ground, with rubble collapsing on top of me. Ulbaron creaked under the weight, though it ate up a good bit of the damage. It couldn't keep me from broken bones, however—the fall didn't come without a cost. My collarbone and a few ribs were knocked out of commission, drastically cutting into my fighting capacity. I wasn't going to be able to run as fast as before. A second wave of fire sent more rubble down on me. Finally, everything went quiet, and the dust started to settle. It was my move.

Tossing the rock aside, I pulled myself heavily to my feet. My chest and shoulder burned; it was hard to breathe. I really needed to boost my regeneration. Limping over to a wall, I hid in the shadow and froze, covering my tracks. *What do you think of that, Nine?*

Half an hour went by before the next drones appeared. In that time, Olson and his helpers had put out the fire, and they were even at work repairing the road. That bought me a couple more minutes. There were only two drones, both of which out of Raptor's reach—my opponent needed eyes in the sky. I assumed they had two invisible friends, so I didn't move. It would have been hard to notice me from that high up even if Nine had spent the time boosting his detection to unheard-of heights. I'd been busy, too.

Suddenly, Raptor's scanner picked up monsters. They were moving in on Aspen. From what I knew, they weren't allowed to cross into the safe zone, though nobody said they couldn't attack it. And as if they were reading my mind, the turrets lit up—Olson was none too happy to see the turn of events. For a couple seconds, it seemed like a dumb idea, but that's when the shells smashed into and detonated the towers. The next shot took out the gate. The thick wood wrapped in steel crumpled like cardboard. Nine made no bones about anything, wiping out anything that stood in its path. The monsters whooped and dashed inside, filling the area with lightning, ice, and fire. Bellowing in pain and rage, I leaped to my feet. *I guess, I'm not going to be resurrecting Grust.* Valkyrie popped out and went to work. A level four automatic pistol was the perfect tool to quickly take out the blood-crazed bastards, though there was one downside. The drones saw me. Nine didn't take long, and a few shells hit the wall next to me, showering me with pieces of rock. The wall held up under the first shot, though it didn't look like it was going to stand a chance against the second. I dashed off to meet the champions. If I was going to die, I wasn't going to be the only one.

The demolished gates and motionless monster bodies flashed by as I struck mercilessly and with deadly accuracy. Catching another flash in the corner of my eye, I dove into the moat. *Just in time!* The approach to Aspen and the monsters left alive on it were engulfed in a series of explosions. But the column of earth and rock sent hurtling into the sky offered me a sliver of a chance. As soon as I hit the bottom, I set off for the bridge. At least, what was left of it. Scrambling up onto the embankment, I wedged myself between two stone columns that were part of the foundation to weather the next volley. Nine aimed it at the moat, digging it even deeper. My cover was buried in earth—I was hidden from the flying observers. Explosions went off left and right, as the robot didn't get the result it was looking for and began riddling the protective embankment. It had apparently decided that I'd run off to one side or the other.

That saved me. I sat there neither dead nor alive, listening to what was going on around me. Raptor caught the drones flying by just a couple meters away, though I didn't risk it. No hijacking—I needed time. The monsters summoned by Nine howled, also flitting by Raptor's radar. They were trying to catch my scent. A little while later, I heard Olson's voice demanding that they stop destroying its city since there weren't any players left in it. I wasn't sure if that worked or not, but I didn't hear any more shots. Something banged over my head, the earth shook, and I lost some of my protection. I was going to panic, but I reined it in—with some vision opened up, I could see that Olson was just executing his function. He'd restored the bridge and in so doing completely hidden me from the observers flying overhead. Monsters dashed through the moat a couple times, even champions with their lightning and ice, but I was able to avoid acquainting myself with them any closer. The stone columns held off the main impact of their sweeping shots; Ulbaron did the rest.

"I can sense the noa here, but I can't figure out how he's able to hide. Where is Mark Derwin?" Just when I thought everything had calmed down, I heard the metallic, emotionless voice. I stopped breathing, afraid to attract any attention. Raptor showed me an enormous red dot representing the player. There it was—Nine had decided to personally see where I'd gotten off to.

"He isn't in Aspen, player!" I heard Olson yell again. "You know I can't lie!"

"But he was in there, function," the robot replied, stopping a few meters away from the restored bridge. "I'll raze your fortress to the ground if I have to, but I'm going to find the noa. The general has already summoned me to assume the seventh number. I don't have much time, so either you give me Mark, or you lose your function. You have ten minutes."

So, Olson had been right. Killing Grust had earned Nine a promotion, and a double promotion at that. Raptor read the monster like a book, though I could only grind my teeth in frustration. There wasn't a single blind spot, not one weakness. Grenades weren't even an option—I didn't have access to them.

Wait a second!

Risking discovery, I pulled the noa out of my chest pocket. Nine moved closer to the bridge as if sensing something. Several drones swooped by, though they couldn't penetrate my camouflage, flying off to be replaced by champions. The latter resumed bathing the ground in lightning, cold, and fire in an attempt to knock my invisibility away. Once I was sure the monsters had gotten far enough away, I opened my hand. Nine came even closer. It was right at the edge of the bridge, practically an arm's reach away, and that was when I made up my mind. Flashing all the colors of the rainbow, with lightning bolts to boot, the stone went flying toward the other side of the bridge.

"Noa!" I got the impression that emotions actually flitted through the metallic voice, but I was too busy to care. At the same time as I tossed the stone away, I leaped up, as well, just appearing at the other side. I only needed a second, and I got it. All of Nine's attention was fixed on the stone that had suddenly joined the party.

A hand on the platform. Shred the defenses. Grab control. Left side drivers boost to maximum. Right side drivers at zero. Help the process along with my hands. A slash with Fang. Bellow as my defenses kick in. Jump forward and wrap my legs and arms around Nine's body. Get a rush of energy as a wave of electricity washes through my body. Yell like a maniac but survive. Hold on. Start hacking.

That all took exactly two seconds. The platform finally toppled over, and Nine and I rolled into the moat. Arms broke under the beast's weight, Valkyrie relentlessly punished its defenses, and Ulbaron tried to buy me at least one more second. But it couldn't. Nine was incredibly strong, incredibly advanced, incredibly protected.

You're trying to hack the defenses of player Ardan-9.

Sum total of your skill levels: 180 (device control: 50, hacking: 40, perception: 40, anatomy master: 50).

Sum total of Ardan-9's skill levels: 174 (hacking protection: 40, resistance: 50, resilience: 44, willpower: 40).

Probability of successful hack: 3.3% (1 — 174/180).

Attempt 1... Unsuccessful.

Attempt 2... Unsuccessful.

...

Attempt 10... Unsuccessful.

Valkyrie started clicking—all six magazines were empty. Raptor did its very best, but it wasn't able to hack in. Another hit slammed into my head, sharp spikes pierced my body, and Ulbaron wasn't long for the world. Barely in control of myself, I activated Fang and plunged it into the robot's body. If I was going to go down, I was going to go down fighting. The blade slipped easily into the steel. Once the hilt slapped against Nine, I jerked the blade up and around, widening the hole. Nine jerked oddly, and I ripped off an enormous piece of armor. My consciousness was slipping away, but with its last shreds, I saw some wires and mechanisms, so I reached out for something small and red. I squeezed it hard. There was a sound, then a scrape, and finally smoke. Fire burst out in my chest, and I was thrown backward, the red bulb still clutched in my hand.

The last thing I saw was the snarling faces of monsters coming at me.

Darkness fell.

"That was a stupid, ill-advised move, Mark Derwin. You have no idea how lucky you are."

"It's the strong who get lucky," I groaned, trying to pry my eyes open. My body ached mercilessly, and I wanted to die, but the fact that Olson's voice was there and sounding calm meant something good. For example, that I was alive.

"The strong?" the function replied with a snort. "Why don't I tell you how strong you are? Your attempt to hack Nine failed, which isn't a surprise—I warned you about that from the beginning. It started chopping you up, though it had a hard time with that because its idiot underlings got in its way trying to bring it the noa. And diffusing it would have been a death sentence for Nine. The general wouldn't have forgiven it. That was the first time you got lucky. Next, the platform overturned, and you rolled into the moat. Nine lost some of its rays and, critically, its protection. Of course, you did help with that. You were able to get it low enough that smacking against the bottom of the moat broke the circuits and robbed it of its mobility for a few seconds. Then, you tore out that fuse. But instead of dying from the threat elimination system, you were thrown against the wall of my fortress. For that, you can thank the champions who threw fireballs and lightning bolts at you. The former sent you flying away from Nine; the latter demolished the circuits and killed the player. The general is furious. It's not going to dig into how its spawn was killed—just the information that simple monsters were at fault was enough. All the changed around Aspen were frozen because of that, which saved you again. An amazing series of events that let you survive. But it was still stupid of you, and the strongest didn't win. If you want, call yourself the luckiest."

"And that's why you're working with me." I somehow found the strength to reply and open my eyes. There I was, lying right next to the Aspen wall. A few superior monsters ready to eat me alive were frozen next to me, and I even jumped. They were an arm's reach away. Fang darted out almost on its own, and there was one less monster looking for my head. But even that simple movement sent pain searing through my body. Ulbaron had already regenerated, so I couldn't see my wounds, but I know there were quite a few of them.

"Yes, that definitely makes you an interesting

player," Olson said. He was up on the wall, outside my field of vision. "The general is deciding what to do with our location right now, so you have time. Again, you're lucky—the three remaining destroyers had to be sent to the north. You earthlings finally got a grip on the rules of the game. There are a total of 149 hexagons on Earth, and only ten of them have humans left alive. But wherever you all are, the owner and the owner's armies are having a rough go of it. Get yourself back together, complete your mission, and we'll talk. But until then, Aspen is closed to you. Having you around is too expensive."

Olson left, and I began crawling down. The red bulb in my hand was useless, so I tossed it aside. It wasn't anything I could sell or use. Slipping off the embankment, I nearly gave up the ghost from the pain, but I gritted my teeth and kept going. There was a small sphere glowing next to Nine—I needed it like oxygen if I was going to stay alive in the world any longer.

"Grust, come back! I need you!" I whispered as soon as I had my hands on the noa. The stone shone brightly before dying away, instantly losing its beauty and power. Then, it completely disappeared without even leaving the usual dark ash behind. But something appeared to the side, and that something was none too happy.

"I hope you get constipated so badly you

explode!" the ghost yelled, kicking the dead robot angrily. "I hope you rust in a junkyard! I hope you..."

As Grust solidified and turned into his new marble-skinned self, he spent the whole time berating Nine. It was only when his foot stopped passing through the body and began banging against it that he calmed down.

"I lost the drone. And the vehicle," he said bitterly, nodding at the robot. "That bastard took them out. Oh, hey! Is that my Swallow? Why didn't you say anything? Give it to me."

He flipped me over and grabbed the gun.

"How'd you pull it off? Is Aspen done? Mark, let's hear it! They didn't cut your tongue out, did they? And where is that bastard's phone? How do I take its coins?"

Grust wouldn't shut up. Closing my eyes wearily, I tried unsuccessfully to relax. My excited partner shook me by the shoulder.

"Mark, wake up! Guess what? They didn't reset me this time! I still have everything I got before I died the second time. Isn't that great?"

"What are you so rambunctious for?" I grumbled, no longer able to take it anymore. "Are you really Grust? My partner only ever talked when he had to."

That worked. Grust's face darkened as if he suddenly heard himself, and the happy, excited expression on his face faded to the usual doom and gloom.

"Absolutely... The nerves, I guess. Okay, I'm back. Are you good?"

"Does it look like it?"

"I've seen worse. Once, I was almost burned alive. But you're breathing, so you'll make it. What do you need me to do right now?"

"Kill all the monsters around here. They're frozen," I said, closing my eyes once more. I was exhausted.

Grust left me alone, and I immediately fell asleep.

When I woke up, my wounds were gone without a trace. I was alive, happy, and livid at myself. Nobody had kept me from fleeing Aspen, waiting the three hours it would have taken to level-up, and then coming back to try again. In that moment, my chances of hacking Nine would have been over 20%. *How did they possibly let me beat them...*

Grust had finished polishing off the monsters and was patiently waiting for me.

"Take your pick." I started materializing the items I'd gotten from Eleven and Ten. "If you can use any of it, great."

"Not bad," my partner said reverently, heading right in to rummage around. I went over to Nine—it was its turn to turn over everything it had.

Devices available for extraction.

There were six level five items, three level four items. It wasn't the best haul, of course, unless you took into account the value. Everything at level five started at a million coins.

"Hey, Grust, give me your phone." I sent him the level five store and storage. Nine wouldn't be needing them anymore, not to mention its 820,000 coins. Surprisingly, Eleven had been the richest of the trio. Although, perhaps Nine had just spent all its wealth on the drones.

You took the first picture of 30 dead superior monsters. 900 coins received.

You took the first picture of 10 dead champions. 18000 coins received.

"Here's your share." I sent Grust half and nodded toward the pile of metal. "Anything to sell?"

"Are you kidding?" My partner even went over to stand between me and the game items. "We can't sell any of this! Once I get to level 100, I'll boost my attributes and show the world how it's done. We're holding on to all of it."

"Okay then," I replied, not about to argue. "What level is Swallow?"

"Four. It was three."

"I took out a larva, so it must have counted toward the group. Okay, ready?"

"For what?"

"Genocide. I owe Olson a mission, so we need to take care of it."

Chapter 22

"WHY DON'T WE BUY A DRONE?" Grust asked for the umpteenth time. "We're really blind without one."

"That would cost almost two million with the invisibility and repair kit. I don't have that kind of money right now."

"I'm talking about level three," he replied with a frown. "We can both pitch in—we're on the same team."

"Would you forget about that level already?" I practically shouted. He wasn't listening to reason. "Drones at that level can't see level four creatures. They won't show up on the scanner!"

"And we really need invisibility?"

"Did your encounter with Nine really teach you nothing? Grust, you have to understand, the game changes so drastically every couple days, and you either keep up or stand out. I don't have two million coins."

And I certainly wasn't trying to pull one over on him—I'd really spent almost all the coins I'd had on getting myself stronger. There had been enough near misses that I needed to make sure I was prepared for whatever might happen. And while I'd thought before that I was spending too much on my attributes, in that moment I realized how stupid and naïve I'd been. Before level 40, you just needed one syringe, but things really got exciting after that point. From 40 to 50, you needed three; from 50 to 60, you needed five; from 60 to 70 you needed seven. I hadn't checked to see what happened at that point, as I couldn't even bear to think about it. It must have been approaching some final value—there was no way to keep going at any kind of solid pace.

"Fine, screw you... I'll buy it myself," my partner said heavily as he started printing out level five items. There was lots of protection, lots of weapons. A nice arsenal that didn't really fit any attributes. Selecting four items he thought he didn't need, he sat down under the nearest tree and started sticking himself with needles. The game gradually materialized a flying dish and the accessories for it. *Whatever*, I thought. At the end of the day, hoarding didn't get you anywhere in the game, and Grust had lost the previous model. And so, I sat down next to him and pulled up my status table. It had been a while since I'd last checked it out.

Status table		
Name	Mark Derwin	
Coins	795 000	Level	260

Titles and ranks		
Title: Hero		
Ranks: Bandit Bane, Lone Wolf, Stone Wall		

Attributes			
Strength	60	Regeneration	60
Stamina	60	Resilience	40
Agility	60	Willpower	40
Necrotica	40	Cartography	40
Fortress	40	Perception	70
Noiseless	40	Concealment	40
Scanner	40	Camouflage	40
Introversion	40	Hacking	70

Skills	
Pistol shooting	70
Rifle shooting	8
Melee weapons	60
Device control	70
Device repair	50
Detection	40
Monster knowledge	40
Anatomy master	60
Consciousness block	40
Trackless	40

While I didn't max myself out anywhere, I made sure I had at least a sliver of a chance if I had to take on Eight. Of course, I could have spent more, but I still had to buy three sets of magazines for Valkyrie and a bunch of energy blocks for Ulbaron. Everything cost coins. And earning them was getting harder and harder. I held onto the flying platforms for the time being, figuring that Grust would boost his device repair and turn them into something. Walking around was a terrible option.

Data flashed on the screen. Next, a map popped up—my partner's drone soared into the sky and rushed off toward our next target.

"I'm not too excited about heading over there," he said nervously as he evaluated the defenses surrounding the third noa concentration plant. While the first one we'd found had relied on concealment and the second on players, the third was all about monsters. Actually, I'd already seen the plant, though I hadn't known what I was looking at. It was right on the border of two locations on the other side of the third farm. A little farther away, over in the next location, was another larva's farm. And the fact that they were located so close together attracted my attention. I took a closer look, only to find that I was right—both farms were on transports, the enormous vehicles whose job it was to carry around their valuable human cargo. The large red splotch indicating the changed spread out a few kilometers away from the station to cover both farms. Whichever way you came from, the monsters were waiting.

But even that wasn't the worst part.

Several hundred flying monsters with champions in the lead circled the anomaly. And they, too, were challenging, but nothing we hadn't dealt with before. The problem was the two enormous constructions sticking out like sore thumbs next to the plant. The first looked like an enormous speaker, and it was labeled simply as Radar, while the second was practically pulled from Star Wars and hurriedly dropped onto our planet. The massive, surprisingly nimble device was capable of wreaking havoc—at least, it looked like an anti-aircraft missile battery armed with the latest in alien technology. The label was appropriate: Liquidator. The general had apparently drawn some lessons from Nine's defeat, setting up something even more powerful to defend the owner's most valued sites. We just about lost the drone as soon as it crossed some kind of line in the sand. Regardless of its active invisibility, the radar installation caught sight of it, and dozens of rockets were sent hurtling in its direction. It was only Grust's flawless marksmanship that kept the drone whole and in one piece—as the rockets chased the drone down, Swallow picked each and every one out of the sky. The thought of what the guy would be able to do once he broke level 100 and started pouring on the attributes warmed my heart. *We need to make that happen.*

"No underground passages. Coming at them through the air isn't an option. A ground attack won't work, either. That's one tough cookie," I grumbled, my voice strained.

"When the drone was above the farm, the radar didn't catch it," Grust said suddenly. "That means the speaker's range isn't that good, and we can use that."

"How?" I asked in surprise. "If we attack, every monster in the vicinity will come at us."

"In that case, we'll need to make sure they don't notice us." He looked at me and continued when he saw the confusion on my face. "You have your concealment pretty high, right? And your hacking, too?"

"So? I can't get anywhere near the radar or the liquidator."

"You don't need to. Really, you don't see it? Come on, Mark! You were able to adapt to the game, but you can't see what's right in front of your nose. The transporter!"

"What about the transporter?" I asked, still staring dubiously at Grust.

"Do you know who Gastello is?"

Gastello? He was a hero of the Second World War, a pilot who was shot down and managed to turn his plane into history's first fiery battering ram by crashing it into a column of enemy armor. I'd read about him at school, but I had no idea how he was supposed to help us fight the monsters. Finally, chills ran down my spine—it hit me. Grust wanted me to jump right into the lion's den.

"The farms are everything to the monsters, so

they won't fire at them unless they absolutely have to. You'll be fine."

"And you're just going to be drinking coffee?"

"If you're talking about this slop," my partner said, pointing at a packet of game food, "then yes, I'll be having my coffee. Mark, do you see any other way? I'll do my best to distract the monsters, though I'll tell you right away that I won't be going all out. Okay?"

"Like I have a choice," I muttered.

"You always have a choice. You can throw up your hands and beg for mercy." It was his turn to guffaw. "Otherwise, shut up and do your job."

I glared at Grust and turned away. *Some motivational speech.* Emotions gurgled in my chest, less anger and more anticipation and building adrenaline. I'd already gotten to a farm once, though there hadn't been a larva. Grenades had been enough to take out the tubs. But right then, I didn't have access to the game explosives even if someone could have activated them and stuck them in my hand. They immediately deactivated—Grust and I had checked. And that just left what my partner was hinting at, a mission I was the only one suited for.

There were no goodbyes. We both knew the job was a dangerous one, though neither of us was feeling at all overwhelmed by the moment. Having turned ourselves into moral monsters, all we cared about was surviving and hurting the beasts around us. Nothing else mattered. There were no regrets, no sadness, just a job to do. *The women can do the whining and moaning.*

Grust's drone stayed with me until I got to the city. Walking along the familiar streets, I stopped next to an equally familiar building, though it was quiet. The eighth floor, the one the player had been hiding on, was empty. Nobody was left anywhere, not in the basement, not in the garage, not even on the roof. Olson had been right—the humans in our location had been wiped out.

A patrol marched by, and I frowned. The mage champion bathed the area in lightning bolts, something I was already used to, but behind it strode a group of players scanning the area with a device I recognized. Twelve's troops had had something like it. After I asked Grust to change some of the settings on the drone, we both cursed—there were players all around the farm in addition to the monsters. Sure, they were low-level, with none of them above level 50, but they were still enough to complicate things. Players were much smarter than the changed beasts.

From the looks of them, the players weren't bored with their monotonous job. Three fighters swept every nook and cranny in the area with their eyes; the technician didn't take its eyes off the device it kept swinging from side to side. I made sure I ventured into the scanner's range, though the device couldn't see me.

But I had to sigh just before I was about to set off—the technician's head had exploded in a brightly colored spray. The next three to drop were the trio of player guards. A couple kilometers was nothing to Grust. And just as I was going to yell at him for his impatience, I bit my tongue. Monsters came swarming out of every opening in the vicinity. The clever bastards had packed the sewer system, staying hidden from scanners there, and Grust didn't know he had to modify how he scanned. And I'd forgotten to tell him. By default, neither the drone nor Raptor scanned underground. One after another, the nimble monsters dropped, heads blown to pieces, but the horde sweeping out of the city was going to be too much for my partner to handle. There were players, too. I smiled bitterly. *Not going all out, Grust? If this isn't all out, what does that even look like?*

Faced with a choice between the mission and helping him out, I went immediately with the former. Grust was equipped well enough to handle himself. Paying closer attention to the manhole covers and adjusting Raptor's settings, I found a convenient tunnel. Yes, it was a sewer, but that was better than trying to dodge the lightning bolts the champions were tossing around. The whole perimeter of the central square featured four tight defensive rings a mouse couldn't have snuck through. The monsters had even knocked down the adjacent buildings so I couldn't get my Spiderman on and coming swinging down from above.

The sewage well dropped me into a fairly wide open area. Ulbaron told me immediately that the city was dead, as was its sewage system—the collecting basin was halfway full of a dark, stinking liquid. The drains were clearly blocked up somewhere, and the crap was just sitting there. At least, there weren't any monsters. Grust deserved credit there for pulling them away. It took me a while to force myself into the liquid, but a distant howl gave me all the incentive I needed. A second later, I was up to my waist in whatever the substance was, having turned on Ulbaron's hermetic encapsulation. I wasn't about to be breathing any of that in. Raptor served as my eyes, and I made my way forward around the boulders and holes hidden by the liquid. And there were a lot of them. My scanner picked up red dots at the edge of the area, all around the outlet I was on my way toward. Moving at the speed of an unsettled turtle, I crept toward the superior monsters. They were up to their necks in the liquid, heads stretched high in the air as they occasionally gifted everyone around them with the sound of their melodious voices. There was a champion, too. It was hanging on the rungs leading up to the surface, unable to force itself any lower. And regardless of the fireballs it sent flying around the area once in a while, it seemed like the creature was more fighting its disgust than worried about the mission at hand. Changed it was, but it still apparently had a squeamish streak.

The central square was right above me, and I was thrilled to see that the obstruction in front of me was the last one I was going to be facing. But I still had to get past the group of monsters as quietly as possible.

Raptor told me that neither the champion nor the superior monsters had any equipment I could block. But there was another option. Slowing my pace even further, I crept closer until I was an arm's length away from the nearest creature. What had once been human was only reminiscent of its past in its thirst for blood. It was difficult to admit, but that was something that had always come naturally to humans. But moving like a sapper disarming a bomb, I clipped a remote-control system on the monster's arm. It didn't even jump when the device snapped into place. Heading over to the wall, I finally let out a breath. I'd never been that close to the changed without either of us trying to kill the other. Grust had given me a few of the remote controls, though I'd sent him the money for it as a workaround to beat the penalties I was dealing with. When I turned it on, I was able to operate other devices. The explosives, for example—the game couldn't lock me out of the device control functionality completely.

After making sure everything had gone off

without a hitch, I sent a short impulse, and the creature squealed and twitched its arm. It was like it had been shocked. Paws started slapping at the liquid as the monsters began trying to find whoever had hurt their friend, even the champion perking up. An enormous fireball hissed right up under the ceiling to light up the area. But all that did was melt the pipes, and the entire space smoked up. Just a few seconds later, visibility had been reduced to zero, so the champion pulled its fireball back. One more shock sent the paws slapping at the liquid even faster. A wave kicked up. The champion hissed something, and we were hit by light from above us—someone had opened the manhole cover. There was an inquisitive snarl, and it sounded to me like the mage responded in some language I didn't understand. They were insisting on something upstairs, but the mage wasn't happy about it. I decided to give him an incentive and shocked the monster I was controlling one more time. It squealed louder, clearly incensed and frustrated it couldn't figure out what was going on. The order came again from the surface. That time, the champion sighed in a way that was almost human. After barking a reply, it lowered itself into the liquid, freeing up the rungs leading to the manhole. And that was what I'd been waiting for.

I climbed up a few rungs and turned on the self-cleaning system. Ulbaron trembled gently, and the liquid clinging to it rolled off as if the surface had suddenly turned hydrophobic. Another mage, that one apparently in charge of the defense, was poking its head into the hole, so I didn't hurry up. While the sooty smoke was concealing me where I was, it thinned drastically just a bit above my head. The champion down below went over to the monster I was controlling, so I erased my tracks by dissolving the remote-control device. That was something the game couldn't erase—I was a master of tricks and tips. After it made sure that everything was okay, the champion went back to where it had been, just a couple rungs down from where I was, to bark up its report. The one at the top stepped away from the manhole cover but left it open so the smoke could dissipate. *Olson was right about how lucky I am!*

I climbed higher, almost to the very edge. Raptor went crazy—the area was flooded with red. If I hadn't known that was going to happen, I would have panicked, but I was ready for it. I didn't even have to climb out of the manhole. Right next to me was a wall of steel, so I placed my hand on it and grinned evilly. *Bingo.*

Transporter Tr-443, a larva-level creature designed to transport level four and higher farms.

Would you like to hack into and take control of it?

You bet! That's what I'm here for.

You're trying to hack the defenses of transporter Tr-443.

Sum total of your skill levels: 250 (device control: 70, hacking: 70, perception: 70, monster knowledge: 40).

Sum total of Tr-443's skill levels: 60 (hacking protection: 15, resistance: 15, resilience: 15, immunity: 15).

Probability of successful hack: 76% (1 — 60/250).

Attempt 1... Successful.

Hijacking control block... Successful.

Hijacking protection block... Successful.

Hijacking attack block... Successful.

You gained complete control of transporter Tr-443.

An enormous spreadsheet of available modules spread out in front of me, all with the *deactivate* button next to them. There wasn't anything else I could do with them—there wasn't any way to stop the birthing process, and I couldn't start taking out monsters with the advanced defense system, either. But there was another option. The transporter was an enormous machine capable of covering long distances, and I was about to leverage that feature. Clutching the body, I made it stand up on its legs.

The feed from the drone was impressive as the entire square suddenly eased upward. The sides closed in on each other, clapping together like a book closing. The tiers of tubs began to collapse, their contents spilling out. And as the crazed larvae ran around trying to save their precious cargo, all they could do was slide down the slick and nearly vertical sides. The transporter didn't close completely, which would have been ideal for me, as it was designed to hold other creatures right in the middle. But the bigger problem was the pandemonium that broke out above my head. Monsters flew to and fro, and that was when I decided to get to work. Continuing to climb up the transporter with one hand, Valkyrie popped out on the other. Closest to me was a larva, and I wasn't about to let the game steal yet another victory from me. The 0.2% damage number meant nothing—that was a paltry five hundred shots from Valkyrie. I was fine with that so long as nobody else got in the way. *Oh, and the most important part!*

You took a selfie with a live larva in the background from less than three meters away. 60000 coins received.
***
You destroyed the larva in location 552, hexagon 118.

Valkyrie, Fang, Ulbaron, and Raptor levels increased by 1 (5).

Level +10 (270).

5 free attribute points received.

***

You took the first picture of a dead larva. 120000 coins received.

The dead hulk blocked the passage completely, meaning that I didn't have a shot at the second larva. But it was definitely there—the drone told me the centipede was working frantically with its feelers to save at least one tub in the chaos.

Fine, screw you. It was time to execute Grust's plan.

The Gastello maneuver.

The transporter started up hideously quickly for its immense size. Just five kilometers separated the liquidator from the city, and so I set a direct route through the buildings. The enormous vehicle made of some impervious alloy smashed through the apartment highrises without a second thought. They fell like houses of cards, all under the watchful eye of the drone. I watched the highest stories collapse into the hull of the transporter, crushing the bodies of the monsters. Still holding on with both hands to make sure I didn't fall off, I pulled up Olson's mission. Each new blow made a big dent in the number of monsters left. Suddenly, the transporter shook, and a column of earth shot up next to it. The liquidator had finally noticed the threat, firing a warning shot—it knew exactly what was inside the onrushing monster. The drone soared higher so I could correct my course. A couple degrees to the right, and there we were. Right on target.

The liquidator's next shot was no warning. The transporter shook so hard that I was shaken off, thrown down three stories. And the drop might have been enough to make me pee my pants if I'd had time. Instead, turning in midair like a cat, I rushed off after the monster. It surged out ahead, and the liquidator took its third shot.

But it wasn't at the crazed transporter with nobody at the controls. The liquidator was shooting at me.

No matter how fast or agile I was, no matter what my stamina was, outrunning and surviving dozens of rockets just wasn't possible. The earth behind me erupted in columns that reached the sky. When the shock wave hit me, I was thrown so far forward that even Ulbaron and its universal protection was powerless about the physics at play. I felt like I was being run over by a steamroller. I was flipped, thrown, and tossed, everything was broken, and I was even buried in a layer of earth to cap it off. Ulbaron informed me of critical damage and got to work rebuilding the hermetic capsule. None of my arms, legs, or body had any feeling. Only the numbers on my helmet's screen and the picture from the drone kept me from falling unconscious—I'd been right on the money. Instead of hitting the liquidator, the transporter crashed right into the radar. That was my primary target. Knocking the installation off its base, the crazed vehicle wedged itself into the dome and finally came to a stop. Momentum had carried it partly inside the force field, leaving just a little outside. *Damn it! I was supposed to play Gastello and end up inside!*

The liquidator flashed again, unleashing a new barrage of rockets in my direction. There was an explosion, a blinding flash, and a piercing pain that traveled through my body. I finally fell unconscious.

Goodbye, Squirrel. I'm sorry it had to end like this.

Chapter 23

"MARK, CAN YOU HEAR ME? Stop playing dead—I can see you in the rankings! You're still alive. Come on, wake up! We need to finish this! Mark, can you hear me?"

Grust really had an unpleasant voice. *You just don't think about it when he isn't talking as much.* But in that moment, with him yelling in my ear, it was all I could think about. Kind of nasally and with a lisp was the best way to describe it. Regardless, I opened my eyes and stared up at the soil filling my vision. Raptor pulled up my status, and I grunted in surprise—just an hour and a half after I'd been buried alive, I was healthy and in one piece. All my systems were at peak condition. I was ready for battle. Looking over, I noticed that the feed from the drone was right where it was supposed to be, and that the camera was staring down at a small hillock. The icon showing a player inside it told me that I was looking at myself. *Wait, how is the drone that close to the liquidator?* That question so intrigued me that I greeted Grust by asking it.

"Because the liquidator is deaf and blind without the radar. I thought you were going to take out the liquidator, but it worked out fine. Can you pull yourself out?"

"I think so." I moved my arms and legs. It was tough but doable.

"In that case, get out of there and take out the liquidator. I can't hack into it, but if you could hand me control, that would be great."

"What about the monsters?" I started digging myself out gently to avoid drawing fire.

"I shot everyone I could find in the city, but you tossed most of them under the dome, so I'm not sure. There hasn't been a message about the larva dying."

It took me five minutes to dig myself free. The enormous hulk of metal stood all alone amid the sweeping field, the tip of the transporter poking out of what looked like nothing. Everything else was hidden behind the protective field. Crawling forward, I checked to see if the liquidator would notice me. *Nope, really is blind.* It swept its rays from side to side like a broken toy, mindless and aimless.

You gained complete control of liquidator LR-32.

Hacking into the thing wasn't much of a challenge. The rocket launchers pointed up at the sky drooped, and I suddenly heard a piercing cry overhead. Looking up, I noticed an entire squadron of flying monsters swooping toward me.

"What the..." I pulled out Valkyrie, but Grust was faster.

"Don't worry, I got you!"

I only had time to take three shots, picking off the fastest of the beasts. Swallow was a menace at level five—each shot took out multiple monsters. *I wish we'd had something like that for Nine!* We would have made short work of it.

"Where are you?"

"Give me a couple minutes. And don't touch anything! If you break my toy, I'll rip your head off."

The scarecrow that showed up was only vaguely reminiscent of my partner. His armor was scorched and battered; he was as dirty as a farm hog. His shattered helmet was hanging on by a thread. At least, the face peeking through the holes was a happy one, and the job was done.

"What happened to you?"

"One of the champions was a little quicker than the rest. I didn't notice it, and it climbed up above me.... Basically, it's my fault. I should have been watching. Okay, what do I do here?"

The liquidator dropped out of my list of equipment, and Grust sat down on the ground to page through the controls. As soon as it found itself with direction once more, the mechanism perked back up toward the sky.

"Ah... So, that's that? Got it! Yep... But what if...? Oh, wow. Did you see that?"

How could I not?! I nearly wet myself when a thick and unexpected burst of pure energy slammed into the ground just a few strides away from me.

"Hey, um... You want to step away? This is my first time here. Ah-ha, that makes sense. Mark, look what I can do!"

The liquidator's launchers aimed up at the sky, and six rockets rushed off in the direction of the city. A fiery mushroom cloud billowed into the air and elicited a happy cry from my partner.

"Got it! Okay, I'm ready—let's do this thing."

The installation wheeled around and jerked. From what I could tell, Grust had activated all the firepower it had at its disposal, and the rockets hurtled out one after the other to turn the next location's farm into ruins. There was a transporter there, too, but it was powerless against our new firepower.

You destroyed 1 of the 3 farms in location 550, hexagon 118.

***

You destroyed transporter Tr-448, a larva-level creature.

Valkyrie, Fang, Ulbaron, and Raptor levels

increased by 1 (6).

Level +10 (280).

5 free attribute points received.

"Take that, you bastards! Bite me!" Grust yelled, flashing both fingers in the direction of the defeated enemy.

"Emotions again?" I replied in surprise.

"I just about died, to be honest," he said with a sigh. "And such a stupid mistake. There I was, on top of the world, and suddenly this monster drops down on me. It really got to me. Anyway, let's finish this. You want to deactivate this thing? I have a bunch I need to do."

You took a group selfie with a live larva-level creature less than 3 meters away. 80000 coins received.

***

You destroyed liquidator LR-32, a larva-level creature.

Valkyrie, Fang, Ulbaron, and Raptor levels increased by 1 (7).

Level +10 (290).

5 free attribute points received.

Unfortunately, I couldn't take a picture of the liquidator once it was dead—the game didn't count the pile of dark ash. We did pull more than ten level four devices from it, however. Grust jumped in front of the pile to announce that he'd be buying a transport and sticking them all on it as soon as he had the cash. All I could do was sigh, pointing over at the hulk of the transport hanging in midair.

"Shall we?"

My partner couldn't get under the dome without cutting loose his inner exhibitionist, and so I went in first. The usual ten hairy guards were on duty, but they didn't stand a chance. I peeked out—Grust was already firing, mowing through the horde of monsters rushing the dome. Everything was so simple and easy. But an uneasy feeling started eating at me. *The game never just hands anything to you. Never!*

Climbing up onto the transporter, I quickly found the frozen larva.

You took a selfie with 2 live larva-level creatures in the background from less than three meters away. 150000 coins received.

You took a selfie with 45 live champions in the background from less than three meters away. 81000 coins received.

Raptor worked fine under the dome, but even the nice chunks of change did nothing for my mood. All I could think about was that something was up.

And there was nothing I liked about that. Valkyrie got to work, and I started making holes in the pinned monsters—at level seven, my automatic pistol went right through them.

> **You destroyed transporter Tr-443 and the larva in location 551, hexagon 118.**
> **Valkyrie, Fang, Ulbaron, and Raptor levels increased by 2 (9).**
> **Level +20 (310).**
> **10 free attribute points received.**
> ***
> **You're the first player on Earth to reach level 300.**
> **10 free attribute points received.**
> ***
> **You destroyed all three farms belonging to the larva in location 552, hexagon 118.**
> **Level +5 (315).**
> **3 free attribute points received.**

Taking the transporter apart earned me another ten level four items, and I dropped them into my storage after glancing over at Grust. He wouldn't have forgiven me if I'd sold them. In the meantime, I'd actually had to replace Valkyrie's magazines—there had been quite a few of the monsters. And it was right about then that I noticed Grust backing up toward and then being pushed against the dome. The wave of onrushing monsters was overwhelming, and he'd bitten off more than he could chew. I was forced to forget about the radar and go cover him long enough for him to get undressed and duck under the dome. Looking around at the ocean of beasts coming at us, I realized that they were from three separate locations. *There's even a larva!*

Suddenly, the trap made sense. To everyone's surprise, the dome disappeared—there were two technicians inside the control block I hadn't had time to get to, and they'd managed to screw us over royally. The entire area froze. The monsters were just as taken aback as we were, though I quickly realized what was going on, grabbed my partner, and dashed toward the plant. I had to grab control before it was too late. With one incredible leap, we found ourselves on top of the big contraption, and I got to work hacking into it. *I have to get the defenses back up!*

"A plane," Grust broke in. "One of ours..."

I snarled, completely focused on the job at hand. *No matter how far you go, there's always someone stronger.* All I had was a 4% chance of hacking into the plant without access to the control center.

"Mark, seriously, it's a plane! And nothing from the game; it's one of ours. Look! The monsters aren't coming after us."

I glanced over. The changed beasts kept surging

forward, but it was like the field was still there—they couldn't get through it. One more unsuccessful attempt later, I gave up. *Yeah, that really is a plane.* It was flying high in the air, beyond reach of my scanner and Grust's rifle. The drone soared skyward, its maximum altitude 5,000 meters. Add on the two-kilometer scanner range, and I figured we just might get high enough. *Are there humans or the owner's monsters inside?*

"Mark, they're ours!" Grust shouted happily when he saw the icons. There were three people in the plane, only with his poor perception, we couldn't see their levels or names.

Suddenly, I noticed a small red dot smack dab in the center of the station. *A laser!* My perception showed me where it was coming from—the edge of the forest a couple kilometers away. My stomach dropped. I knew what the plane was doing there.

Leaping to the ground and checking my scanner, I saw two red dots moving away from the plant at a depth of ten meters. Two humans. *Damn it, humans, level 14 and level 15.*

Stay right there. Block!

No such luck—they didn't have anything from the game on them. Not even phones.

"Grust, time to go. Hurry! That's a bomber up there, and we have less than a minute."

There was no way we were going to shove our

way through the monsters, and that left us just one escape route: into the center of the earth. Where all the noa came from.

Fang dug into the wall of the plant as I started hacking away. We had to get inside. Seconds ticked away, and I worked as fast and as hard as I could. Both our lives hung in the balance.

When we got to the controls, the bad feeling in my gut wasn't just yelling; it was screaming at me that we had to go. But no sooner did we get to the room, than my heart skipped a beat—the level was raised, the hole closed. And I'd been counting on getting out that way. Still, I wasn't about to give up that easily.

"Grust, open the hatch!" I shouted, shoving him toward the controls. "Hurry!"

The picture from the drone showed a rocket dropping out of the belly of the plane. Grust took a while to pick through the unfamiliar interface. *Taking too long!* As I watched death flying toward us, I realized that we weren't going to make it. Even if we got the shaft open, the explosion would incinerate us.

"Got it!" my partner shouted happily, and the hatch started to open. "Take care of this, and don't you even think about not resurrecting me!"

Before I could figure out what he was talking about, he thrust Swallow into my hands and shoved me into the opening. I fell in, unable to react. And as I flailed around for something to grab onto, Grust gave me another hit that sent me flying downward. I hurtled toward the nothingness below. At the same time, the hatch nearly closed, there was an explosion, and I felt the plant shudder. Enough fire made it through the remaining crack that both my legs were seared right off. The picture from the drone disappeared, as did Grust.

My vision faded as the intense pain rushed through me, though I twisted around and buried Fang into the wall. I jerked, my arm yanked right out of the socket. Screaming, I let go of the knife, though it was stuck so deeply in the wall that my fall was arrested on the spot. The fire above me died away to leave me in complete darkness.

Locations 552, 551, and 550 in hexagon 118 was cleared of monsters and declared a safe zone.
Notification sent to all players.
***

Clear the location complete.
You completed an additional mission condition and will receive a bonus from Olson.
***

Valkyrie, Fang, Ulbaron, and Raptor levels increased by 3 (12).
You are unable to use your named items as you do not meet the requirements.

Ulbaron's air conditioning kicked out instantly, the suit turning into a heavy, immobile deadweight. My phone slipped out of Raptor and disappeared into the gloom. Twisting back around, I held out my free hand to summon it back. In the meantime, I was just lucky Fang was attached to my wrist, as it was the only thing keeping me from dropping into the deep abyss. *Damn, there's that word again—lucky...* Grust, on the other hand, hadn't been as lucky, having stayed to close the hatch. My arm crunched, and I screamed in pain as the joint slipped back into place. Regeneration worked whether I liked it or not.

Clutching my phone between my teeth, I slammed my fist into the wall. That gave me a handhold. Repeating the blow to dig the hole deeper, I was able to jam a fist inside and free Fang, useless as it was. The wall held up under my weight. Stretching higher, I buried the blade well above my head. I was going to have to pull myself out of my suit before my legs regenerated. That began a long ascent.

An hour later, my legs were back. By then, I'd gotten to the tunnel dug by the pair of humans who'd gotten away. It was caved in, but it still represented the only way out. The massive hatch locked above me meant I wasn't getting out that way.

I decided to see what was going on with my named items before continuing. Pulling up my phone, I dug into the descriptions. *Damn it, so close!* Their attributes had all risen, though the requirements had risen in parallel with their destructive power, defense, and everything else. And though I matched up to most of the new requirements, there were a few I had to boost. *Are you serious?* It turned out that the better I played, the stronger my equipment got, and the better the chances were that I wouldn't be able to use it. Sooner or later, it would be impossible to get my attributes any higher.

Monster knowledge +10 (50).
Resilience +10 (50).
Necrotica +10 (50).
Fortress +10 (50).
Detection +10 (50).
Scanner +10 (50).
Cartographer +10 (50).

It killed me to boost cartographer, a useless attribute I needed for Raptor. I would have been blind without it. Level twelve meant 120 meters of scanning for anything and everything, along with the ability to connect to devices. Anyway, it took a mere 210 syringes to get myself to where I needed to be. *The next bump had better be at level 20, otherwise there's no way I'm going to clear any more locations.* What had just happened was bad, anyway, but it could have been worse. *On second thought, it's actually a good thing.* It meant that humans were alive and fighting back, even counterattacking. They knew about the noa concentration plants, they'd managed to tunnel under mine, they'd taken out the guards, and they'd probably grabbed the noa stones. I was going to have to find the pair and demand my share. *I wonder if they saw us.* If they did, why hadn't they warned us? They were interesting questions I was going to start tracking down the answers for three hours later.

However, life, as it always does, decided that I needed a curveball. My phone suddenly lit up, and I saw a message that just couldn't be true. But it was.

Incoming call from Squirrel Derwin.

"Squirrel?" I asked in surprise once I'd accepted the call. *Why did she wake up?*

"Mark, he's a mutant!" I heard a hoarse groan in the background. My sister. That was followed by a blow, a gurgling sound, and then a rough male voice in the phone.

"Surprise, you bitch! Thought I was dead? Screw you! And now, you're going to answer for everything. For the metro collapsing, for the fact that I didn't die, and for the fact that the radiation just about did me in. You're going to pay for every minute I've had to spend working on this coffin. But I did it. I broke into it and found your darling sister! And you have ten minutes to send a hundred thousand coins to this phone—if I don't get them, I'm going to take a much closer look at our little sweetie-pie here. It's been a long time since I've had one this juicy!"

The line went dead, and I saw stars. My head felt empty. Suddenly, all I wanted to do was keel over the edge and drop into the emptiness—everything I'd worked so hard for had been in vain. In that moment, I realized what I'd been hearing when I'd called Squirrel. It was that bastard, the one I'd thought was a goner, trying to break in. The player by the name of Wart. And what was in store for my sister was far worse than if she'd simply died.

With shaking fingers, I transferred Squirrel the coins. My search for the other humans was off, as was my plan to resurrect Grust. It was time to head into the city. *Oh god, I hope nothing happened to her!*

End of Book One

Want to be the first to know about our latest LitRPG, sci fi and fantasy titles from your favorite authors?

Subscribe to our NEW RELEASES newsletter:
http://eepurl.com/b7niIL

Thank you for reading *No Mistakes!*
If you like what you've read, check out other sci-fi, fantasy and
LitRPG novels published by Magic Dome Books:

Reality Benders LitRPG series by Michael Atamanov:
Countdown
External Threat
Game Changer
Web of Worlds
A Jump into the Unknown
Aces High

**The Dark Herbalist LitRPG series
by Michael Atamanov:**
Video Game Plotline Tester
Stay on the Wing
A Trap for the Potentate
Finding a Body

Perimeter Defense LitRPG series by Michael Atamanov:
Sector Eight
Beyond Death
New Contract
A Game with No Rules

**League of Losers LitRPG Series
by Michael Atamanov:**
A Cat and his Human

**The Way of the Shaman LitRPG series
by Vasily Mahanenko:**
Survival Quest
The Kartoss Gambit
The Secret of the Dark Forest
The Phantom Castle
The Karmadont Chess Set
The Hour of Pain (a bonus short story)
Shaman's Revenge
Clans War

The Alchemist LiTRPG series by Vasily Mahanenko:
City of the Dead
Forest of Desire
Tears of Alron

Dark Paladin LitRPG series by Vasily Mahanenko:
The Beginning
The Quest
Restart

Galactogon LitRPG series by Vasily Mahanenko:
Start the Game!
In Search of the Uldans
A Check for a Billion

Invasion LitRPG Series by Vasily Mahanenko:
A Second Chance
An Equation with one Unknown

World of the Changed LitRPG Series by Vasily Mahanenko:
No Mistakes
Pearl of the South
Noa in the Flesh

**The Bard from Barliona LitRPG series
by Eugenia Dmitrieva and Vasily Mahanenko:**
The Renegades
A Song of Shadow

Level Up LitRPG series by Dan Sugralinov:
Re-Start
Hero
The Final Trial
Level Up: The Knockout (with Max Lagno)
Level Up. The Knockout: Update (with Max Lagno)

Disgardium LitRPG series by Dan Sugralinov:
Class-A Threat
Apostle of the Sleeping Gods
The Destroying Plague
Resistance
Holy War

World 99 LitRPG Series by Dan Sugralinov:
Blood of Fate

Adam Online LitRPG Leries by Max Lagno:
Absolute Zero
City of Freedom

In order to have new books of the series translated faster, we need your help and support! Please consider leaving a review or spread the word by recommending *No Mistakes* to your friends and posting the link on social media. The more people buy the book, the sooner we'll be able to make new translations available.

Thank you!

Till next time!